HARBOR
ICE

To Leslie and Paul
All the Best
Enjoy!
K. Mason
11 '12

HARBOR
ICE

K.D. MASON

SEAPOINT BOOKS
AN IMPRINT OF SMITH/KERR ASSOCIATES LLC
KITTERY POINT, MAINE
WWW.SMITHKERR.COM

Distributed to the trade by National Book Network
Generous quantity discounts are available through
Smith/Kerr Associates LLC, 43 Seapoint Road,
Kittery Point, ME 03905
(207) 439-2921 or www.SmithKerr.com

Cataloging-in-publication data is on file at the Library of Congress.

ISBN-13 978-0-9786899-9-5
ISBN-10 0-9786899-9-2

Cover and book design by Claire MacMaster
  Barefoot Art Graphic Design | deepwater-creative.com
Cover photo: W. Douglas Zechel
Back cover photo: Richard G. Holt

Dedicated to my mother, Caroline Morrison.

* * *

In the beginning, I thought writing would be a solitary pursuit. This couldn't be further from the truth. Without the kindness, the inspiration, the encouragement, the patience of so many good friends, this project never would have been possible. Thank you. Thank you. Thank you.

Nancy
Caroline
Paula
Mary
Deb
Barbara
Chip
Byron
Sue
Brigid
Chuck
Joanne
Ann
Courtney
The New Mexico Attorney General's Office
My friends, editors, agents, and publishers Jean and Spencer

If I forgot anyone, please accept my apologies and know it wouldn't have been possible without your help.

Prologue

THE ICY BLACKNESS closed in on her as she sank into the nearly frozen water. Panic, pain, fear, disbelief, all obliterated by the killing cold. Her last sight, the silhouette of that man standing above her on the side of the road. Her last emotion, unbearable grief, because now, she could not keep the promise made to her lover. Her last awareness, the ring on her finger, the ring she had failed to deliver.

The man shivered in the sharp wind, as he struggled to catch his breath. She had been stronger than expected, and now as she sank out of sight, he began to plot his next move.

"Damn bitch! Who did she think she was? Trying to fight me! Nearly pulling me in! Goddamned bitch! F …!"

He cut his words short. It was a point of pride that he didn't ever lose his temper, so as quickly as his temper flared, he regained control and a calm came over him. Softly, he swore to himself, "This isn't over; I will get that ring."

He shivered and turned, then walked back to his car. As he climbed in, he glanced back one last time and swore softly.

CHAPTER ONE

THE GALLERY

"FABULOUS. MMMH … these hors d'oeuvres are fabulous," gushed Lillian. "Have you tried the mushroom and pickled cactus canapés yet?"

Meredith shook her head and rolled her eyes slightly as she continued to chew on the grilled southwestern teriyaki rattlesnake skewer that was in her hand. She had never quite developed the knack for chewing and conversing at the same time so she just nodded with a slight smile.

"I'll be right back," said Lillian, and she was gone, off stalking the waiter who had just emerged carrying a new tray of trendy hors d'oeuvres.

She watched Lillian move across the room and thought to herself, "I wish I could do that. No fear, completely at home in the present." Lillian moved out of sight so Meredith turned her attention back to the sculpture she was standing in front of and continued chewing, her thoughts elsewhere.

It was fifteen years ago today that Lillian had come into Meredith's life. Before then she had thought her life complete. She and twenty or so other free spirits lived on the commune. It wasn't easy, but it had its rewards. She remembered that morning. The sunrise had been particularly beautiful. She remembered how the deep blues and grays of night were overcome by the brilliant pastels of the rising sun. She remembered how her early morning tea had burned her tongue. The day was hot like most days in the high desert at that time of year, and it was her turn to go into town to pick up the few things that they could not provide for themselves on the commune.

By the time she reached town, her t-shirt was damp with sweat, and beginning to stick to her back and cling to her breasts. Parking the truck in front of Sadie's Emporium, she sat for a moment looking at the deserted street. As she got out of the truck, she pulled the shirt away from her body—holding it out and letting the hot, dry breeze blow over her skin. For a moment she felt the coolness from the evaporating sweat. The brightness of the sun and the swirling dust made her squint. It wasn't until she was in the shade of the porch roof that she saw she was not alone. Sitting on one of the chairs Mabel kept on the porch, a backpack next to her, was a woman. She had the look of a lost dog who knew exactly where she was. Meredith blushed, realizing how silly she must have looked flapping her t-shirt in the breeze, and stammered, "Oh, hi." The stranger appeared to be about her age and returned the hello. Then before either could say anything else, Mabel stuck her head out the door and said, "Oh good, you've met." That was where it all began. That was the moment when Meredith's life truly became whole.

Lillian returned to the commune that day with Meredith. The two women were as different as night and day, yet there was a deep connection. Soon they became inseparable, first as friends, then as lovers and soulmates.

So Meredith stood quietly, chewing and studying the work before her. She wasn't sure what it was exactly, and its title gave no clue. Ever practical, she just did not understand things that seemed deliberately obscure. Her thoughts wandered again. Crowds of people made her uneasy. She preferred the familiarity and comfort of the farm. It was all she needed, but for Lillian, it was different. This trip to Taos was Meredith's anniversary present to Lillian, and in spite of her unease, the past two days had been truly special. The women explored the city, experienced new restaurants, browsed through stores filled with more things than Meredith could imagine ever needing or using. For Lillian, it was a chance to get out of well-worn boots, dungarees, and work shirts; put on real clothes; and absorb the kinetic energy of the city. It wasn't New York or San Francisco, but it was enough.

Her feet aching from two days in shoes more fashionable than she was used to, Meredith sat on a bench in front of a large, brightly colored abstract painting. She glanced in the catalogue she carried and saw that it was called *Desert Light*. "Lillian's really happy here," thought Meredith. It was at times like this she sometimes felt doubt about her relationship with Lillian: Why does she love me so? She needs this. This is where she belongs, here, in a city, surrounded by crowds and activity.

"A penny for your thoughts?" asked Lillian as she sat down next to Meredith, facing the other way.

Meredith looked over. "Lil, you startled me."

"You were looking so pitiful, sitting here all alone. I was beginning to feel guilty for abandoning you."

"Don't. I'm fine. My feet are just a little sore."

"I'll rub them for you later."

"That would be nice. Now go, enjoy the show. I'm fine, and besides this weekend is my gift to you."

Lillian leaned over and gave her a gentle kiss on the cheek. "I'll be right back. Maybe later, after I rub your feet, you could do my shoulders."

Meredith smiled. "I'd like that." And then she was gone, leaving Meredith sitting on the bench, lost in her thoughts, staring at *Desert Light*.

An hour passed, and Lillian was beginning to feel guilty for abandoning Meredith and was getting tired. She scanned the crowd in the main room and didn't see Meredith sitting on the bench where she had left her. As Lillian went from room to room, her anxiety increased. Finally as she entered the last room, she saw Meredith standing in front of a large canvas chatting with a man. Lillian paused, watching. They were talking, pointing at the picture and laughing. As her anxiety dissipated, it was replaced by embarrassment. It was not like her to panic like that, and she needed a moment to compose herself. It was as if their roles had suddenly reversed; she was now the fish out of water and Meredith seemed right at home. Taking a deep breath, Lillian chided herself for being so silly. "Meredith!" she called out as she walked toward them.

Meredith turned toward her voice, a smile on her face. "Lillian, there you are."

Before she could answer, the man turned toward her as well. His glance lasted but a second before he turned his attention back to Meredith. As brief as that glance was, it was enough. There was something familiar about him. What it was didn't come to Lillian immediately, but she saw in his eyes that same recognition and it was unsettling. "I know him," she thought to herself as she walked toward them. It was obvious that he was saying something to Meredith even though Lillian couldn't hear them over the other voices in the room. As Lillian came within earshot, he took Meredith's hand, gave it a slight shake, and she heard him say, "Thank you again for your company." As he turned to leave, he nearly bumped into Lillian. For a second time their eyes met, and this time there was no doubt, he knew her and she him. Then, without a word he strode off.

The two women looked at each other, silently, surprised by the abruptness of his departure. Lillian turned and watched him disappear around the corner, leaving her with that nagging feeling of familiarity. Turning back to Meredith, trying to not show her discomfort, she said with a teasing tone in her voice, "So what gives? I leave you alone for a few minutes and you start picking up guys?"

Meredith was defensive; then as she began to respond, she realized Lillian was teasing her. "Nooo. I was doing no such thing. I was just being polite, and besides, he seemed quite nice."

Lillian looked away again in the direction of his departure.

"Lillian, are you all right?"

"Yes. I'm fine," she said, her voice drifting away.

"You're not. What's bothering you?"

"Nothing."

"Bullshit. I know you too well. Something is bothering you. What is it? Was it him?"

"No, it wasn't him ... well maybe it was. I feel like I know him from somewhere only I can't remember where. Come on. Let's get out of here."

"Good idea." Meredith took Lillian's hand.

Meredith's touch was reassuring and the dark feeling Lillian had began to lift. "It's been a long day, and I promised you a foot massage." Still holding hands, they turned and walked toward the exit.

As they entered the main gallery and the door was in sight, Lillian stopped short. Jerking her hand out of Meredith's, Lillian looked down at the ring that was on her finger. Meredith, surprised by this, turned and looked at Lillian. With concerned eyes, Meredith asked, "Lil, are you all right?"

"No ... yes ... no," Lillian's voice tailed off.

"What is it?"

"It just came to me why he seemed familiar."

"Who? What?"

"That man. The one who you were talking to. I remember him." Lillian looked down at the ring again. Meredith saw that and suddenly things didn't feel right, and she hadn't felt that in many years. There were parts of her past she had never shared with Lillian—it had never seemed necessary—but now those old feelings were surfacing, and she reacted. They were still standing in the middle of the room and suddenly Meredith felt very conspicuous. "Come on, let's go over there and you can tell me what this is all about." She took Lillian's arm and guided her over to a corner where there was a tall floor plant. It wouldn't hide them, but it felt more private there.

Neither spoke. They just stood there facing each other. Lillian didn't move. Meredith stepped in, wrapped her arms around Lillian, and whispered, "Lillian, love, what's wrong? Tell me."

Lillian sniffled. Meredith felt Lillian shudder and gave her a reassuring squeeze. To anyone watching it was an innocent hug. Lillian pulled back, reached into her pocket for a tissue, wiped her eyes, then blew her nose. "I'm sorry. I'm being stupid. Let's just get out of here."

"No." Meredith was firm in her response. "Something is wrong, and you need to tell me what. What about that man?"

"Remember the story I told you about this ring?" Lillian held her hand out for Meredith to see.

Meredith took Lillian's hand and held it with both hands, "Yes. It was your grandmother's, wasn't it?" Meredith asked.

"That's right. Do you remember when my mother died and I went home for the funeral? I told you how a man approached me during the calling hours and wanted to buy it from me."

"Yes … ," Meredith said hesitantly as she tried to remember the story.

"Well, I didn't tell you everything. He had seemed so nice at first. He told me he was an old family friend, and I had no reason to doubt him. He then told me that he was a collector of estate jewelry and that when he saw my ring, he had to know more about it. He began asking me questions about it, most of which I couldn't answer. Finally, he asked me if I would be interested in selling him the ring. I said no and thought that was the end of it."

"I remember that much of the story. You never told me there was more."

"It was after the service. Everyone was leaving and he came to me again. He first repeated his condolences, then he asked me again about the ring. I told him that it was not for sale, and then I remember this dark cloud came over his face. His eyes went black, and his voice was like ice. He told me that he wanted the ring and that he intended to have it. Again he offered me money for it, a lot more, and when I said no, he grabbed my arm. His grip was like a trap and it hurt. He spun me around so our faces were inches apart. I managed to pull away from him and run off. He didn't follow. I ended up with bruises on my arm where he had grabbed me. I didn't see him again, and I came home as quickly as I could. I was terrified, and I just needed to be home, here, with you, safe."

"Oh Lillian, why didn't you tell me?"

"I don't know. By the time I got back here, the bruises on my arm were gone, and I guess I didn't want to worry you."

"And you think it's him?"

"Yes, I'm sure it is."

"Come on, we have to go." Meredith took Lillian's hand and began to pull her away like a mother would a child who was in danger. There was an urgency in Meredith's plea that Lillian had heard only once before, many years ago. They had been hiking in the desert and Lillian didn't see the snake that was about to strike. She was saved by Meredith's warning. That moment flashed through Lillian's head and scared her.

"No! Meredith, what's wrong?" Lillian resisted, pulling out of Meredith's grasp.

Meredith grabbed Lillian's hand again, pulled, and said, "Nothing, we just have to leave right now."

"Merry, you're scaring me."

"Lillian, please, we have to go. Trust me." Again Meredith tugged on Lillian's hand. "Come on. We have to go. Now."

Holding hands, they made their way through the gallery crowd, all the while Meredith kept looking for the man with whom she had been talking. She didn't see him but she knew he was still around.

Before exiting the gallery, Lillian tugged on Meredith's hand, pulling her to a stop. "What's going on?" Lillian asked, facing Meredith. "Why are you acting like this?"

Meredith glanced around quickly then pulled Lillian into the ladies room. Thankfully the room was empty.

Meredith faced Lillian, looked deep into her eyes, and said, "Lillian, there are things about my past that you don't know. There isn't time now, I need you to trust me."

"I don't understand."

"You couldn't. Listen, that man I was talking to, if he is who you think he is, then we have to get away from here. He's not here for his health. He wants something, and I'm guessing that it's that ring."

"What? How do you know that?"

"Lillian, trust me. I have a feeling that I haven't had for many years, and we have to leave."

"Okay, but you have to tell me everything on the way home."

"Fine. Now let's get going."

"Promise."

"Okay, I promise."

CHAPTER TWO

Desert Highway

MEREDITH DROVE AS USUAL, and their departure from the city was un-eventful. There were no further sightings of him. The sunset was spec-tacular, and as they drove silently toward home, they began to relax.

"Meredith?"

"Yes."

"Tell me again how you ended up talking to that man."

"It just happened. I was standing there looking at that canvas, and suddenly he was there standing next to me. He didn't say anything at first, then he asked me what I thought of the painting. I said it was nice but too large for our house. He seemed quite pleasant."

"Did you tell him where we live?"

"No, I didn't. We really didn't say much else. That's when you ar-rived and things got a little weird."

"Yeah, it did, didn't it?"

"I saw how you looked at him and his reaction to you."

They rode in silence for many miles, each lost in her own thoughts before Lillian broke the silence.

"Meredith?"

"What is it, Lil?"

"Promise me that if anything ever happens to me, you'll get the ring to Max."

Meredith said nothing for a few moments as she tried to make sense of the request. Lillian's niece, Max, lived in New Hampshire and was her last remaining relative.

"What are you talking about?"

"Just promise me."

"Of course. I promise."

Meredith wasn't sure, but she thought she heard Lillian say thank you, and it was obvious there was nothing more to be said, so they drove on in silence.

It was late and the night very dark as they drove through the desert. The stars and the new moon were the only witnesses to the moving cocoon of light created by their car's headlights when Meredith noticed another set of headlights far behind them. "Lil, are you awake?"

"Yes. Why?"

"There's a car behind us."

"Well, we're not the only people who live out here."

Meredith looked in the mirror again. The lights were closer.

"They're coming up really fast."

"You know how fast people drive out here in the desert. You are the only person I know who drives anywhere near the speed limit."

"You're right, but ..." Meredith said, glancing in the mirror again.

By now her face was back lit by the reflection from the lights behind like a scene from an old movie.

The car was now close behind, too close, and there it stayed, its headlights blinding her eyes. Lillian turned and looked back, all she could see were the two bright lights boring into their car. "Merry, what're they doing? Why won't they just pass us?"

"I don't know." Meredith tried to sound unconcerned. She tapped the brakes. No change. She sped up. No change. She slowed down. No change. The car stayed close behind as if on a tether.

"Meredith?"

"Yes?"

"I'm—"

It was at that moment that there was a loud crash as their car was hit from behind and lurched forward. Meredith fought to maintain control. Lillian screamed.

"What the fu—" Meredith said, her words lost as they were hit from behind again. She managed to retain control of the car even as the terror threatened to paralyze her.

Crash. They were hit a third time. Glancing to her right, she could see tears of fear and panic beginning to cloud Lillian's eyes. When Meredith looked back, those bright, burning lights were no longer in her mirror. For a split second, confusion hit her, then she realized that the car had now pulled up alongside matching their speed.

Both women looked left, and time froze as they saw the face of the man from the gallery staring over at them with cold, dark eyes. Before either woman could react, he yanked his steering wheel toward them and the cars came together one last time. Meredith screamed as she fought for control of the car as the tires caught in the soft shoulder. Then they were rolling, tumbling, and it was over. Silence.

The car came to rest upside down, far enough off the road that it would be hard to see unless one were looking for it. Still holding the wheel, Meredith opened her eyes. It was dark. Her head throbbed, her stomach and shoulder hurt, and she could feel something warm and sticky running up her face. It took a moment for her to realize that she was hanging upside down, suspended by her seat belt. "Lil?" she heard herself say, but there was only silence. "Lillian?" she repeated, her voice loud in her mind, but again there was only silence. "Lillian!" she tried to scream but nothing came out, and the silence was overwhelming. As her eyes began to adjust to the darkness, she could just make out the lifeless form of her mate. Lillian was still next to her, but she looked like a crumpled ball of paper.

Hanging upside down, staring at Lillian, Meredith saw flashes of what had just happened. The man at the gallery, Lillian's fear when she saw him, their escape from the gallery, and the relief felt as they began the long ride home, each mile bringing them closer to their sanctuary.

Meredith remembered when the headlights first appeared behind them and she didn't give them another thought. It was only when those lights seemed to gain on them faster than reasonable that doubt began to creep in. Doubt turned to fear as the distance closed. The fear turned to dread as they were hit from behind. Then the final moment of terror when they saw him next to them. Time froze as he looked at them with a sick grimace on his face with eyes like burning embers. That's when she saw him wrench his steering wheel in their direction. It only took a second before his car crashed into theirs, but it felt like an eternity. And now, as she hung suspended upside down, those eyes filled her memory. Fighting for consciousness, she saw those eyes again through the shattered windshield. She wanted to cry out, but she couldn't.

She blinked and wiped at the tears that were filling her eyes and running down her forehead. Then blackness swept over her. She didn't know whether it was minutes or hours when she woke to see two white lights coming toward them. "Thank God. Someone's coming to help." Lillian didn't reply. Meredith looked at Lillian again and, seeing her lifeless body, she knew that Lillian would not answer her ever again. That's when something caught her attention in the faint glow created by those lights. As if reaching for Meredith, Lillian's arm was extended. Her hand had fallen open and in the palm was the ring. Lillian's last act was to try to hand it to her lover and life mate.

The lights came closer, and Meredith could hear the sound of tires crunching slowly over gravel. Finally the sound stopped and the lights went out. "They're here. We'll be all right," she thought to herself. Then the other car's door opened, the interior light came on, and she saw him. Help was not on the way. Fear gripped her. His shoes began to crunch on the gravel as he walked toward their overturned car. She could see the light from a flashlight as he swept it back and forth as he approached. The pain in her shoulder was beyond any that she had ever felt, but she endured it as she reached for Lillian's outstretched hand. She touched the ring; it still radiated Lillian's warmth. Meredith grabbed it and put it in her mouth, tucking it between her cheek and gum as his footsteps became louder. It was at that moment the pain, the fear, and the shock of what had happened overcame her. She didn't hear any more steps.

The black silence of the desert night was broken only by the thin beam of his flashlight as he approached the overturned car. Then, without even realizing it, he started whistling. It was a simple tune, one that he used to whistle as a child to chase away the demons of the night. He could see the car. It was upside down, all the windows were either cracked or broken. The light from his flashlight reflected off the bits of glass that were scattered in the sand like so many diamonds. The car's body was a mass of crumpled, crushed metal. Walking slowly around it, he swept the beam over the wreck as he inspected the results of his handiwork.

There was no movement and no sound save for his whistling. The passenger door was ajar. He leaned over and shone his light inside the car. He could see two shapes that he knew were the two women. The one nearest the passenger door was twisted into a grotesque shape, her neck obviously broken. The other one was hanging upside down, suspended by her seat belt. She didn't interest him. He knelt down next to the passenger door and leaned into the car. "Okay, bitch. Come to Papa," he mumbled under his breath. Then, putting his flashlight in his mouth, he grabbed one of her arms and began to pull her out of the car. Not being able to hold the beam steady as he pulled, the shadows created by the light seemed to bring the corpse to life and were made all the more eerie by the lifeless movement of her head, her neck broken.

As soon as she was mostly out of the car, he dropped her arm, took the flashlight out of his mouth and washed it over her looking for the ring. It wasn't on either hand. He searched her clothes with the same result. "Son of a bitch. Where is it?" He pulled her farther away from the car, then lying on his belly, he snaked his way into the car where she had been. His flashlight created and dispelled shadows around the interior. His hands ran through the broken glass and debris, and found nothing.

The other woman—the one upside down behind the wheel—appeared to be dead as well. He checked her hands and pockets and noticed she was warmer than the first one. He felt for a pulse. It was faint. She was still alive. Wriggling back out of the car, that feeling of not being in control began to overwhelm him; he kicked at the ground in frustration, sending gravel flying into the night. That kick returned him to sanity, and he began to consider his options as he walked around the car. "I should kill her," he thought. Then as he reached the door on her side of the car, he stopped and reconsidered. It was one thing to cause a death by creating an accident and quite another to do it deliberately with one's own hands. "No, I'm not a murderer." His decision made, he squatted by the door and pointed his light on her lifeless upside-down form. "If you live, I'll find you, and I will have that ring," he said softly. Then he stood, turned, and walked back to his car. The inky darkness of the desert night was beginning to give way to the pre-dawn light as he drove off.

CHAPTER THREE

DARK DAWN

SHE WAS SPINNING AROUND, first upside down, then sideways. The great beast was tossing her around like a rag doll. Everything hurt, she cried out in pain. The sound of her voice startled her. The violent shaking stopped. Suddenly she was in a tree suspended upside down. She couldn't see what had hold of her, then she felt something in her mouth followed by a buzzing sound. It was hot. Her mouth was dry, and that something stuck to the inside of her cheek. It hurt to move. Meredith tried to open her eyes. A bright light blinded her, forcing her eyes to squeeze shut. In the sanctuary of darkness, she found herself driving down a highway, then a face appeared, staring at her. She gasped.

Despite the brightness, she began opening her eyes for a second time, hoping the light would make the face go away. The bright light bore into her brain like a drill, and the image faded. The intense pain forced her to scrunch her eyes closed again and after a long moment she began to open them for a third time. The bright light was only the sun, but it was in the wrong place. She thought to herself. "That's weird. Where am I?" She stared at the sun and began to remember. The crash, his face, then nothing.

Her head was pounding as she turned to where Lillian had been sitting. The pounding became almost unbearable, and bright lights flashed behind her eyes. She had to close them tightly and take a deep breath before opening them again slowly. Lillian wasn't there. That's when she saw a shape outside the car in the sand. Meredith called out, "Lillian." She heard it in her head, only no sound came from her lips. Her mouth was dry as a bone, and there was something stuck to the inside of her cheek. She moved her tongue around in circles, searching for the slightest bit of saliva where there was none. Her tongue hit the object that was stuck to her cheek, and suddenly all the events of the past hours came flooding back to her. Her tongue dislodged the ring, and she spit it out, then managed to croak a feeble "Lillian!" That squeak of a sound sounded like a freight train in her head, and she had to close her eyes again and breathe deeply. There was no reply. All she heard was the buzzing of flies as she tried frantically to lick her lips, to swallow, to find some trace of moisture. "Lillian," she cried again, this time with more force, her increasing panic overcoming the pain in her head. There was no movement, save for a small lizard that skittered across the sand and over Lillian's leg.

Meredith's senses were returning. She was hanging upside down, suspended by her seat belt. She tried to open the buckle. The pressure on it made that nearly impossible. She tried moving her legs. She didn't feel anything. She began to panic. "Lillian. Help me." Her cry was met with silence, then to herself she said, "Okay … Stop it … Think … You're alive … Lillian needs you." The sound of her voice was somehow comforting. She tried the buckle again, only this time, she tried to push herself up to take some of the pressure off of it. It took several tries before the buckle released and she landed on her head and shoulder. Her legs were still on top of the steering wheel, and she now could feel them. Catching her breath, she slowly wriggled her legs free of the wheel and fell in a heap onto the roof of the car. Because her door was jammed shut, she began dragging herself toward the missing door and Lillian. Small shards of broken glass cut at her arms as she pulled herself out. As soon as she was free of the car, she rolled onto her back, exhausted, and rested for a moment. She could feel the heat of the sand, and she had to press her arm over her eyes to block the blinding sun. It felt so good, so comforting.

She was on a beach. The one she and Lillian had visited in Mexico, years ago. They were lying next to each other in the sand, feeling the warmth of mother earth on their backs and the sun baking their faces. The cry of a bird brought her back to the present. Lillian! Meredith turned her head and saw Lillian, face down, just a few feet away lying there, no sign of life. "Lillian," she said, softly at first as she struggled to sit up. "Lillian." This time louder, more forceful. There was no reaction. Meredith's heart began to pound, and she scrambled to her knees and crawled over to the limp body. As soon as she was near and saw the way Lillian's head lolled to one side, she knew. From her experiences living on the commune and having killed many a chicken, she knew that Lillian's neck was broken.

Overwhelming despair washed over Meredith as she cried out and fell on top of her friend and lover, sobbing uncontrollably. "Why?" she kept crying out over and over. She ran her fingers through Lillian's hair, caressed her lifeless face. For those few moments, it was as if Meredith were dreaming. She did not see or feel the dirt and dust from the violence they had just endured. Instead she saw her lover as if still asleep on the next pillow, her hair smooth and silky. A large bloody tangle in Lillian's hair brought Meredith back to the present, and the horror of the night flooded back. It was as if some primeval instinct of survival suddenly surfaced.

She sat up. The ring. Where was it? She remembered taking it from Lillian's lifeless hand. She remembered spitting something out as she hung upside down in the car. Crawling back to the car, she peered through the broken window. Bits of shattered glass and debris covered the inside of the roof of the overturned car. The ring has to be here, she thought. Question turned to doubt, then to panic when she didn't see it. Wriggling through the window, she frantically felt around for the ring. Dust mixed with sweat. In a hoarse whisper she hissed, "Come on. Where are you?" Then her fingers touched something smooth and round. Gingerly she picked up the object. Sweat dripped into her eyes as she looked at the ring. She stopped, and a calmness flooded over her. Slowly she slid back out of the car and returned to Lillian's lifeless body.

Her voice, shaky, yet firm, broke the silence of the desert morning as she spoke to her dead companion. "Lillian, I have the ring. He didn't get it. It's here with me."

Almost expecting an answer back, she sat next to Lillian. Studying the ring, Meredith remembered her promise made those few hours ago. It seemed like a lifetime had passed since that moment in the dark of the car as they drove through the desert night. Now all she could remember was Lillian's voice, asking for a promise that if anything were ever to happen to her, the ring must be given to her niece Max.

The cry of a bird brought Meredith back to the present. She stood, and as she did, the world went black for a moment. She covered her eyes and, before opening them again, took several deep breaths. The head rush had passed. She dragged Lillian's body back to the car and covered her in a blanket. It just seemed the right thing to do. Kneeling down, she kissed Lillian one last time, then she spoke the last words she would ever say to her life's soulmate: "Forgive me, my love, but I can't stay here; it's not safe. I've got to go now. I'm taking the ring to Max."

With the ring in her pocket, Merdeith stood and began the hike toward home.

Memories of a long forgotten past surged through her as she walked. Her every move was reactive. There could be no police, not yet. The car was well off the road, and chances were good that it would not be found right away. Only after she was safely away would she call and report the accident. But not until she was safe. She walked on, oblivious to the heat as well as the aches and pains that coursed through her body. She was in survival mode. She had a promise to fulfill. She would find Max and deliver the ring. Then they would grieve together.

The fear she felt those many years ago, before Lillian, before the farm, was back and it kept her going. Its cause was different today, but the fear was the same. As the past mixed with the present, a confused picture formed inside her head. She knew what she had to do, and instinctively she knew how to do it.

As soon as the farm was in sight, she stopped and allowed herself to rest for a moment, gazing over the tranquil scene. It looked so peaceful and welcoming. In that moment, she imagined Lillian stepping out onto the porch with a glass of ice cold lemonade in her hand welcoming her home. "No. Lillian's gone. There will be time to rest later," Meredith thought as she shook the image out of her head, willing her exhausted and bruised body to continue. Her pace quickened as she neared their home, their place of sanctuary and comfort for all those years where she could … a place where she could what?

Reality returned as she stepped onto the porch. Something was wrong, very wrong, and suddenly her legs felt like lead as if some unseen evil force was smothering her, sucking the life out of her. The door was ajar, and where the knob and lock should have been, there was just a hole. Her heart pounded as she approached the door. All at once that numbing weariness that was consuming her was transformed into anger and rage.

Her companion had been taken from her, that was enough. She was not going to allow their home and the memory of their life together to be desecrated. She picked up a shovel that leaned against the house as she approached the door. She paused, listening for any sound, looking for any sign that would indicate the presence of an intruder. Her focus was so intense that she didn't feel the soft breeze caressing her hot skin nor did she hear the cry of the eagle soaring above. She only felt her heartbeat pounding in her chest and echoing in her ears as she pushed the door open.

The scene that greeted her was one of total chaos. Shelves had been swept clear, their contents all over the floor. Furniture had been torn and shredded. Drawers were pulled out, their contents on the floor. It was as if a tornado had gone through the house. She was numb. She began to walk gingerly through the physical remains of her life with Lillian. In a trance, she would stop now and then to pick up some object, a memory of her life with Lillian. Meredith began talking to herself. "That miserable son of a bitch. Why? Why did he do this?"

She reached in her pocket, felt the ring, and the answer came to her.

"He wanted the ring. That's why."

"What was so special about this ring?" she wondered. She couldn't remember if Lillian had ever told her.

"Who are you?" Meredith asked to the silent room.

As she made her way through the destroyed house, the numbness began to wear off and was replaced by her determination to survive. She thought of the irony. "I wasn't the only one who had secrets. Lillian never told me the whole story of the ring. And now she's dead because of it."

Meredith knew what she had to do. She would get her things, those special things she kept for such an emergency, and she would leave. She had to before the body was found and the police showed up. When she was safely away, she would make the call, disappear, and go find Max. Then, she would go find the bastard who did this and … Her thoughts ended there.

A quick shower, some aspirin, and a change of clothes made her feel more human, and after some food and a cup of coffee, she was ready. She went to the spot in her bedroom where hidden under a floorboard was her secret stash that even Lillian hadn't known about.

CHAPTER FOUR

FRIENDS AND LOVERS

THE EARLY MORNING BREAKFAST CROWD that had filled Paula's General store had already begun to thin out by the time Jack arrived and took a seat at the counter.

"Mornin,' Jack."

"Mornin,' Beverly."

"What's with the face?" she asked as she poured his coffee. But as soon as she asked the question, she knew the answer. Before Jack could respond, she said, "He's back, isn't he?"

"Yes. Is it that obvious?"

"Sorry, it is."

Jack picked up his cup and took a sip of the steaming liquid. He said nothing as he put the cup down and looked away.

Andy had returned, and Max had gone back to him as she always did. No one particularly liked Andy, especially Jack. Andy was probably closer to Jack's age than Max's, but that didn't matter. Andy had a slight accent that was impossible to identify. His clothes were always nondescript, yet stylish. He was one of those people who just always seemed at home no matter where that was. Upon meeting him, he seemed like an old friend, and then when he was gone, the question of who he was remained. But more than the mystery of who Andy was, it was the effect he had on Max that Jack despised.

Whenever Andy showed up, any lingering animosity that Max held for him after his last departure would wane quickly and she would fall into him again. Then suddenly, without any warning, he would disappear again, leaving Max crushed and Jack to pick up the pieces.

Andy's absences were sometimes short, only weeks, and the longest had been almost a year. His departures never came with explanations or goodbyes and now he was back.

Beverly wanted to say more. Jack didn't deserve this, but she knew Jack wouldn't listen. So she just turned away, walked toward the other end of the counter to greet a new customer, leaving Jack sitting there with his thoughts and coffee.

Jack Beale had come to Rye, New Hampshire nearly twenty years ago at the insistence of his friend Tom, who was now the town detective. They had met back in their twenties while Jack was bartending in one of Miami's hottest clubs. Jack had moved to Miami right after college to escape some bad memories and start over. His college sweetheart had dumped him on graduation day and after the obligatory pity party he decided that he needed a fresh start as far from home as possible. He packed up his car and drove, finally coming to a stop in Miami, and that's where he stayed.

Back then, Tom was on the vice squad in Miami and often visited the club Jack worked in. Tom befriended Jack as a potential source of information. Eventually they became good friends, and Jack became a part of Tom's family. Tom's wife took it as a personal challenge to find Jack a woman. Her efforts resulted in Jack having a very active social life, many friends who happened to be girls, but no girlfriend.

"Hey Jack." Tom's voice startled Jack as much as the clap on the back, as Tom took the seat next to Jack.

"Hi Tom," came the unenthusiastic reply.

Tom looked at him with concern.

"You okay?" he asked as Beverly filled his cup. Looking up at her, he caught the look on her face. "Oh," he said and glanced over at Jack again.

"Yeah. I'm fine," mumbled Jack.

Tom knew from Beverly's look that Jack wasn't and there was only one reason for this kind of malaise in Jack. It was Max. More specifically, another man and Max, and it had to be Andy.

"Sorry man," Tom said. "Max?"

"Yeah."

Even though Max and Jack were friends, they really were more without being so. Jack was in love with her, but he couldn't go there. Whenever he approached that place where you are totally exposed, where you have nothing to hide, where you are at one with another, he would see Marie and retreat. Even after all these years, he had never recovered from her death.

For Max, Jack was a safety net. He was always there for her. He would help her pick up the pieces whenever an affair went wrong. They were best friends, they hung out, they shared secrets, they were lovers in every way save the final one. Jack always backed away, and Max needed more. So she lived her own life simultaneously with Jack and without Jack.

As crazy as it would make Jack whenever Max would go out with other guys, there was only one who could put him into such a funk: Andy. "You want to talk about it?" asked Tom.

"Not really." Jack took another sip of his coffee and continued to stare straight ahead. Tom got the hint and backed off, joining Jack in silence.

Memories flooded Tom's head. He remembered how he and Jack had met in Miami all those years ago.

Jack was bartending, and Tom was working vice. Vice had a lot of interest in many of the patrons of that club, one in particular: Markus Ravenowicz. Often Jack or one of the other bartenders would be asked to work at private parties by the patrons of the club. These parties were a welcome change of pace and could be very lucrative. The prize was when Ravenowicz would host a party on his sailing yacht, *Raven*. His parties were legendary. Sometimes they were dockside, and very formal with seemingly hundreds of guests coming and going throughout the night and often ending at dawn. Other times, his parties were more intimate and relaxed as guests would spend a day out on the water under sail. These parties were Jack's favorites because he had the opportunity to help the crew in sailing the *Raven*. For Tom, the parties were an opportunity, and he took advantage of Jack's friendship to get information about Ravenowicz. Occasionally, these sailing parties would last several days while the *Raven* sailed to the Bahamas or the Keys. After the first time Jack had gone on one of the extended parties, he confided in Tom that his goal in life was now to own his own boat and to spend his life sailing around the Caribbean and maybe even the world.

"Why does she do it?" Jack's voice broke the silence of cups clanking, eggs cooking, and the general din of a busy breakfast place.

It took Tom a second to come back to the present. "Do what?"

"Why does Max keep going back to him?"

"I don't know."

"He treats her like shit. He shows up out of the blue. She gets angry at him, for what, all of thirty seconds, then she just melts, and off they go back to his place and she's gone for days. He hangs around for a few weeks, she's all googly-eyed and in another world, and then one day, he just takes off without so much as a goodbye. She then comes to me crying, and I have to help her deal with it."

"I know, man. That sucks."

CHAPTER FIVE

Miami Vice

JACK HAD BECOME Ravenowicz's favored bartender, and one day Jack's dream took a large step toward becoming a reality. Ravenowicz came into the club and asked if Jack would like to join his crew for an extended cruise around the Caribbean. The offer floored Jack. He probably would have done it for free, but when Ravenowicz offered to pay him, Jack couldn't say yes fast enough. They were to sail in two weeks.

Jack couldn't wait to tell Tom. That night, they went out for drinks and Jack was so excited he couldn't shut up. He kept talking about what a great opportunity it was. Tom listened in polite silence, but finally the look on his face caused Jack to stop and ask what was wrong.

It took a minute before Tom was able to answer. He didn't want to be a wet blanket so he asked Jack what he knew about Ravenowicz.

Jack sat there, staring as if Tom had three eyes, then said, "Not much other than the fact that he is ridiculously rich, he throws great parties, and he wants to pay me a lot of money to go sailing."

Tom didn't want to crush Jack's dream, but wanted to make sure that he understood. There is a difference between knowing something to be true but not being willing to admit it, and having someone actually say the words, giving them substance.

Before Tom could say anything else, Jack said with a touch of sarcasm, "Okay, you're the cop and now you are going to tell me that Markus Ravenowicz is some kind of a drug lord and that it would be a bad idea for me to do this."

Tom's silence answered his question.

They argued well into the night about what was or wasn't true about Markus Ravenowicz. In the end, Tom couldn't change Jack's mind. All Jack saw was blue skies, bluer water, fair winds, beautiful women, and exotic ports of call. Before they parted, Tom gave Jack a special number he could call anytime day or night.

Weeks passed with only one quick call from Jack. He was in Martinique and had called to say hello and how wrong Tom had been about everything. Shortly after that call things began to change for Jack.

After Martinique they sailed west to Belize. Their first stop was Placencia Village where they bought some lobsters and bread from a local fisherman and his daughter. Another boat joined them and after a couple of days of partying, the other boat sailed off leaving one person behind on the *Raven*. They sailed to Belize City immediately.

Anchoring near the city, south of Swallow Caye, Ravenowicz, several members of his crew, and the man who had joined them in Placencia left the yacht. It would be several days before they were to return. In their absence, life on the yacht was pretty relaxed. While there was work to be done in preparation for the next leg of their journey, the crew also found time to get off the yacht and explore. Provisioning the bar and wine cellar was fairly easy, so Jack got a little more time off than some other crew members. A day was spent exploring some of the cayes out by the reef, St. George's, Caye Caulker, and Ambergris. It was paradise, and he vowed to return someday.

The next day, his employer returned to the yacht with several new guests. The relaxed atmosphere vaporized, replaced by a palpable tension. Whenever Ravenowicz was not present, his guests' conversations were whispered and punctuated with furtive glances. In his presence, their smiles seemed forced and their pleasant banter strained. Jack and the crew could feel and see this change, so they just went about their jobs preparing for the next day's departure and tried to remain as invisible as possible.

That night it was hot and the air still. Jack went up on deck for some air. At first he didn't see anyone else, but he could hear muffled voices. The moon had not yet risen. He knew he shouldn't be there, but he couldn't bring himself to leave. Hidden in the shadows, his eyes adjusted to the darkness, he could see that the man who had joined them in Placencia was seated in a chair and Ravenowicz was standing in front of him. Their voices rose and fell, but the words remained unclear. Jack could see their silhouettes against the city lights. It was obvious this was not a social conversation. Suddenly there was a bright flash followed by a sharp pop. Blinded by the flash, Jack didn't have to see to know what had just happened. The sound of something being dragged across the deck followed by a splash was confirmation enough for Jack. He remained hidden in the shadows, not daring to breathe until he was sure he was alone on deck. It was only then, with his heart pounding, that he slowly, carefully, and silently made his way back to his quarters. He lay in his bunk, awake, for the rest of the night, hoping and praying that no one had seen him.

The next day the guests, minus one, left the yacht amid feigned smiles and cold handshakes. No one knew that Jack had witnessed the murder, so he just had to stay cool and get back to Miami alive. When they finally returned to Miami, he reported to Tom what he had witnessed and quit bartending.

CHAPTER SIX

PARADISE FOUND AND LOST

BEVERLY CAME BY with some more coffee. "You guys want something to eat? You look like you're at a funeral, and you're bumming me out. How about some of our special stuffed french toast? That'll make you feel better."

Jack looked up. "Sure, that would be good. Thanks."

She looked at Tom, and he nodded yes as well.

"What should I do?" Jack asked without looking at Tom.

"I'm not sure what you should do, but I do know what you shouldn't do. You shouldn't keep beating yourself up like this. You know you two belong together."

"Your opinion."

"I know." Stalemate. Their heads turned back forward and silence followed. Tom's thoughts drifted.

It had been shortly after leaving the *Raven* that Jack's grandmother died, leaving him a modest estate. It was enough, combined with what he had been paid by Markus Ravenowicz, to allow him to buy his dream boat, and if he didn't live an extravagant lifestyle, he wouldn't have to work either. He found an old fiberglass sloop. He named her *Irrepressible*. Thirty-eight feet of sweat and toil became his new home as he began to live his dream. Jack and Tom still maintained contact, even though it was sporadic.

Tom glanced over at Jack who was still staring straight ahead, holding his cup of coffee. So much had happened since those days. He smiled as he pictured Jack, the swashbuckling young lad, sailing across the deep blue Caribbean all those years ago. While Jack lived out his dreams, Tom's life changed also. His job had become increasingly dangerous, and his wife convinced him to leave Miami. The end result was a move to a much quieter Rye, New Hampshire. Unable to reach Jack to tell him about his departure from Miami, Tom didn't know if he would ever see his friend again. As the two friends sat in silence sipping their coffees on this cold winter's day, Tom remembered that day when he answered the phone and it was Jack.

One day a call came through from the islands. After the initial greetings and small talk, Jack blurted out the real reason for his call. He had met the girl of his dreams and he had to tell someone. He had been anchored off Jost Van Dyke in the British Virgin Islands near a little beach bar. There were dozens of other boats in the anchorage, and all crew members must have had the same idea: go ashore, have some dinner and a few drinks. As it turned out, it was beach barbecue night. The rum was flowing freely, music was playing, and before long, there was a full blown party in progress. That's when he met her.

She was dancing with a group of other revelers to some Bob Marley song. Her dark, tanned skin glistened in the soft light of the tiki torches. Her movements were slow and sensuous as she closed her eyes and felt the beat of the music. He couldn't stop staring at her.

He had never seen anyone so beautiful, so desirable, and so free. The song ended, and she opened her eyes, looked in his direction, and caught him staring at her. She smiled and walked straight toward him. He froze. Blame it on the rum, blame it on the moon, blame it on whatever you want, but he couldn't move.

Her name was Marie, and her French accent was even sexier than her dancing. They danced, they drank, and they went back to his boat and made love until sunrise, then slept in each other's arms. He woke first and laid there watching Marie sleep. He hadn't been dreaming. She was perfect. Her skin was soft and smooth, the color of coffee, unblemished by tan lines or any other evidence of civilization. Her face was so peaceful and relaxed. It was innocent, like that of a young child not yet schooled in the realities of life. When she woke, they made love again.

Marie moved onto *Irrepressible* and they lived each day as if it were the last. They spent their days sailing, swimming, and snorkeling as they explored the islands that made up the British Virgin Islands. Nights were reserved for each other. Jack reveled in the exuberance with which Marie gave of herself, nothing was hidden, no secrets, no fears. With her, his heart was full and he was content.

Because of two past events, he had built a wall against ever becoming close to another woman. The first was when his college love had abandoned him on graduation day, and despite the many attempts of Tom's wife to find him another girlfriend, Jack's defenses remained impenetrable. The second was the cold-blooded execution he witnessed on the *Raven*. He had lost his capacity to see goodness in people. Marie changed all that.

Jack had discovered things about himself that he had never known, and felt no shame or embarrassment in sharing them with her. He had never felt such comfort and trust with anyone in his whole life. Jack never asked anything of her nor she of him; each seemed to know exactly what the other needed and all was freely given. It was as if their souls had been searching for each other and now they were complete. They were about to sail easterly to St. Martin, then begin the slow turn southward visiting St. Kitts, Nevis, over to Antigua, Guadeloupe, Dominica and Martinique. He just wanted Tom to know.

"More coffee?" Beverly's question brought Tom back to the present.

"Sure."

As she filled his cup she looked toward Jack who was still sitting there silently staring straight ahead, lost in his thoughts. "Him?"

"Might as well," responded Tom and she topped off Jack's cup.

Jack didn't move. He just sat there. Tom took a sip of his coffee and remembered the next call.

The next call from Jack, or rather about Jack, was from the police in Martinique. It was a confusing story about a shooting. Marie had been killed, and Jack needed his help. Tom left immediately, and it seemed to take forever, but finally he arrived in Martinique. Jack had not left his hotel room since the shooting, and he was a mess. It took a while before Tom was able to piece together what had happened since all Jack kept repeating was, "She's gone. Marie's gone."

Jack and Marie had been sitting in an outdoor cafe, enjoying a perfect tropical night when down the street, there were some loud shouts followed by a loud popping sound. The same popping sound Jack had heard only once before. Nearly forgotten memories flashed through Jack's head and his heart raced. He looked at Marie; she looked back at him with a strange surprised look on her face and said, "Je t'aime toujours." As she slumped forward, he saw a red stain coming through her white blouse. He screamed, and as he jumped up, he knocked over the table and caught her limp body as it crumpled to the street. They fell together, he holding her, screaming for help, which would do no good. He didn't remember much else. The police filled in other details. A stray shot from a violent argument up the street had taken her.

The next several weeks were a blur as Tom convinced Jack to return to New Hampshire with him. Jack wouldn't even consider leaving his boat behind, so they sailed north. It would be a long, slow healing process, and the sail north would be a good place to start.

"Breakfast," Beverly announced as she placed two platters of special stuffed french toast in front of the two men and refilled their coffees.

"You know Jack, it doesn't have to be this way," said Tom.

"I know."

"You want me to take care of Andy for you?" Tom asked with a slight grin and a touch of sarcasm.

"No. I don't want you to take care of him. I'll deal with it," replied Jack.

"Mmmm, this is good," said Tom as he swallowed his first bite. "Oh by the way, when's Courtney leaving on her vacation?" he asked, changing the subject.

"I'm taking her to the airport in a couple of weeks."

"Where's she off to this time?"

"Not sure. Somewhere warm, the Caribbean I think. You know how she is. Winter comes and she needs warmth, so she takes off in search of sun, rum, and men."

"We should all be so lucky."

"Yeah."

CHAPTER SEVEN

BEN'S

OTHER THAN TOM, COURTNEY was about the only other person in town who really knew the details of Jack's past. She was his landlord and the owner of Ben's Place, a local restaurant and bar on the harbor. It had been there for as long as anyone could remember and was one of several local watering holes. Its founder, Ben Crouse, had died shortly before Tom's arrival in town, and his nieces Courtney and Kara inherited the place. They were fresh out of college but had worked at Ben's since before high school so they knew the business. They moved into Ben's house across the street, an old, two-story cottage with a wraparound front porch and rocking chairs. Out back there was an old barn.

The cottage's first floor was one large, open room with a kitchen area in one corner. Upstairs, there were two small bedrooms and a bath. Ben had never married nor had he ever thrown anything out, so before the girls were able to move in, mountains of old stuff had to be cleaned out. There were yard sales, work parties, and many trips to the dump. Eventually bare walls and clear floors emerged, and the house's potential could be seen. After refinishing the floors, and painting the walls and trim, the transformation from decrepit old house to an airy, quaint, seaside cottage was complete.

The girls always had their own ideas about what the restaurant should be. They quickly changed Ben's from the small, summer restaurant into a much larger destination showplace. An outdoor deck was added, and in the summer, it was the place to be. Winters, the old woodstove kept the bar cozy and warm. Kara eventually married and moved to a farm in Vermont, and Courtney continued to run Ben's.

Even though Tom was new to town, he made friends quickly. Courtney was one of the first, and as soon as he received that call from Jack, he went to her and told her what he knew of the happenings in Martinique. Then he asked for her help. After listening, she couldn't say no. With that conversation, Jack's future was planned. She wanted to build an apartment in the barn behind her cottage. Jack needed a place to stay, he was handy with tools, he could keep his boat in the harbor, and as a bonus, he knew how to bartend.

Tom and Courtney became Jack's closest friends as he settled into town. He fit right in, and as outgoing as he seemed to be, there was a private side that few were allowed to see. He didn't discuss his past, and people around town didn't ask. Only Tom and Courtney knew the truth; whenever the subject came up, their reply was always, "I know what you know. If you're that curious, why don't you ask him yourself?" This always led to speculation that his two friends knew more than they let on, but no one ever asked Jack.

While he never had a formal job, he always was busy, if not working for Courtney, then helping someone else with something. Word around town was that he was well off, as evidenced by his boat and his lifestyle that was modest but comfortable. He never had a girlfriend although he had many friends who were girls, Max being the primary one. The fact that he ran nearly every day added to the mystery. Most locals couldn't understand why anyone would want to do that. Sometimes he ran alone, sometimes with his running club. The weather didn't matter—hot, cold, windy, rainy, day or night, he ran. For that, locals thought him crazy, although there were some women in town who would discreetly admit he did have great legs and a nice tush, as a result of all that running.

CHAPTER EIGHT

MAX

A DEEP FREEZE had descended on the seacoast in the weeks since Tom and Jack had shared breakfast. The temperature had barely risen above zero for several days despite the sun's best efforts. The salt marshes around Rye Harbor were capped with ice. The creek feeding the marshes was at a standstill, and the harbor was nearly solid. The landscape looked like a picture of the Arctic in *National Geographic*. The boats in the harbor were blocked in, and the fishermen hadn't been able to go out for a week. If you did brave the outdoors, your lungs hurt the minute you inhaled. The hairs in your nose would freeze with your first breath, and the intense cold would penetrate your forehead and your eyes would ache with the same kind of ache you would get when eating ice cream too fast.

The usual crowd was at Paula's General Store for coffee and the day's local gossip. You could go there for some basic groceries or supplies, a quick breakfast, a sandwich to go, or just a cup of coffee and good conversation. Fred and John, two of the local fishermen, were there. Beverly was behind the counter. "Hey Fred. Harbor still frozen? Coffee?" she asked, waving a pot in his direction.

"Hi Beverly. Nearly so. Yes, black" was his cryptic reply.

"John, how about you?" she asked, as she filled Fred's mug.

"Please." She poured.

Both men had been down at the harbor early checking their boats. There was no way to actually go out to the boats since the harbor was frozen and their dinghies were locked in the ice at the wharf. All they had been able to do was stand there in the cold and look out at their boats, an activity which didn't last too long. Now, holding their cups as hand warmers, the two men sipped the steaming brew.

"Good coffee Beverly," said Fred, but she was already off taking care of someone else and didn't hear him.

At the end of the counter, the new guy was sitting, reading his *Boston Globe*. Beverly stopped to refresh his cup. "Anything good in the paper?" she asked, as she refilled his cup.

He looked up at her and in a quiet voice said, "No. Not really."

"Usually isn't," was her reply, and she moved on.

He never had much to say, but you could tell he was taking it all in. He had been seen at Ben's Place every day this past week around four o'clock by everyone who made the rounds. His name was Franz, but everyone called him Scotch and Soda Man because that's what he drank.

Coffee and breakfast at Paula's, split up and go about your daily business, then meet at Ben's to recap the day before drifting home or to another bar for a nightcap. This was the circadian rhythm of Rye Harbor. There were probably another dozen or so people at Paula's that morning when Jack walked in. He made the rounds, said hi to John and Fred, chatted about the cold snap, kissed Beverly good morning on the cheek, nodded to Scotch and Soda Man, and took a seat at the counter as Beverly poured his coffee.

Jack had just returned from taking Courtney to the airport for her midwinter vacation. It was an early morning flight, and now he was looking forward to breakfast. Beverly was pouring him a cup of coffee as he was taking off his coat when the door slammed shut, followed by a wave of cold air. Everyone turned to see who had just come in.

It was Max. Andy was finally gone again. Jack was back to being the "good" friend, and although she was almost back to normal, he wasn't. He looked at her for a moment while she stamped the snow off her feet and began removing her mittens. He could feel his heartbeat quicken. She looked great. Her red hair cascaded out from under the large fur hat she was wearing. Her nose and cheeks were pink from the cold, and her eyes were aglow. She was visibly excited. She pretty much knew everyone and everything that goes on around town, and as she began looking around, Jack turned back to his coffee, trying not to give away his excitement at seeing her.

At five-feet-four-inches with an athletic figure, a head of red hair, and an independent spirit, there was something about her that made her irresistible to men. Max, the head bartender at Ben's Place, came to Rye about five years after Jack. When she arrived, all the men around the harbor acted like fools trying to be the first to get to know her. That initial frenzy didn't last too long, and Jack won the competition for her friendship. Others would win her heart from time to time, but Jack became the trusted friend. He was safe. A part of him had never fully recovered from Marie's death and that kept him from being able to open up to Max in the way that his heart wanted. So he remained on the sidelines, ready to help her pick up the pieces when things didn't work out, and it killed him.

Most of the time Jack was able to deal with her affairs, since that's all they were, but Andy was different. He and Max had dated off and on for years in a relationship of extremes, alternating between passion and loathing. Throughout, Jack stood by and watched as Andy played her, over and over. She deserved better, but where Andy was concerned, she wore blinders.

As soon as she saw Jack, she rushed over to him, and asked "Did you hear?"

"Good morning Max," Jack said, ignoring her question.

With a slight huff, she started again, "Good morning Jack. Did you hear?"

Conversations lulled as everyone paused to overhear what Max had to say.

"Hear what?"

"About the abandoned car that was found up the road early this morning."

"What car? I drove Courtney to the airport early this morning, and I didn't see any car."

"Neither did I," chimed in Fred.

Max shot him a look. He looked back and shrugged, "I was just saying: I drove down to the harbor before sunrise and I didn't see anything either. What's the big deal?"

"Fred, give her a chance. I'm sure that this must be big," Jack said, with a bit of teasing sarcasm in his voice and the beginnings of a smile. "Go on Max."

By now the conversational lull had turned into silence save for the occasional clinking of a spoon or fork against glass. Everyone's attention was focused on Max.

"Okay, you remember how last week I got a ticket from one of those new officers in the PD when I was on the way to work? It was totally bogus, and he was just being a jerk about it. Well anyway, I stopped by the station this morning to see if Tom could help me out with that ticket. He didn't have much time to talk because he said he was busy. There was a car found abandoned on the boulevard early in the morning. Of course, I couldn't let him off that easy. You know how it is, and he's such a nice guy—too bad he's married," she said teasingly as she looked at Jack. He motioned for her to continue with the story.

"Anyways, he told me about how this car was found abandoned on the side of the road right near where the boulevard crosses that creek, just before the turn into Ben's. All that was in the car was a pocketbook in the front seat. Nothing else. No luggage, nothing. There wasn't much in it, just a wallet with some cash and a driver's license."

Jack interrupted asking the obvious question. "So if there was a license wouldn't that make it easy to find out who belongs to the car?"

"That's what I thought," said Max. "But Tom told me the license turned out to be a fake."

"What about the car's plates?"

"They were from New Mexico, and he was waiting to hear back on them."

"Where's the car now?"

"It's at the station," Max said.

"When did you say they found the car?" asked Jack.

"He said it was really early in the morning, before sunrise. I guess one of the cruisers was, well, cruising around, and he saw this car on the side of the road. Remember how cold it was? No one was out and there wasn't much of a moon so it was really dark. Anyway, he saw this car sitting by the road. It was unlocked, the stuff was on the front seat, and there was no one around. It seemed strange, so he called it in and then had it towed," answered Max.

Jack thought about this for a few seconds, then asked, "No luggage? Nothing?"

"Apparently not."

"You said the car was from New Mexico?"

"Yeah. Strange, huh? You'll have to ask Tom if you want to know more. I'm just trying to tell you what I found out."

"You're right Max. It is pretty strange."

This story set the tone for the morning's gossip and conversation at Paula's. It was too cold out to rush off anywhere so the crowd stayed and replayed the story over and over. Theories abounded, and Jack could see this would keep the rumor mills fueled for at least a week.

CHAPTER NINE

UNHAPPY HOUR

DESPITE THE FRIGID TEMPERATURE, Jack had decided to go for a short run. It was about noon when he finally laced on his running shoes and headed out the door. The sun was at its peak and the temperature was maybe ten degrees, but the wind chill made it feel well below zero. He didn't plan to run very far, only three miles or so, just enough to break a sweat and feel refreshed. As he ran, Jack, like everyone else, kept thinking about the story Max told everyone that morning. Who was the driver? Where did she go? Why was the car abandoned? Was there more than one occupant? Was there some innocent explanation, or was it something else? The one thing Jack was sure of was that this mystery would keep everyone going for quite a while. After all, New Hampshire winters are long and slow, and diversions are needed.

After a shower and short nap, Jack was sufficiently rejuvenated and headed over to Ben's Place for some late afternoon post-run rehydration. When he arrived just after 5:30, it was almost dark and Max was behind the bar serving all the usual suspects. Although this was not the same cast from the breakfast crowd at Paula's, the characters were much the same. The only person who had been in Paula's when Max broke the news was Scotch and Soda Man, and he was in his usual seat at the end of the bar.

Jack nodded a silent hello to Scotch and Soda Man, who nodded back. Besides Scotch and Soda Man, Leo, Ralph, and Paulie were at the bar, as they were every day. The routine was the same: three or four light beers, a lively but not always coherent debate, and gone by seven. Tonight Max was retelling what she had heard in the morning while

Leo and Company chimed in with penetrating comments and observations. The power of beer to make one smarter, faster, and more perceptive and to make everyone a friend is remarkable. Jack sat at the end of the bar near where the waitstaff picked up their drinks and just enjoyed the show while sipping the cold draft Max had put in front of him.

By 6:30, the dinner crowd had begun to fill in, and the waiters and waitresses were taking turns picking up their drinks at the bar from Max, who was now getting into the rhythm of the night.

"Hi Jack."

When he heard his name, he turned toward the voice.

"Hey Patti. Busy tonight?"

"Not bad. On my way in, I saw you out running."

"Yeah. I went out for a short one."

"Jack, you're crazy. It must have been freezing."

"It wasn't bad."

"Hey, what do you think about that car that was found on the boulevard last night. Strange, huh?"

Before he could answer, Patti's drinks were ready; she loaded her tray and said, "Hold that thought. I'll be back."

Jack watched her leave, and he must have been too obvious because Max said to him, "Jack Beale, what are you looking at?"

He blushed slightly as he turned back toward Max. "Nothin'."

"Nothin' my ass. You were checking out Patti. She's too young for you."

"Is not."

Max put another beer in front of him.

Patti had worked at Ben's for a couple years as a waitress. She's younger than Max with a head of curly blond hair, mischievous eyes, and a band of freckles across her nose. Her natural exuberance and ever-present smile affected everyone she met. She also was a terrific photographer. Some of her photos were on display on the walls in

Ben's. They were mostly pictures of life at Rye Harbor, boats at anchor, sunsets, tuna landings, and winter storms. She and Max got along really well and had become close friends and through that friendship, Patti became one of Jack's good friends. Like Max, Patti could trigger the "male pig gene" and sometimes Jack would have to catch himself before he did something stupid.

The evening got busier, and he and Patti never got a chance to finish their conversation. Max also was too busy to talk, although she did get him a third beer that he took to the table in the corner by the woodstove. Leo, Ralph, and Paulie paid their check and left to continue the circuit. A young well-dressed couple took two of their recently vacated seats. From his table in the corner, Jack sat and watched the choreography of a night in the busy restaurant and bar: the ebb and flow of patrons in and out of the bar; the way the staff would go from moments of total frantic activity that verged on panic and then just as quickly have nothing to do. Jack marveled at how Max kept it all together, drinks for the dining room staff, conversation with those at the bar, running the register, and serving meals. Just remarkable.

His thoughts returned to the car that was abandoned on the side of the road. There was something about that car that just didn't feel right to him. What would cause someone to abandon a car on a deserted stretch of road on one of the coldest nights of the year? A car with New Mexico plates no less. It had been brutally cold, barely above zero, for five days now. The latest weather report said the pattern would break tomorrow and warm up considerably over the weekend. "So much for global warming," he thought.

Jack was about to leave when he looked up and saw Andy walk in. "Son of a bitch. What's he doing here? I thought he was gone," Jack thought.

It had been only a month or so since Andy's last disappearance, and Jack knew Max was not yet fully recovered from that last departure. "This can't be good," Jack said under his breath as he sat back to see what would happen. He watched as Andy took the last seat at the bar, next to the couple who had just come in. Max was at the register with her back turned to the bar. She hadn't seen him come in. Jack saw Scotch and Soda Man take a quick look at Andy as he sat down. Andy was focused on Max, so he didn't notice Scotch and Soda Man looking at him. Seconds later, Max turned around and saw Andy. Jack held his breath and watched. The shock of suddenly seeing him sitting there stopped her dead in her tracks. It took a moment for the stunned look on Max's face to harden. She finally said, "Hello Andy."

"Hi Max."

"Is there something I can get you?" asked Max icily.

"Sure, a beer would be fine. How's things?" asked Andy. Max paused, fire still in her eyes. "Fine." Then she turned away from him to get his beer from the cooler.

As smooth as silk he replied, "I missed you."

Max turned back with his beer and silently placed it on the bar in front of him.

"Thanks."

Jack couldn't hear their words from his seat across the room, but he knew what was being said. It was obvious that Andy had no idea how pissed she was at him; he never did. From the tension in her face and the set of her shoulders, Jack could tell she was livid. At the same time, he also could see a twinge of relief that Andy was okay, but that was well hidden behind her anger and rage.

As she looked up from placing the beer on the bar in front of him, Jack caught her eye and signaled for another; and she nodded in his direction, picked up a glass and went out to get his draft.

"She doesn't deserve this," he thought. Before he could finish his thought, she returned with his beer in hand. Andy sat there, staring straight ahead, and finished his beer as Max walked past him. He didn't move. She left the safety of the bar and brought the beer to Jack. As she put it down on the table, he looked up at her and his thoughts must have been written all over his face. She looked into his eyes and said, "I know. Don't say anything. I'll be fine." And with that, she turned and walked back to the bar. Jack finished his thought, "Why can't she just tell him to fuck off?" Unfortunately, he knew the answer.

Jack watched as she replaced the empty bottle in front of Andy with a full one. Patti came in to pick up more drinks, and when she saw Andy sitting there, she dropped the glass she had been holding and it shattered on the floor. The entire bar turned and looked in her direction. As she bent down to pick up the broken glass, Andy said, "Hi Patti. Long time."

Obviously flustered, Patti stammered, "Hi Andy. When did you get back?"

"Just now."

Before he could say anything else, Jack came up to her and said, "It's okay Patti, you're busy. I'll clean this up for you."

"Thanks Jack," and with that she grabbed the rest of her drinks and left.

"Well, if it isn't our hero. Hello Jack."

"Andy," was his terse reply.

Max came over and said to Jack, "You don't have to do that."

"It's okay Max. You're busy too." Jack turned and went in search of a broom and dustpan. Max returned to the bar and glared at Andy.

"You get more beautiful every time I see you," was his response.

The excitement over, everyone went back to whatever they had been doing before Patti dropped the glass. Jack returned and swept up the broken glass while Andy watched silently from his barstool.

As Jack returned to his seat in the corner, Andy turned toward the couple next to him and said to no one in particular, "You know, Max and I go way back."

There was no response, so he turned back to his beer and took a sip. Then he turned in the other direction until he was looking at Jack. With a grin, Andy touched the neck of the bottle he was holding to his forehead as if offering a salute. Jack made no move to acknowledge the gesture so Andy turned back around to face Max and signaled for another beer.

Jack noticed that Scotch and Soda Man would occasionally look over in Andy's direction. At first Jack didn't think anything of it. After all, you always check out any new arrivals. But after catching Scotch and Soda Man looking over several more times, Jack realized it wasn't quite the look of idle curiosity. There seemed to be some kind of recognition going on.

"Hey Max, how about another?" Andy's voice rose above the background noise of the busy bar. Max placed it in front of him without saying anything and quickly turned away. He turned again toward the couple to his right.

They tried to ignore him, but his voice continued getting louder. "You know, she's a very special lady. She definitely has something for me. I can leave, and be gone for … oh … two, three months at a time, and whenever I return, she's right here, waiting for me."

Andy's voice was now loud enough for everyone in the bar to hear. With this last pronouncement, Max spun around in front of Andy, faced him, and with a look that would wither a rose, in a quiet measured voice, said, "Andy, I think it's time for you to leave."

Conversations in the bar paused as eyes turned in his direction. Jack shifted in his seat ready to get up. Scotch and Soda Man put his drink down and turned toward Andy. The couple he had been talking at glanced over nervously. Andy was silent as he glowered back at Max. "I'll have another beer," he said.

"No. You won't. You've had enough, and it's time for you to leave," Max said in a calm matter-of-fact voice.

Andy looked at her, not quite believing what she had just said. Before Andy could react, Scotch and Soda Man got up, went over to Andy, and in a muffled voice said something to him. Andy turned and stared at him. Jack watched the look on Andy's face as it went from anger toward Max, to defiance, to … to what? It was subtle and only lasted a split second before Andy slowly slid off his barstool, shot Max one last look and left. All eyes turned toward Scotch and Soda Man. Jack still was trying to sort out what had just happened when Scotch and Soda Man threw some money on the bar; said to Max, "I'm sorry for the disturbance"; and then left as abruptly.

The tension that had built eased immediately as customers in the bar went back to their conversations. Jack could tell Max did not feel this same sense of relief, even though she continued working as if nothing had happened.

Jack stayed for the rest of the evening. After the last customer had gone, he got up, walked over to the bar, and said softly to Max, "Are you all right?"

She said yes, just like he knew she would. Jack knew she wouldn't want to talk about it for a few days, but he'd be there when she was ready.

Patti had finished for the night and came in to cash out. "What was with Andy tonight? I thought he was gone."

"So did I," answered Max.

"Are you all right?"

"Yeah, I'll be fine."

"Perfect timing," thought Jack. This was a girl moment when all men would be considered scum, so he said good night and went home, leaving the girls to vent.

CHAPTER TEN

AN EVENING OUT

THE NEXT DAY REMAINED COLD, but the temperature was now in the twenties. The sun was brilliant in the cloudless sky, and Jack spent most of the day puttering around in his shop. There are several unwritten rules for working in one's shop. First there must be at least a half-dozen unfinished projects. A dozen would be better, but a half will do. Second, a stream of new projects must be continually added to the list even as works-in-progress are being finished. Third, no matter what your original intent when you started working on any particular day, you should not expect that to be what you are working on when you end the day. Working in the shop is a process of discovery and rediscovery.

Today Jack intended to finish building a small bookshelf he had promised Max several months ago. As he started, he found that one of his chisels needed sharpening. While doing this, he found that several chisels needed new handles, which he made. Before he knew it, his afternoon in the shop was over, and he had spent a very busy and fulfilling afternoon there. The bookshelf remained a work-in-progress, but his chisels were ready to go.

Jack had just closed up the shop and was climbing the stairs to his apartment when he heard the phone ringing. He could have let his machine answer the phone. He could have calmly entered his apartment. He could have given Cat a hello head scratch first, listened to the message on the machine, and returned the call. He could have done any of those things, but he didn't. Jack was one of those people who just couldn't let a phone ring without answering it if doing so was at all possible. So he took the remaining stairs two at a time, nearly falling as he cleared the top step, flung the door open, scared Cat as he narrowly missed kicking her across the room, and grabbed for the phone. "Hello," he croaked as he caught his breath.

It was Max.

"Hey Max. What's up?"

"Were you out running? You sound out of breath."

A little embarrassed, Jack said, "No, I was just coming up from the shop and I wanted to catch the phone. What's up?"

"Listen, I never got a chance to thank you for what you did last night."

"I didn't do anything."

"Yes you did. You were there, and well, it was easier dealing with Andy just knowing you were there. I'm off tonight. Would you like to catch a movie or something?"

Jack was caught a little by surprise. "Why sure, that sounds great."

"Okay, I'll pick you up around seven. See you then. Bye."

As Jack said, "Sure," she hung up.

As he hung up the phone, Cat began rubbing his leg and begging for dinner. He was grinning as he picked Cat up and said, "Well, Cat, I'm going out tonight. Let's get you some supper." Cat thought this was a good idea, and while she ate, Jack headed for the shower.

He stood under the rush of hot water—eyes closed, head bowed —and felt its warm soothing spray cascade over his head and down his back. The effect was almost hypnotic. His mind drifted as if he were being transported to another time and place. Random thoughts and memories flashed and mingled in his head. He was with Marie, they were holding onto each other tightly. He remembered her touch, her smell, and the softness of her skin. She pulled back from him and looked up into his eyes, he could hear her voice, "It's okay. I'll always be a part of you. It's okay." Silently he looked down at her, then realized that she now had red hair. He opened his eyes with a start and shook his head. The water was still hot and the room was now filled with steam. "Woah, that was weird," he said to no one.

Then the voice in his head began to lecture him. "Last night when Andy came into the bar you were angry. It makes you crazy every time he hurts Max. You are the one she goes to. Admit it, you're in love with her."

The water was beginning to get cold, and that was probably a good thing. He climbed out of the shower, shaved, and dressed.

He was just putting on his coat when he heard the toot of a car horn. Max was right on time. "See you later Cat," he said as he closed the door. As he climbed into the passenger seat, before the interior light went out, he glanced at Max. She was bundled up in a fur-collared coat with a brightly colored scarf around her neck. The cold had put a fresh glow on her cheeks, her eyes sparkled and she looked great. In the seconds it took him to get in and close the car door, he took all of this in. As soon as he closed the door, he got a whiff of her perfume and the male-pig gene woke up. "Hi Max, you look great."

"Thanks, you too. I'm hungry, how about we skip the movie, go downtown, and get a bite to eat?"

"Sure," was Jack's reply. He needed a second to get his feelings in check. He rubbed his hands together and blew on them for warmth as he thought to himself, "Slow down. Don't get all worked up. Girls naturally like to dress up and smell great. Stop reading more into this than is there. You've been out with her before. You know the drill." The pig gene went back into the sty, but the gate didn't completely close. "Boy is it cold. Where do you want to go?"

"I don't know. Let's decide when we get there."

Parking was almost nonexistent downtown. They drove around, and after several circuits, they finally found a spot near the park. That meant a bit of walking, but hell, it was in the teens now and almost felt warm. Maybe the weathermen would be right and the real warm-up would happen tomorrow. As they walked, Max asked, "Jack, what do you suppose really happened with that car they found?"

"I don't know," he answered.

"Do you think it has a simple explanation?"

"I have no idea. Maybe she was lost, stopped to look at a map, and was abducted by aliens."

"Stop, be serious."

"All right, I'll be serious."

Max pressed on. "The car wasn't broken down; it was abandoned. Why would someone just leave everything behind on such a bitterly cold night?"

"Max, I really have no idea ..."

Max continued, "Wait, I know. There was someone else in the car—a kidnapper who wanted something from her. ... No, no, she was fleeing from someone, and was run off the road and kidnapped."

"Max ..."

"No, no, just listen, she was murdered ..."

"Max, you watch too many soaps."

Defensively she replied, "I do not."

"I'm starting to get cold, and I'm definitely hungry," Jack said as they arrived at the door of The Rusty Hammer.

"How about we eat here?" Max suggested, as she looked through the frosted windows on the door.

"Fine by me."

They were given a table by one of the front windows. They sat and, with drinks in hand, watched the few people out on the street hurrying along, like so many puffing steam trains. The warmth of the room and the effect of her drink put a glow on Max's face that Jack found irresistible.

"What are you looking at?" her voice snapping him out of a place where he wasn't sure he should be going.

"Oh, nothing." He tried to be nonchalant, but he could feel his cheeks warming.

"Jack. Don't tell me that. You were thinking something, and now you are blushing. Come on, tell me." Her teasing tone was making him uncomfortable.

"I can't. It was nothing. Really. How about we order?"

"You're avoiding my question," Max pressed on, with an exaggerated pout.

"Yes I am."

The waitress appeared at that moment, saving Jack from making a complete fool of himself. They ordered and proceeded to enjoy the meal, which was accompanied by several more rounds of drinks. As the evening went on, Jack and Max relived stories from the past, laughing, joking, and teasing as only two very good friends could.

The mood continued as they bundled up for the walk back to the car. Even though it was considerably colder than it was when they arrived, it wasn't readily apparent, probably due to the effects of the food and alcohol. About halfway to the car, the cold was beginning to penetrate and Jack put his arm around Max. She pressed closer, and their steps quickened. His heart was pounding. As they walked along arm in arm, a jumble of thoughts went through his head: "Jack, what are you doing? Don't get all worked up. You've been drinking. It's cold. You're just friends. Chill out."

Max was just as silent, and he wondered what she was thinking but didn't dare ask. When they reached her car, Jack thought he sensed a slight hesitation before they separated. Before he could react, she handed him the keys. "Here, you drive," she said and climbed in on the passenger side. He smiled as he walked around the car and got in.

Cold car seats had a way of shocking the system. They were the perfect antidote to that moment that may not have been a moment. He wasn't sure.

"How long before we have heat?" asked Max as she sat on her hands for warmth.

He was gripping the wheel tightly, trying to control his shivering as he answered her. "Soon. I'm sure it will be toasty warm by the time we get home."

"We get home?" Jack began to panic when he realized what he had just said. He peeked over toward her to see if she had any reaction. He couldn't tell and took that as a no. "Good," he thought.

The heat had began to overtake the cold as they neared Rye Harbor.

"Jack?"

"Yeah Max?"

"Before we get to your place, could we go by the place where that car was found?"

"Sure. Why?"

"I don't know. I just can't get it out of my head. Why would a car just get left on the side of the road like that? What happened to the woman?"

"Max, you're starting again. You're making assumptions about things you don't know."

"Sorry. I can't help it."

Jack made a detour off the boulevard and drove south past the spot so he would be coming back up the boulevard in the same direction that the car had been traveling. As they neared the spot, he slowed and then stopped. There weren't any other cars on the road. It was dark, save for a ribbon of moonlight over the frozen landscape that magically appeared and dissappeared as clouds raced across the sky.

"Here we are."

Max didn't say anything. She just stared out her window, looking out over the ice-covered marsh while Jack watched her.

The wind gently rocked the car as they sat in silence, their thoughts kept private in the small confined space of her car, kept barely warm by its tiny heater. The intimacy of the moment created by the combined effect of the late hour as well as an evening of too much food and too much drink was beginning to affect Jack. He could smell her perfume, he could hear her breathing as his heartbeat echoed in his ears. Jack wondered if Max felt it too. "You deserve better than Andy," he thought. He wanted to tell her how he felt, but he couldn't.

"Okay, let's go." Her words broke the silence.

"You sure?"

"Yeah. I'm all set."

"Okay then."

He shifted into gear and drove away. It took less than five minutes to reach his place. When he stopped the car, a moment of awkward silence filled the car. He wanted to ask her in. That would have been nothing new. They were friends, and she had been to his place many times but never after a night like tonight. He was filled with emotions he wasn't sure he could control if given the opportunity. Before he acted, she said, "Thanks Jack. Dinner was great, I needed tonight. You are the best friend a girl could have."

Then she opened her door and got out. The blast of cold air and the "friend" moniker brought him out of his fantasy world and back into the present. He too opened his door and got out. Each walked toward the front of the car, and with the harsh light of the headlights washing over them, stopped. She stood in front of him, looked up into his eyes, then leaned up and gave him a gentle kiss on the lips. He could feel her warmth and smell her perfume as he accepted the kiss. As brief as it was, to Jack it was more than a simple goodnight peck. It lingered just enough to tell Jack that there was something there. They separated, she got in, they said good night, he closed the door behind her, and she backed down the drive. As he walked toward his apartment, he could still feel the touch of her lips.

CHAPTER ELEVEN

HARBOR ICE

SUNRISE THE NEXT MORNING was spectacular. Without even going out Jack could tell the cold had broken and this day would be special. He could see the harbor from his window, the tide was high, the ice cover was cracking, and the outgoing tide would probably take away much of the arctic ice fields that everyone had been looking at all week. He was still smiling about last evening with Max. Even though it was mid-January, with the rise in temperature and bright sun, it looked like spring. It's amazing what a few degrees of temperature rise will do to one's disposition. Jack got in his truck and headed out to Paula's.

Coffee, a muffin, and the Sunday paper were his immediate priorities. Then, maybe he would putter around the shop or climb under the cover on the boat to see how it fared during the freeze of the past week. Even midwinter, on a sunny day, there are a couple of hours midday when you could sit on the boat in comfort and imagine you were somewhere much warmer. Today would be one such day. He really wanted to see Max, but he didn't want to seem too eager, so he would wait until later in the day.

Beverly was working the counter. "Hi Jack," she said when she saw him come in. He returned the greeting, took a paper from the rack, and said hello to the others who were already enjoying their coffees and breakfasts. As Beverly poured his coffee, she asked with a mischievous grin if he had seen Max over the weekend. Jack completely missed the innuendo and matter-of-factly told her about their night out. "Have you heard anything new about that car that was found?" she asked.

"Nah and I haven't seen Tom to ask."

It was at this moment that the door opened and Scotch and Soda Man came in. "Mornin' Franz," said Jack as he walked past.

Franz nodded a silent hello, and took a seat at the end of the counter. Beverly headed over to get him his coffee. As Jack began shuffling through his paper while trying to decide what to read first, he overheard Beverly asking Scotch and Soda Man how he got the scratch on his cheek. The answer was lost to the clinking of spoons in coffee and the background murmur of overlapping conversations. Curious, Jack glanced over in Scotch and Soda Man's direction. Jack didn't remember seeing a scratch when Franz walked in and didn't see anything. "Must be on the other cheek," he thought to himself and went back to his paper. He was in no hurry this morning.

A blueberry muffin and several cups of coffee later, Jack finally closed the paper. The place was nearly empty, even Franz had left. Jack had been so engrossed in the paper that he hadn't noticed how much time had passed. He paid his tab, said bye to Beverly, and walked out the door. It was warm, the sun felt good on his face, and there was already a steady stream of traffic on the road.

On the New England coast, there are some things that are totally predictable. One is that when a stretch of severe weather, in this case the cold, changes suddenly, the whole world has to drive to the shore to look at the ocean. It took a few minutes before Jack was able to pull out and become part of the endless stream of traffic. Progress was steady but slow. No one was in a hurry. Everyone was enjoying the day, even Jack.

As the line of cars reached the long, straight stretch by the marsh just before the harbor, Jack understood why everyone was driving so slowly. The temperature had risen enough that the ice was breaking up, and the outgoing tide was taking the ice floes out of the marsh and into the harbor. It was spectacular. Many cars were turning off and heading toward Ben's. "Max is going to be busy today," he thought as he made that same turn. Crossing the bridge over the creek that fed into the harbor, he too slowed, mesmerized by the moving ice that was like a cold, white lava flow. Mini bergs were already drifting out among the boats.

As he drove past Ben's, he took note of the fact that the parking lot was already full. He'd return later. First there were some unfinished projects in his shop that he wanted to work on. Pulling into the driveway, he looked up at his boat—wrapped in its cocoon of white plastic—and decided that before he began anything, he would climb up under the cover and check on her.

It was warm under the cover, and when he closed his eyes, he could almost imagine being back in the islands, only this time with Max. It was tempting to spend the afternoon sitting there, but there were too many unfinished projects awaiting him in the shop. So after a quick look around and finding everything in order, he climbed off the boat and went into the shop.

Around four o'clock, Jack decided he had accomplished enough for one afternoon. As he headed for the door, he glanced about the shop, making some mental notes about projects started and others nearly finished. He left the shop, went upstairs, showered, and headed over to Ben's. It was a short walk, and the air felt good. It was no longer that dry, bitterly cold air that you didn't want to breathe. This was a warmer, more moist air, laden with those wonderful rich saltwater smells previously frozen and now re-emerging. It felt good to take a deep breath.

The closer to Ben's he came, the broader the grin on his face. As he opened the door and stepped inside, he took a deep breath and thought to himself, "Will you quit acting like such a kid? It's Max, and you've known her forever and you're making more out of last night than you should. Grow up!"

The bar was not as busy as he had expected, judging from the number of cars in the parking lot. Max saw him come in.

"Hi Jack."

In the split second before he answered, he tried to glean whether there was anything different in the way she looked at him and in the tone of her voice. He couldn't be sure. "Hey Max. Where is everyone? I thought there'd be more people here."

"Look outside."

He turned and could see a wall of people lined up at the deck railing, looking out over the harbor.

"Oh. What's the attraction?"

"The ice. Go out and take a look. Your beer will be waiting when you come back in."

He joined the crowd at the rail, and what he saw was like nothing he had ever seen before. The tide was out and the entire flat in front of Ben's was covered with huge slabs of ice that were stacked up like fallen dominoes. Some were at least a foot thick and the size of small cars. The sun was getting lower in the west, which was creating the most spectacular effect. The low angle light had boats lit like they were under spotlights, and the play of shadows and light on the ice chunks was mesmerizing. He stood there silently with everyone else.

Patti arrived for her shift just after Jack. As she came into the bar from the kitchen, she was adjusting her necktie and said to Max, who was looking out the window, "What's going on?"

"Go see."

Patti went outside. Max watched her stop and stare for a moment, and then she turned and came running in. She ran right past Max and shouted as she went by, "Have someone cover for me. I'll be right back. I have to get my camera."

Max's reply was lost in the hubbub. "Sure, no problem."

Patti returned in moments, her face flushed from the sprint to her car, and she headed straight out onto the deck. She hadn't even bothered to put on a coat. Immediately, she began snapping pictures. As the sun touched the horizon, the bright, even light of day was replaced with the ever-changing colors and textures of the sunset. This rapidly changing atmosphere created a dance of shadows that made the ice seem as if it were alive and moving. Not satisfied with only shots from the deck, she began climbing over the railing.

"Patti, be careful. You're going to slip and hurt yourself," Jack yelled at her.

"Nonsense, I'm fine, and I'll be careful," she replied as she dropped down onto the ice. With her tie flapping over her shoulder, she began climbing over the slabs of ice, snapping pictures as she moved. Before she had moved too far out on the ice, she turned and pointed her camera at the crowd along the railing. "Smile," she shouted as she snapped several pictures, then she turned and headed farther out onto the ice.

The crowd began to return to the bar. The temperature was dropping, and Jack pulled his coat closed. "She must be freezing," said a voice next to him. Turning toward the voice, Jack was surprised when he found himself facing Scotch and Soda Man. As often as they had seen each other in the bar, they had never really spoken before.

"Probably. But she'll freeze to death before she quits if there is a picture to be taken," Jack said as he turned his gaze back toward Patti.

"I see."

Even from his distant vantage point, Jack could tell that she was breathing hard. Her breath was creating a halo of vapor around her head.

"You watch. She's going to land on her ass before too long," Jack said and then realized that he was speaking to no one. He was the sole remaining spectator to Patti's mission.

That's when it happened. She was focusing for one last picture when her foot slipped. She yelped and fell ass over tea kettle behind a particularly large piece of ice. Jack's first reaction was to laugh. He heard her scream as she went down, her arm extended upward holding her camera high and out of harm's way. "Are you all right?" he shouted.

"Yeah, but my ass is all wet," she yelled back.

Chuckling, Jack turned, went to the bar door, stuck his head inside, and said, "Hey Max, Patti slipped and landed on her ass in a puddle. She says she's okay. I'm going to go help her in."

That was enough to get everyone's attention again, and the more curious returned to the deck to watch. Just as Jack lifted his leg over the railing, Patti screamed. Louder, more primal, it was unlike any scream Jack had ever heard before. His reaction was immediate and instinctual. He dropped to the ice, and in a leaping, slipping, scrambling sprint he raced toward her.

The scream and Jack's reaction to it was all it took. The bar immediately emptied as everyone rushed back out onto the deck. Even Max came out to see what was going on. Jack was so focused on his mission that he didn't realize several people had followed him out onto the ice.

"Are you all right?" he wheezed. Patti just looked at him with a strange look on her face. She was cold, wet, and shaking. He took his coat off, put it over her shoulders, and looked deeply into her eyes. In a shivering voice just above a whisper, she said, as she pointed behind him, "Hand ... body ..." It took a moment for Jack to comprehend what she had said and another moment for what he saw to sink in. There was an arm hanging out from under the slab of ice.

A plaid flannel shirtsleeve covered the arm. It was torn, exposing the bluish white flesh beneath. From the size of the arm and the hand, the right hand, he knew it belonged to a woman. The hand was more delicate than that of a man, although he could see real strength in the fingers. The knuckles were cut and bruised, several fingernails were broken, and there was a gold ring on one finger. "Shit." Then he stood, faced where he had come from, and yelled back, "Call 911."

He heard the message being relayed back to Ben's. That's when the first person who had followed Jack out onto the ice arrived.

"She okay? What happened?"

Jack turned to him, "She'll be okay. She's just cold and wet, but there's a body under that slab of ice in front of you."

"What!?" he jumped back a step.

"A body. At least I assume it's all there, only one arm is visible."

"No shit. Really?" as he began to maneuver around for a look.

The message to call 911 electrified the crowd on the deck. It took only a moment for the crowd to react. While some rushed inside to make the call, the rest began climbing over the railing, rushing out onto the ice to see for themselves. The crowd oozed over and around the ice floes, forming and reforming as if it were some kind of a giant amoeba come to life. The jumble of ice made footing treacherous, and the way things were going, someone was destined to fall and get hurt— or at least very wet. Too much was happening too fast.

As the amoeba pressed in, Jack shouted out in frustration, "Hey! Back off. The police will be here soon."

As soon as the words left his mouth, he felt his face flush. "Where did that come from?" he wondered. Not only did he surprise himself, but the crowd began to quiet and most people moved back. As they moved, he heard a low voice ask with a touch of sarcasm, "Who put him in charge?"

Before he could respond, he felt a tug on his sleeve and a shivering voice said, "J-J-Jack. W-W-Will y-you m-move?" Patti tugged on Jack's sleeve. She was shivering.

Jack turned back to Patti. "You have got to go in. You're freezing."

"N-No. I-I'm f-fine. I-I n-need-d t-to t-take s-some m-more p-p-pictures. M-Move o-o-over." With that she raised her camera and began taking pictures of the arm hanging out from under the ice. The hand and ring received extra attention. "Jack, have you ever seen a ring like that?"

He bent over and took a closer look. "No."

Sirens could be heard in the distance, and Jack stepped back while Patti's camera kept clicking away as she recorded the entire scene.

He saw the flashing blue lights of one of the town's cruisers as it crossed over the bridge and turned into Ben's. It was followed moments later by the red lights of the ambulance. Because of the snowbanks around the parking lot, the lights were no longer visible, but the reflections betrayed their presence. Jack finally heard a familiar voice.

"Okay, could everyone please move back?" It was Tom.

"Tom, am I glad to see you."

"Hey Jack. What's this about a body?"

"Right here." He pointed toward the arm. Tom worked his way around the ice, and when he saw the arm, he murmured to himself. "Son of a bitch." Then he moved closer to get a better look and slipped, nearly landing in the same puddle Patti had fallen into. He caught himself, and only his hand went into the water. As he stood and shook off his hand, he heard a camera click followed by a slight chuckle. He looked around and saw Patti. She looked wet and cold, and had her camera pointed in his direction with a mischievous smile that said "Gotcha."

"I'll need that film," said Tom as he turned his attention to directing the rescue team.

"Sure," was her reply.

As the fire-rescue team went to work, the crowd was pushed farther back, and with axes and chainsaws, rescuers went to work freeing the body from the ice.

"C'mon Patti. Let's go up and get you into some dry clothes. You're freezing," said Jack.

She shivered back, "N-no. I-I'm st-staying."

"Fine, suit yourself." He was beginning to shiver as well.

That's when Max showed up. After all, everyone had to get a peek.

This kind of thing didn't happen very often in small towns in New Hampshire. She was bundled up and had with her Patti's coat along with a hat and gloves. "Here, Patti. You look ridiculous in Jack's coat."

"Thanks." Patti gave Jack's coat back to him and slipped into her own along with the hat. The gloves went into her pocket so she could use the camera.

Rescuers worked fast. The shouts, grunts, and groans of many men working very hard were punctuated by the sounds of axes thumping into the ice and the ear-splitting whine of a chainsaw. Steadily the mini berg that covered the body was reduced until all that remained was the part directly over the corpse. The work slowed, but the sense of urgency increased. The tide had turned, and the sun was rapidly disappearing. Through it all, Patti kept shooting while Jack and Max stood and watched.

The last piece of ice was finally removed, and for a moment everyone stood and stared silently at the dead woman. Except for the gentle lapping wavelets of the encroaching tide and the shushing of the light breeze, there was silence.

She looked to be in her late sixties and although plain, she was attractive, even after having been under the ice for who knows how long. She was wearing work boots, khaki slacks, and a plaid shirt. Sand as well as bits of marsh grass and seaweed could be seen between the frozen folds of her torn clothing. There were scratches and bruises on her arms, some recent and others, healed reminders of past events; her hands gave testament to the violence of her death.

Max leaned in to get a better look at the body while Jack held on to her hand, steadying her so she wouldn't slip. Her gaze moved over the body, finally coming to rest on the face. She stared at it. There was something familiar. The eyes drew her in. They seemed to be looking straight at her with an intensity that made her shiver. It was as if they were pleading with her for something. Then, just as quickly, that anguished gaze seemed to soften, replaced by one of peace and serenity that seemed to say, "I've found you. You're here."

Max shook her head as if to clear it. "It's just the changing light from the setting sun," she thought as the click of Patti's camera brought her the rest of the way back. Then Max looked at the face again.

"I know her. Why do I know her?" she thought. Then it came to her, and she stiffened, nearly pulling Jack off balance. "Oh my God," she murmured.

"Max. Are you all right?"

Silence. She just stared.

"Max?" Jack squeezed her hand.

Slowly she moved her head, her eyes searching for something that would disprove what she just came to know. But that didn't happen. Instead she saw proof of what she had hoped was not so. She saw the ring. Memories flashed through her head.

CHAPTER TWELVE

THE GOLD BAND

IN 1975, MAX HAD BEEN ELEVEN when her father died. Even though he had been diagnosed with cancer five years earlier, there had been remission and a return to a seemingly healthy life. While her mother devoted most of her energies to caring for her husband, Max had grown to rely on her Grandma Ruth more and more. Whenever life at home became very bad, the two of them would sit together and Ruth would tell Max stories. Her favorites were about the ring that her grandmother always wore.

It was a simple gold band, but having only one side. Max remembered tracing her fingers around the band and how they would go all the way around inside and out without ever leaving its surface. What did Grandma Ruth call it? Max couldn't remember. The ring also had an inscription on the face that would be hidden against her finger. Written in ancient Hebrew, it said, "Wherever thou goest, so will I." Then in German: "Ruth -1918 with all our Love." The stories her grandmother would tell were magical, and were always about the ring and how it was the key to great treasure. Those stories helped her get through those difficult times, especially when her father lost his battle with the cancer.

Her mother, Dorothy, was devastated by the finality of her husband's death. Max, Grandma Ruth, and Dorothy still had each other and drew upon their combined strengths to get through. The funeral was a blur; Aunt Lillian visited; friends and strangers called with condolences; and through it all, the three generations held onto each other. As life returned to normal, as if there could be such a thing, Grandma

Ruth became an even more important part of Max's life. She was going into her teenage years, and the natural friction between mother and daughter many times were soothed over by Ruth.

One day, Max saw her grandmother speaking to a stranger. When asked who he was, she quickly changed the subject. It was during this time that Max noticed some subtle changes in her grandmother's behavior. She sometimes seemed distant, sometimes nervous, and always more cautious. It was more a feeling that Max had, but it seemed real. Max let it go because it didn't seem important.

In 1978, only three short years after Max's father died, Grandma Ruth became very sick. The cause of her illness was unknown, but the result was serious enough to warrant hospitalization. Max spent many hours with her grandmother. Max tried to retell the ring stories to her grandmother, thinking they would be a happy diversion. They weren't. Each time Max tried to tell one of the stories, her grandmother would change the subject. Nothing helped, and her health continued on its downward spiral. Ruth asked Dorothy to find her sister, Lillian, and to have her come home; it was important. Dorothy did. While waiting for Lillian's arrival, Ruth seemed to improve. After a week or so, Lillian finally arrived, and she went to her mother's side with Dorothy and Max. Ruth wanted to talk to her daughters alone, and afterward Max noticed that Lillian now wore the ring and that her mother and aunt seemed even more somber. It was the next day that Ruth died.

The process of the funeral was all too familiar to Max: the hushed tones as arrangements were made, followed by the calling hours when friends and strangers came by to offer condolences. The moments of feeling totally alone when the only sound you heard was the beating of your own heart even though you were surrounded by conversation. During the evening calling hours, Max saw a man talking to Aunt Lillian. Max didn't know who he was, but he seemed familiar. She saw Lillian's posture change. Suddenly she seemed nervous as she clasped her hands, not in a sorrowful way, but as if she were hiding something. After the man left, Lillian was pale and shaking.

The next day, after the burial, Aunt Lillian left. She tried to make it seem normal, but Max knew it wasn't. Her mother also seemed more guarded in her grief. It was all so strange.

CHAPTER THIRTEEN

QUESTIONS

THE SUN WAS NO LONGER VISIBLE, and only the last reflected light remained. A low, almost whispered voice broke the silence, "Bring the stretcher over here. We have to get her out of here now." Gently, almost reverently, she was placed on the stretcher, a blanket wrapped around her as if she needed the warmth and the straps tightened.

The reverence and care exhibited as she was secured to the stretcher quickly changed. She was now an awkward, heavy object that required a great deal of brute force to be dragged, lifted, pulled, and manhandled over the ice and back to dry land.

Patti followed, still recording the event. Max looked up at Jack and said in a quiet pensive voice, "Jack, I know who she is."

It took a second for that simple statement to register. "You what?"

"I know her."

"C'mon."

As they climbed over the last rocks of the seawall into the parking lot at Ben's, a scene of organized chaos greeted them. It almost had the feel of an outdoor carnival. There were flashing lights. Crowds of people milled about, all talking and pointing excitedly at the harbor then at the body, which by now had been placed on a gurney and was sitting next to the ambulance. The rescuers were putting away their equipment, and Tom could be seen talking to Patti. Jack and Max made their way through the crowd and approached Tom.

"Tom," Jack said as they neared the ambulance.

Tom turned, "Hey Jack. Patti was just telling me about what happened. You were out with her?"

"Yeah, I was. Listen, Max says that she recognized the bo–," he caught himself, "… the woman."

Turning toward her, Tom said, "Max?"

"Hi Tom. She's my Aunt Meredith. Well, she's not really my aunt. She and my aunt lived together out in New Mexico, but I always thought of her as my aunt. I haven't seen her for a long time, but it's her."

Tom stepped over to the gurney. "Are you sure?"

"Yes."

"Would you mind taking another look?"

"Sure, I mean no, I wouldn't mind." She clutched Jack's hand as he walked with her over to the gurney. Tom slowly peeled back the blanket, and as he did so, her arm flopped off the gurney and dangled as it had when it was in the ice. Max jumped and clutched at Jack. "Sorry," said Tom. Were it not such a somber moment, Tom might have chuckled at her reaction. He gently picked up the arm and tucked it back next to the body. "Is it her?"

Max was staring at the hand that Tom had just placed back on the gurney. "Max, do you recognize her?"

She looked up. "Oh, sorry." She looked at the woman's face, said nothing, and looked back down at the hand.

"Max. Are you all right?"

Jack, his arm still around her, squeezed her shoulder for support.

"It's her."

"Are you sure?"

"Yes. But the ring. It's gone."

"What ring?"

"My aunt's ring. I saw it on her hand when she was down on the ice. That's how I knew for sure."

Tom lifted the blanket and examined both hands. There was no ring.

"Are you sure?"

"Yes. She was wearing the ring, and it's gone now."

Jack could hear her voice beginning to tremble. She was on the edge of panic.

Before she could become completely unglued, Jack gave her another reassuring squeeze. Then he looked at Tom. "Tom, the ring was there. I saw it; Patti took several pictures of it."

Tom paused, then replaced the blanket, looked at Jack, and said, "Why don't you take Max and Patti inside where it is warm. I'll be right in."

"C'mon ladies," said Jack, and he guided them toward the door.

As soon as the ambulance was gone, Tom followed the last of the onlookers back into Ben's. This was the most excitement that Rye Harbor had ever seen. The bar was packed and one of the other bartenders was busy behind it. Tom scanned the crowd for Jack, Max, and Patti. It took a moment, but he finally saw Jack and Max sitting at a corner table. Tom worked his way through the crowd and finally reached the table.

"Hi guys. Where's Patti?"

Jack looked up. Max was still visibly upset, and she just looked down at the table and sniffled. "She went up to change into dry clothes. She'll be back down in a minute."

"May I sit?"

"Of course. Pull up a chair."

"Thanks. Listen, I'm going to need to talk to all three of you." Then he looked over at Max.

"You okay?"

"Yeah. I'll be okay. I just can't believe that she's dead," Max sniffled.

"Max, do you have your aunt's number?"

"Not here. I'm pretty sure I have it at home."

"Do you know what town in New Mexico she lives in? I'd like to try and get in touch with her."

"Dry Gulch," was Max's reply.

Tom wrote the name in his note pad then said, "Excuse me for a minute."

Moments later Tom returned and asked Max if she was up to talking with him.

Max sat motionless.

"Max?"

"Sure. Why not," her voice flat.

Turning to Jack, Tom said, "Peggy set up a room for us. We're going to get away from all this noise to talk. When Patti returns, could you let her know I'll need to talk to her as well."

"Sure." Then looking at Max, Jack said, "Go on. I'll be right here," and he gave her hand a squeeze.

She stood and walked off with Tom.

Just as they left the room, Patti arrived. She was rosy cheeked and with her curly blond hair, she looked like Shirley Temple. "Is Max okay? Where're they going?"

"He needs to talk to all three of us, and Max is first. Peggy set up space out in the restaurant. It'll be a little less distracting than if we talked here."

One of the waitresses came over to the table and asked if they would like drinks.

"Sure. I'll have an ESB draft," said Jack. ESB is a locally brewed amber ale that was Jack's favorite brew. Patti ordered an Irish Coffee.

As the waitress turned to go order the drinks, she paused, turned back, and asked, "Is it true?"

"Is what true?"

"Is it true that Max knows the woman they found out there?"

"Yes," was Jack's terse reply. The expression on his face put an end to any further questions.

"Right," she said and turned to go get their drinks.

"Boy, news sure travels fast," said Patti.

"Sure does."

It took only a few minutes for the waitress to return with their drinks. Jack picked up his beer, tipped it in Patti's direction, and said, "Cheers."

She picked up her Irish Coffee and clinked it to Jack's glass. "Cheers."

Tom and Max returned just as they finished their drinks.

"Hey Patti," said Tom.

"Hi Tom. Hey Max, you okay?"

"Yeah, I'm okay." Her voice was still subdued. She pulled a chair over from the next table and sat down next to Jack. His eyes softened, and he gave her a reassuring look and a little smile. It was the kind of look you would give someone at a funeral that says, I feel your pain and I'm here for you.

"Patti, do you have those pictures for me?"

"I do." She stood and squeezed her hand into her jeans pocket and pulled out a little plastic square and handed it to him.

He looked at it. "Thanks."

"No problem."

"How about we go talk."

"Sure."

Patti excused herself, and she and Tom walked out of the bar.

"You're not really okay, are you?" Jack asked Max.

"No."

"I'm sorry …"

She turned to face him and at the same time cut him off. "Don't apologize. It's not your fault. It's just … I don't understand. What was she doing here? Where is my Aunt Lillian?" She paused as her eyes began to well up with tears.

Before Jack could say anything, Max sniffled. While wiping her eyes with her sleeve, she asked in a quivering whisper, "The ring? She was wearing my aunt's ring and it wasn't on her hand in the parking lot. Jack, what happened to the ring?"

"Max," he said taking her hand in his, "I don't have any answers for you. I can only say that I'm sure that everything will work out. Tom's good, you'll see. And I'm here for you."

Then he thought, "I've always been here ..."

"I know. ... Thanks."

The waitress returned, and Jack ordered another beer and Max, a glass of wine.

"Max, tell me about the ring."

"It was a ring that my Grandma Ruth always wore. It was a gold band with an inscription, and when I was little, she would tell me stories about the ring, about how it was magical and had special powers. They were just stories, of course, but they helped me through a very bad time in my life. My father had cancer, and during his last few years, my mother spent all her energies taking care of him; Grandma Ruth took care of me and told me those stories."

"How old were you?"

"I was eleven when my father died."

"That must have been rough."

"It was."

"How did your aunt get the ring? Why not your mother?"

"I'm not really sure. What I do remember was that after my father's death, I saw my grandmother talking to a stranger. He upset her, and after that, she was different."

"Different how?"

"I don't know, just different. Then she got sick, and I remember trying to cheer her up by telling her the stories about the ring, just like she had for me. She would cover it up with her hand as if to hide it and would change the subject. She wouldn't talk about it."

"You still haven't told me how your aunt got the ring."

"I'm getting there. She was my mother's twin, not identical, but they were twin close, even though very different. My mother was the homebody; her sister, the wild child out to save the world. After my grandfather died, Lillian took off. We were never exactly sure what she was up to, but she did come home for my mother's wedding and that was when they found out Lillian was living in a small community in the New Mexico desert."

"Max, the ring?"

"I'm getting there. My grandmother got very sick three years after my father's death. Lillian was still living in New Mexico, and she came home. For a few days, my grandmother seemed to get better, she was so glad to see her two daughters together again. I remember one day she called both of them to her bedside. I wanted to be there also, but they asked me to leave the room, and when they came out, Lillian was wearing the ring and my mother had an envelope in her hand. They were very somber. The next day, Grandma Ruth died."

"So you have no idea why Lillian was given the ring?"

"None." Neither spoke for a few minutes. Then Max looked at Jack with a far-off look in her eyes and said, "I do remember that at the funeral, I saw a man talking to Aunt Lillian. She seemed upset and until now I never made the connection, but I think he may have been the same man I saw talking to my grandmother after my father's death when my mother and I were having problems. I remember how he upset her. Lillian went back to New Mexico right after the funeral, and I haven't seen her since. But I know it was her ring that I saw today."

Patti returned from her interview with Tom and it was Jack's turn; he corroborated everything Patti and Max had already told Tom. Just as they were getting up to return to the bar, Tom turned to Jack and said, "Jack, I don't know what happened to the ring that Max saw on our victim. It's doubtful that it just fell off. That usually doesn't happen with dead bodies. Somebody probably took it, and what worries me is Max. She's pretty upset, and I don't want her doing anything stupid. We'll find it."

"Tom, you know that I'll help you in any way I can. And don't worry about Max."

"Thanks."

As Jack put his hand on the door to open it, he turned back to Tom. "What do you think?"

"Think about what?"

"You know. The body. Accident or murder?"

"Jack, the investigation has just begun, we don't even have a cause of death yet. How can I possibly have any answers?"

"Because I know you."

"Off the record?"

"Off the record."

"I don't think it was an accident."

"Me neither."

"So, now that we agree off the record. There's nothing more to say right now."

Jack rejoined Max and Patti at their table while Tom left with his next interviewee. The two girls seemed much more upbeat than when Jack had left with Tom. One glance at the tabletop, and Jack knew why. There were several empty glasses, and he could tell Max was now drinking "halvsies." That was her code word for a half-sized White Russian, even though they sure looked full-sized to Jack. "Hi Jack," Max and Patti said in unison.

"Hi ladies," he said as he sat down and signaled the bartender for another beer.

"So what did you tell Tom?" asked Max.

"I just answered his questions and told him what I saw, which was probably just what you told him."

"I don't think he believed me about the ring."

"I think he did. He'll find it."

"I took pictures of it," chimed in Patti.

"Yeah, Patti took pictures," Max said. "He has to believe me. Poor Meredith. I liked her. Did you know she and my aunt were lesbians?"

"We guessed," said Jack. It was time to change the subject. "Are you working tomorrow?"

"I'm not in until four."

Tom finally finished his interviews. As he said goodbye to the last person he noticed that Jack, Max, and Patti were the only ones left and that they were now sitting at the bar.

"Hey Tom, come join us for a drink," said Max.

"Where is everyone?"

"While you were talking, everyone left and they closed. I told the bartender that I would lock up for him since he covered my shift tonight. So here we are. Waiting for you. Come on, have a drink."

"Sorry, can't. I'm still working, and you should go home."

Then looking at Jack, Tom said, "Don't let them drive anywhere. I don't want to find them in our holding cell in the morning."

"I won't. I'll take them home with me."

"Good. Good night."

"C'mon girls, it's time to go." It took some effort. Actually it was like herding cats to get them both going in the same direction, but Jack persevered and, in the end, Ben's was locked up and they walked to his place. He ushered them upstairs, scaring Cat in the process. Max and Patti managed to get their coats and shoes off, then Jack maneuvered them toward the bed. Max and Patti would have his, and he would sleep on the couch. He barely managed to get the covers pulled back before both girls flopped onto the bed. Patti pulled the covers up and over her head, and fell asleep instantly. Max didn't move, so he pulled them over her. Then on an impulse, he bent down and gently kissed her on the forehead. "Good night Max," he whispered.

"Good night Jack," came back the slurred reply. He swore she was smiling.

He wished he were beside her, but tonight the couch in the other room with Cat would have to do.

CHAPTER FOURTEEN

THE MORNING AFTER

JACK AWOKE MONDAY MORNING with a stiff neck and the sunrise streaming in through the skylight, right into his eyes. It took him a moment to remember why he was on the couch. When he did, he smiled, got up, and went to peek in on the girls. They were gone. He padded back out into the living room. Their coats were gone, and he saw a note on the floor at the top of the stairs. All it said was, "Thanks, Jack. Love and kisses, Max and Patti."

"Humph. They snuck out on me without even a goodbye. Cat, did you see them leave?"

Cat looked up, then closed her eyes and put her head back down. She had no intention of moving.

"Fine, be that way." His stomach was beginning to grumble. He knew he didn't have much on hand so it would be off to Paula's for breakfast after a quick shower.

When he walked in, he could feel the buzz. Beverly waved a quick hello. It seemed like the whole town was there. Fred, John, Leo, Ralph, and Paulie were all crowded around the end of the counter. Jack couldn't see who was holding court, so he made his way over.

He did not expect it to be Max, and when he saw her, he smiled. "Good morning sunshine," he said to her before she saw him. As soon as she heard his voice, she lost her train of thought.

"Jack. What are you doing here?"

"I might ask you the same thing. You didn't even say goodbye this morning when you left."

That brought a hush to the crowd gathered, and all eyes turned toward Jack. For years they had watched him be the good friend, always there to help pick up the pieces, especially after Andy would leave. Jack knew, everybody knew, that Andy was bad news, and yet Max would keep going back to him after he would disappear for weeks, even months at a time. It was common knowledge that Jack was head over heels for Max, even though he never told her so. Now, he just said in front of everyone that she had spent the night at his place.

Max blushed. "It wasn't like that," she protested. "Patti was there. We had too much to drink last night, and Jack let us sleep at his place. We're just friends."

"Ouch. The 'F' word," someone in the crowd whispered under his breath.

Jack was enjoying this too much to end it so soon, so he added, "All you had to do was nudge me. I would have gotten right up."

That did it. Max glared at him. "Jack Beale, tell them. Tell them that Patti and I stayed at your place because we were too wasted to drive. You even slept on the couch; we were in the bed."

Everyone turned their attention toward her in mock shock. Max, realizing what she had just said sounded wrong, looked over at Jack and pleaded. "Jack."

She was so darn cute when flustered, but he wasn't ready to let her off the hook yet. "It's true, guys. She and Patti slept together."

He paused before continuing while Max glared at him, her mouth open and gave his arm a slap. Someone in the crowd chuckled, and he continued.

"Last night, by the time Tom had finished all of his interviews, Patti and Max were, shall we say, very relaxed, and Tom suggested they should not be driving anywhere. I put them up at my place, and I did sleep on the couch. I'm surprised that Max made it up so early today."

Max interrupted and spoke to Jack, "About dawn I woke up. I couldn't sleep any more. I kept thinking about Meredith and what could have happened to her. So I woke Patti, and we left."

Then for the crowd listening, she added, "I didn't want to leave her alone with Jack." She said that last part with a wink and a grin. Payback. She turned back to Jack and continued, "We walked back to Ben's, got in our cars, and left. First I went home and tried calling Aunt Lillian. There was no answer. I know I saw her ring on Meredith's finger, and it's gone. My head hurt, and I was getting really hungry."

As if on cue, Beverly came over and placed in front of Max a plate of scrambled eggs, bacon, toast, and home fries. It looked so good that Jack said to Beverly, "Can you bring me one of those also?" As Max took her first bite, everyone said goodbye, and moved farther down the counter to continue their discussion, allowing her to eat her breakfast.

"Mind if I join you?" asked Jack as he took the stool next to her.

"Of course not."

"Quite the night last night." It was a statement as much as a question.

"It sure was. Thanks Jack."

"Thanks for what?"

"You know. Taking care of me the way you do." She was going to add, "You're such a good friend," but decided not to.

"You're welcome."

"What do you think happened?"

"I really don't know."

"Why would Meredith have been here in the middle of the coldest night of the year? Something had to have happened. There was no answer when I called early this morning. And the ring. She had my aunt's ring. Why? And now it's gone."

Beverly brought Jack his breakfast, and little more was said while Jack and Max ate. Of the early morning crowd, only Fred and John remained by the time Jack and Max had finished eating. They were about to leave as well when John walked over and said, "Max, we're all sorry about your aunt's friend. I'm sure everything will work out."

"Thanks," said Max.

Then, as he turned to leave, Jack asked, "Goin' out today?"

"Gonna try, now that the ice is out of the harbor."

"Good luck," said Jack.

John left, leaving Jack and Max as the last two customers.

Jack turned toward Max. "Come on Max, I'll walk you out to your car."

He left money on the counter for the check and called out a good-bye to Beverly who wasn't in sight.

Jack helped Max with her coat, then before they reached the door, Jack stopped and turned toward Max. "Did you notice who wasn't here this morning?"

"No, who?"

"Franz."

"Franz?" She paused a moment then said, "You mean Scotch and Soda Man?"

"Yeah. He'd been here every day all during the deep freeze, and just when it begins to warm up and we have some excitement to talk about, he's MIA."

"I guess. He told me the other day that he was going to be around for a few more days. He said he still had some unfinished business to take care of," said Max. "What made you notice?"

"I don't know. I mean he was there last night. I saw him helping with the stretcher when they brought it over the rocks and up into the parking lot."

Max was silent for a moment, "Now that you mention it, I do remember seeing him."

"Probably means nothing."

Max agreed, but now she couldn't get him out of her head. As soon as they stepped outside Max was forced to shield her eyes from the brilliant sun. Bright sunlight and a severe hangover did not make for a pleasant combination. "Jack, do you remember seeing him in the bar afterward?"

"Come to think of it, no."

"I don't either."

"I wonder if Tom talked to him?"

When they reached Max's car, they paused and stood facing each other in silence. For a moment it seemed that both had something more to say to the other, then the moment passed. Even though the sun was out, the wind was still cuttingly cold so Jack made the first move. He reached for the door handle and pulled on it. As the door opened, he said, "Get in Max, it's freezing out here. I'll see you later at the bar."

"Bye Jack. Later."

CHAPTER FIFTEEN

PICTURES

JACK SPENT HIS DAY constantly going somewhere and rushing to do something, none of which he would remember later, only that he had been busy. He did run into Tom at one point and asked him how the investigation was going. Tom didn't offer much, except that he was still trying to get in touch with Max's aunt.

As they parted, Jack turned and asked, "Hey Tom. Did you talk to Scotch and Soda Man last night?"

Tom looked back at him questioningly, "Who?"

"Franz; we call him Scotch and Soda Man. At least that is what we call him at the bar. He's been staying in the area for the last couple weeks, and has kind of become a regular at Paula's in the mornings and then at Ben's in the late afternoons. He always orders scotch and soda. He will sit at the end of the bar, sip his drink, and read a newspaper, but always seems to be observing everything that goes on, especially Max, but in a very subtle way. He was at the bar last night when the excitement started and the body was found. He helped bring the stretcher into the parking lot, but I don't remember seeing him there after."

Tom said he hadn't talked to Franz and thanked Jack for the information.

In the late afternoon, Jack made his way over to Ben's. Max was behind the bar when Patti came in to work. Jack saw her talking to Peggy, the hostess. Then Patti breezed by him, offering only a quick hello, grabbed Max, and pulled her out back behind the bar.

"Patti," said Max, a little annoyed at being pulled away from Jack.

"I have the pictures."

"What pictures? ... Oh! The pictures. I thought you gave them to Tom last night."

"I did. But I made a copy first."

"You better not let Tom know. They're evidence, and I don't think you should have them."

"Well, I do. Do you want to see them or not?"

"Of course. Hold on while I get someone to watch the bar."

Patti went upstairs while Max went over to Jack. "Jack, will you do me a huge favor and watch the bar?"

Instantly suspicious, he asked, "Why?"

"Pleeease. It's important," she asked again, not giving an answer.

"What's up Max? What are you and Patti up to?"

"Jack, come on."

"Why?"

"You are impossible."

"I know," and he sat there.

"Okay, I'll tell you, but you have to keep quiet."

"We'll see. Talk."

"Patti made a copy of the pictures she took last night before she gave them to Tom. You can't say anything."

"Fine. I'll watch the bar."

Max ran upstairs where Patti had already loaded the pictures onto Courtney's computer. Max and Patti began to look at them, but when they got to the first picture of the ring, Max had her stop. She studied it silently. "It's hers. It is my Aunt Lillian's ring."

They looked at the rest of the pictures, and Max asked Patti to print out several of the ones of the ring.

Finished, the girls went back down to the bar. Max had the printouts in her hand. Jack had everything under control.

While the girls were upstairs, Leo, Ralph, and Paulie had come in, and were now well into their third beers and still talking about last night. Fueled by the power of beer, they had solved the mystery at least three or four times while sitting there with Jack. He marveled at what those three could accomplish with a few beers in them.

"Jack, look at these," Max said, pulling him aside. The boys stopped their deliberations when they saw her do this.

"What do you think?" asked Ralph in a hushed tone.

"I don't know," replied Leo.

Paulie, the master of the obvious, then said, "Look, she's showing him something. Looks like pictures."

Ralph looked over at him and said, "Duh."

"I was just saying."

"Maybe they're pictures from last night," chimed in Leo.

Ignoring the boys, Max continued showing the pictures to Jack. "Jack, look. It's my Grandma Ruth's ring. I was right."

Silently he studied the pictures. "You sure?"

"Yes, I am. My Grandma Ruth's father had the ring made especially for her. It was a one-sided gold band …"

"What do you mean it was one-sided?" he interrupted.

"There was a twist to it and if you traced your fingers around it you could go around the outside and around the inside without ever taking your finger off of it."

"Oh."

"There was an inscription in Hebrew and the translation was 'Wherever thou goest, so will I,' then 'Ruth' and a date or something. Look, you can see some of it in Patti's picture. That's not English. Tomorrow I will take the picture in town and see if I can get it translated. I bet it's Hebrew."

Jack continued to study the picture. "You said your great-grandfather had the ring made for your grandmother?"

"Yeah, from what I remember of the stories that Grandma Ruth told me, he had it made when she was born. He was a diamond broker in Switzerland. She always told me that the ring was magical and was the key to a great treasure. I always thought those stories were just that, stories. Maybe they were more than stories? Maybe … ?"

"Max, stop right there. You know how you can get carried away. Why don't you give Tom this information and let him do his job."

"Okay."

Jack watched her as she looked at the picture again and thought, "That was too easy …"

Before he could complete his thought, she looked up and, as she turned away, said to no one in particular, "But first I am going to have someone look at this picture and translate the inscription."

Then as an afterthought Jack said to Max, "You know, it might be a good idea not to let Tom know you have those pictures."

She paused and then walked out into the back room behind the bar leaving Jack and the boys alone.

Leo, Ralph, and Paulie heard most of what Max was telling Jack and, fortified with another round of beers, began again to solve the mystery.

When Max returned, she didn't have the picture and no more was said about it for the rest of the night. Jack stayed, waiting for Max to finish for the night. Finally, everyone was gone and he helped her close up. When it was time to leave, she looked at him and said, "Ready?"

"I guess." Then he hesitated. "Max, about this morning."

She cut him off. "It's okay. It was nothing. I should have let you know we were leaving."

"Max …"

She cut him off before he could finish what he wanted to say. "Don't worry about it. Let's get out of here."

He walked her to her car. As he opened her door for her, she turned and paused, just for a second. Then, slowly, they leaned into each other and kissed. Just once. Then, as if embarrassed, they both pulled back. Jack exhaled and spoke first. "Come on. Get in. It's late, and if you don't get home, you won't get any sleep."

"Thanks Jack. I'll see you tomorrow."

"Good night." He closed the door. She started the engine, gave him a little wave goodbye, and drove off. He walked home alone, feeling like some kind of lovesick teenager. He loved it.

CHAPTER SIXTEEN

MISSING PIECES

THE NEXT MORNING after the ritual coffee and gossip at Paula's, Jack stopped at the police station to see Tom. The secretary let Jack in, and he walked down the hall to Tom's small cramped office where he was sitting behind several piles of manila folders. As Jack knocked on the doorframe, he wondered how such a small town could generate so much paper. "Hi Tom, got a minute?

Tom looked up and said, "Of course, come on in. Actually I'm glad to see you, and this saves me the trouble of tracking you down later." He motioned to the chair in front of the desk, and Jack sat down. Even though they were best friends and Jack had visited Tom many times at the station, Jack still got that funny feeling when he sat down. It was the same feeling that you got when you were in grade school and were called to the principal's office. You knew that you hadn't done anything wrong, but just the fact that you were summoned to The Office put a knot in your stomach and you began reviewing your recent past, trying to figure out why you were there. This feeling lasted only a blink, but it was there nonetheless. "What's up?" Jack asked as soon as he was seated.

"Max came in to see me earlier. Man, is she wound up," said Tom.

"You really can't blame her can you? Her aunt's friend is found dead under a slab of ice in the harbor. Max sees what she thinks is her aunt's ring on her finger, and when the body is retrieved, the ring is gone."

"I don't blame her at all. I just wish I had answers for her."

"So what do you have?"

"I still haven't been able to get hold of her aunt so I called the Dry Gulch Police Department. The woman I talked to said I would have to talk to Officer Ruben Martinez, so I'm just waiting for a call back. She told me a car was found out in the desert and that he should be back soon."

"Oh. So what about Max?"

"Like I said, she came in this morning all wound up. She wanted to know if I had contacted her aunt yet, and then went on and on about the ring. I told her I was still trying to get hold of her aunt."

"And the ring?"

"She asked if she could see the pictures that Patti had taken. She seemed to know exactly which one, which I thought was a little bit unusual. Anyway, I showed them to her. Then she proceeded to tell me the whole story and asked for a copy of that picture."

"Did you give it to her?"

"I did. She thanked me and suddenly couldn't wait to get out of here. As she left, she said something to the effect that I'd see that she was right."

"She didn't waste any time," murmured Jack.

"What did you say?"

"Nothing. Anything on that car that was found abandoned?"

"Nope. It was a rental, and even though it was from New Mexico, there is no direct tie in to the body, at least not yet. The IDs that were in the wallet were all fakes, and there were no credit cards, no clothes, nothing else. We shipped it to the crime lab, and now they are trying to see if they can find anything. I contacted the FBI with the information from the IDs and they are doing a reverse search. I'm still waiting to see if they come up with anything."

Jack took all of this in. Tom probably had told him more than he should have, but they went back a long way and Miami would always temper their relationship.

"Can I ask you something?" Tom asked.

"Sure. What's up?"

"I could use your help. There is a lot of crap floating around town. Everyone has an opinion as to what happened, and quite frankly, it's becoming a bit annoying. I wanted to see if you would help me tone it down some. I'll keep you updated as to what's going on and maybe you can slow down the rumor mills."

"So you want me to be your press secretary. Just like those politicians." Then, Jack, imitating a presidential press secretary, said, "Ladies and gentlemen. Thank you for coming today. I have been asked by this office to make the following statement: 'We are concerned about the recent events, and we are doing everything possible to resolve the situation.' Yes, you over there. Like I said, we are working hard, and we will work harder if it is necessary. Thank you for coming in today, and we will let you know if anything happens. No more questions. Good day."

By the time Jack finished his impersonation, Tom was laughing so hard, he had tears coming out of his eyes. He caught his breath and said, "Yes, that's sort of what I had in mind, only not quite so formal."

"Sure. Any way that I can be of help, I will. Just promise me that this won't become another Miami. I don't need that."

"I promise."

As Jack got up to leave, he turned to Tom and asked, "Anything yet on how she died?"

"Nothing definitive. The body was clean, meaning she wasn't shot, stabbed, or strangled. She probably drowned. I'm still waiting for the coroner's final report, even though I did talk to him earlier. All he could tell me for certain was that her death was recent, but because she was frozen solid in the ice, an exact time of death is impossible to determine. In addition to the expected bruises and scrapes consistent with the way we found the body, she had other scars on her arms of unknown origin that were recently healed. There were several broken fingernails, and we are having them tested by the crime lab."

"So she was murdered?"

"Off the record, probably."

"Do you think she and the car are connected?"

"Good chance, but again we don't know yet."

"What about the ring?"

"I don't know. There was no ring on her hand when we got her up into the parking lot, although the photos clearly show it had been on her hand when she was found. Maybe it fell off. Maybe it was taken. We don't know, and without the ring, it's hard to prove that it is Max's aunt's. Max is convinced, but we need more than just those pictures. I'm keeping an open mind, but without proof ..."

The phone began to ring before he could finish. It was Max. She was talking so loudly and quickly Jack could almost hear everything she was telling Tom. Finally he hung up, looked at Jack and said, "If you hadn't figured it out, that was Max. She took the photos to the temple in Portsmouth, and the rabbi translated what little could be seen of the inscription on the ring. It read "... r thou goest, so ..." Not conclusive, but it's enough for now."

Jack had a lot to think about and that meant a run. The day was turning out to be another sunny, mild one, and when days like this come in mid-January, you take advantage of them. As soon as he opened the door to his apartment, Cat dashed out. She intended not to let the day go to waste as well, and she had some time to make up for since Jack left before she got up.

He started out at a leisurely pace and turned north on the boulevard. The one thing good about running this time of year was that the traffic was light, not the bumper-to-bumper traffic of the summer. As his breathing became more regular and he fell into the flow, his mind began to wander: What Tom had told him, the dead woman, and Max.

Mostly Max.

He smiled. Tom was right. She was the one. And last night.

On some elemental level, he had known from the moment he first saw her. It was her red hair that he first saw as she walked into Ben's looking for a job. He was working outside doing something, he couldn't remember what, when Courtney came out and called him over. She had just hired Max as a bartender. Introductions were made, and then Max asked Jack if he would be willing to help her find a place to live. As he said yes, he found himself grinning like a schoolboy who had just been spoken to by the most popular girl in class for the first time. Her smile was infectious, and the rest of the package was, well, all there. She looked about five-feet-four-inches, slender with bumps and curves where there should be bumps and curves, and he had found it hard not to stare. What really got him though were her eyes. They were the most amazing green he had ever seen, and in them, he saw a spirit that was both wild and free but tinged with a touch of sadness and a longing for something not yet found.

As she told the story, her mother had just died so she had no reason to stay in Connecticut. She settled her mother's affairs, packed her car, and headed north. Portsmouth, New Hampshire—located on the Piscataqua River, which divides New Hampshire from Maine—was one of her first stops. It just felt right, and so she stayed, got hired at Ben's and … .

His pace quickened as he began his third mile. "I should have asked her out then." Jack chided himself, but he knew the answer.

She fit right in at Ben's, and it wasn't long before most of the single men were asking her out. Jack would have been one of them, except he thought he was too old and the memories of Marie still haunted him. So he was content to be the good, safe friend. Then Andy came into her life.

"That son of a bitch." Jack's pace increased as all of the frustration that he kept under control began to emerge. He never understood what Max saw in Andy. Their relationship merely confirmed Jack's pet theory that beautiful, strong women seem to fall for dangerous, controlling losers far too often. Why? He just didn't know. Was it because these women thought they could change the men? Was it the challenge, coupled with a woman's ability to nurture and care for a wounded spirit, that surfaced when they were with these men? Was it a desire for risk and excitement? It seemed to Jack to be a genetic flaw that some women possessed.

Max and Andy had dated off and on over the years. During the on times, Jack remained on the sidelines watching Andy's antics, waiting for that inevitable moment when he would suddenly disappear. Max would go from anger to frustration to acceptance, and then Andy would reappear and she'd be back at anger. He was smooth and he'd play her like a cheap fiddle; she'd fall under his spell again; and they'd be back together. It drove Jack crazy to see her treated this way, but there wasn't a whole lot he could do about it except be there for her. He had to let her figure it out for herself if he were ever to have a chance.

His anger was abating, his lungs hurt, and he could feel the effort in his legs, so he slowed his pace some as he thought about Andy's most recent appearance. "Man, was Max pissed at him when he showed up the other night. What the hell did Scotch and Soda Man say to him to get him to leave so quickly?" Jack wondered. "I'll have to remember to ask Franz when or if I ever see him again. I wasn't going to be so diplomatic. Probably good that he got there first."

As Jack made the final turn toward home, he slowed to a jog. The parking lot at Ben's was beginning to fill, and he saw Max's car. His memory flashed back to last night. He grinned as he relived the moment. They had kissed, only once and … "And what?" he thought. As much as he needed to see her, to find out if he had made a fool of himself, he was also scared to. Was he being completely foolish or was there something more? His pace quickened as did his heartbeat as he hurried home to shower and change. Then he would go over to the bar for a bite to eat, for a beer, and to see Max.

CHAPTER SEVENTEEN

THE GOOD FRIEND

"HI MAX," HE SAID as he took a seat at the bar,

"Hey Jack. Beer?" she asked as she went past him while preparing to make a frozen strawberry daiquiri. He didn't know what he was expecting, but whatever it was, it didn't happen. No reaction, no special look; it was as if last night hadn't happened.

"Sure. That'd be great." He could hear the blender running out back, then she reappeared with a pint of ESB, and placed it in front of him. Before he could say thanks, she was gone. The blender stopped, and she returned with a perfect frozen strawberry daiquiri.

Sipping his beer, Jack remembered his bartending days in Miami and marveled at just how good Max was. She looked happy. It was good for her to be so busy because it distracted her from all that had happened in the last few days. Tom still hadn't heard anything from New Mexico about her aunt, and since Max hadn't said anything, Jack assumed that she hadn't either. Whenever there was a pause in activity, she came over.

"How was your day?" she asked during one such pause.

"Busy. I ... "

Before he could finish his sentence, she was gone. As he watched her, he thought that he was just spared from making a fool of himself. Then she returned, "You were saying?"

"Oh, nothing." The moment had passed.

The order printer started again, and she was gone again.

He wanted to talk to her, but he realized that it was not going to happen here or now, unlike the movies where the bartender is polishing a glass while talking to a customer and occasionally making a drink. The reality was that of nonstop action punctuated by brief moments of fragmented speech, not always in any set order, and the result, over the course of an evening, was something you might be able to call a conversation.

Things were beginning to quiet down in the bar. Max had gone out back for a few minutes, and Jack was alone at the bar when Andy walked in. "Oh shit," thought Jack as he watched Andy stop and look around the now nearly empty bar.

He had that look of supreme confidence that Jack hated. It was as if he were better than anyone else and it was a gift that he was there. He also looked like he might have had a few drinks already. His arrogance was such that as soon as he saw Jack, he walked over and sat next to him. "Hey Jack," Andy said.

Before Jack could say anything, Max came around the corner and stopped dead in her tracks. Jack saw the color drain from her face and anger flash in her eyes. Andy turned away from Jack and focused his gaze on Max. Looking at her with a cocky smile, he said, "Hello, Max."

Jack looked over at him, then back at Max, barely daring to breathe. Jack could see the tension in her face as she managed to reply with an icy "Andy."

"How about a beer?"

"Sure." She turned away, making no attempt to hide her contempt for him, took a beer from the cooler, placed the bottle in front of him, and walked away. He took a long pull on the beer, then sat silently watching her.

In an attempt to ease the tension by distracting Andy, Jack said, "So Andy, what have you been up to?"

"Not much, Jack." Then Andy turned his attention back to Max. Another long pull on his beer, and he turned back to Jack. "I understand there was a little excitement around here over the weekend."

"You might say that."

"I heard that a body was found out in the harbor."

"You heard right. Patti found her while taking pictures of the ice."

"Who was she?"

Jack paused before answering. He wasn't sure how much Max could hear, and if he could shield her from Andy, he would. She was upset enough with Andy's presence, she didn't need to have to deal with his questions. "She was a friend of Max's aunt."

"Really? ... How's that?"

"Max recognized her."

Then with a slightly raised voice, so Max would be sure to hear, Andy said, "That's too bad. I wouldn't wish that on anyone. I'm sorry."

Jack thought his response was a little bit odd, but then, it was Andy. As long as Andy was there, Jack wasn't going to leave, so he ordered another beer. Jack nursed his beer while Andy drank several more. Conversation was sparse, and when it did occur, it mostly focused on what had happened last weekend. Andy asked the questions, and Jack answered them. Finally the last customer left, and only Andy, Jack, and Max remained.

Max gave Andy his check and said it was time to leave. "I'd like to talk to you," Andy said with a bit of a slur in his voice as he glanced at the check then reached in his pocket for some cash.

"Well, I don't want to talk to you. Good night."

"Max, we have to talk," he insisted.

"No. We don't."

"Max, come on, it's important. And what about all those good times we used to have?" he said with a slight whine in his voice.

" 'Used to' is correct. Now please pay your tab and leave."

Andy looked over at Jack, stared for a moment, then forced a smile, and said, in a voice meant to provoke, "I see. So now you're doing Jackie here."

Jack had kept quiet to this point—he didn't want to give legitimacy to Andy's antics by reacting—but now a line had been crossed. He started to get up, but before he could say or do anything, Andy threw cash on the bar and headed for the door. As he reached the doorway, he stopped, turned back, and—with steel in his eyes and a voice neither had ever heard before—said, "We're not through yet. That goes for both of you." Then he turned and was gone.

When Jack and Max were finally alone—the doors locked, the cash put away, and nothing remained that could delay the inevitable—they stood there, or rather Jack continued to sit in his seat and Max stood behind the bar, looking at each other. After an awkward few moments while staring at Jack, she finally just said, "What?"

Jack stared back in silence. He tried to keep a straight face as the absurdity of the whole evening came ever more into focus.

She stared.

He stared.

She said, "What?" again. Jack held his stone face for a few more moments and then felt the first small twitch at the corner of his mouth. She must have seen it because she had one too. Then there was that muffled half giggle. All at once the tension broke, and they were both laughing uncontrollably.

When their breaths returned and were able to speak, they both said at the same time, "Wow, that was weird," prompting a new round of laughter. Max poured herself a glass of wine, Jack had another beer, and they sat there talking too far into the wee hours of the night.

"Jack, I'm worried."

"Why?" he replied.

"Because he's back again. I've had it. I can't keep going through this with him. You saw him last week and again tonight. He comes in as if nothing had happened and was expecting everything to be all right. How can I get it across to him that I don't want to have anything to do with him anymore?"

Jack didn't have any good answers for her, so he just tried to be supportive and let her find her own answer.

"Max, I think you need to get away from here even if only for a day."

"I can't."

"Why not? You have tomorrow off, don't you. I heard Patti say she had it off also. Why don't you two go on a road trip? Up north or to Maine. Somewhere, anywhere, so you can just forget about all of this shit for a while."

"You might be right."

Nothing more was said for a few minutes. Then Max said, "You know, I still haven't heard from my aunt. I'm really beginning to worry."

"I'm sure she's fine. I know Tom called the Dry Gulch police to have them check on her."

"He didn't tell me."

"Probably because he hadn't heard anything. Doesn't the saying go 'No news is good news'?"

"I guess."

Max was feeling better. She decided that the idea of getting away for the day was a good one and she would call Patti in the morning to see if she would go with her.

"Max, it's time to call it a night," Jack said, glancing at his watch. Max agreed. Once outside, as she turned to lock the door, a movement or something caught Jack's eye. He turned to look more closely but didn't see anything. He thought he heard a car driving off from the lot behind the commercial wharf. He couldn't be certain and he didn't see any taillights. Max finished with the door, and Jack walked her to her car. He opened the car door for her. They paused and looked at each other. Neither moved; then Max said, "Good night Jack, and thanks for being such a good friend." She got in and drove off.

As Jack walked home, her last words echoed in his ears. "Thanks for being such a good friend." That was twice now in two days she had laid the "F" word on him, but then, what about the kiss last night? Briefly he wondered if last night had really happened or if he imagined it. No. It had happened, and it was more than a friendship kiss. Of that he was sure. Maybe it was too soon? As he thought about it, he knew that was wrong as well. She had kissed him as much as he had kissed her. Then the past few hours flashed through his head. What did he think he saw and heard over at the harbor? What about Andy? What did Andy mean when he said, "It's not over yet"? The walk was short, and Jack was tired. As soon as his head hit the pillow, he was asleep, his last thoughts of Max.

CHAPTER EIGHTEEN

ANOTHER LOSS

HE COULDN'T SEE HER. "We'll be back tonight. I'll call you … ." Her voice was near and he ran toward it, but she was always just out of sight. Her words were lost as he felt something hit him. Then he wasn't running, he was lying on the ground and felt a weight pressing on his chest.

Opening his eyes, he found himself staring into Cat's face. That's when he heard the beep of his answering machine. Cat began tap dancing on his chest making it very clear that he was to get up. "Okay, okay, I'm getting up," he said as Cat jumped onto the floor. Swinging his legs over the edge of the bed, he sat there while Cat rubbed up against him, purring loudly. He looked over at his machine, the message light was blinking. He hit the play-message button and listened. "Hi Jack. Since you didn't pick up, I assume you're still asleep. I'm taking your suggestion and am going away for the day. Patti's going with me. We'll be back tonight. I'll call you tonight when we get back. Thanks for everything. You're such a good friend."

He didn't move as he thought about what he had just heard. "Good. She took my advice, but there was the 'F' word again."

Cat continued rubbing against his leg, purring. He reached down and picked her up; she settled into his lap as he scratched her head. "Cat, can you explain to me what is going on?" She just looked up, squinted, then closed her eyes and purred.

He needed coffee. As soon as he got a cup into the microwave, Cat ran for the door and he followed her down the stairs to let her out. It was cold and gray, a typical dismal winter's day when weather patterns were changing. He shivered as she ran out. He closed the door and went back upstairs to his now hot coffee.

An hour or so later, he drove over to Paula's for a bite to eat. It was midmorning and most of the breakfast crowd was gone. He picked up the paper and was about to open it when Tom walked in.

"Hi Jack."

"Mornin' Tom."

"You seen Max?"

"No. Why?"

"I just thought that …" Tom began to grin and that's when Jack cut him off.

"You just thought what, Tom?" he asked with feigned indignation.

"I just thought that maybe you had talked to her this morning."

"No I haven't."

"Any idea what she's doing today? I need to talk to her." Tom's face clouded over and his voice became serious and official.

"What's wrong?"

Tom didn't say anything right away as he searched for words.

"Something about her aunt?"

"Yes."

"What."

"The Dry Gulch PD just called and told me that they found her aunt."

"That's good."

"Not really. Remember I told you that when I first called them, no one was there because of a car accident?"

A chill went through Jack as he guessed what was next.

"Her aunt?"

" 'Fraid so."

"Shit …" Then he asked the question, even though he knew what the answer would be. "Is she all right?"

"No. She's dead," was Tom's somber reply.

"When did it happen?"

"As best they can figure, a couple weeks ago. The body was a real mess, and it took a while to make the ID. I told them about finding Meredith. They couldn't believe it."

Jack was silent as he thought about what Tom just told him. Then he said, "She's gone away for the day. Andy was in the bar last night. He upset her petty good, and she needed to get away. Patti went with her. This is really going to freak her out."

"I know. You said she'd be back tonight?"

"Tom, maybe I should tell her. She said she'd call me when she got home."

"Sure, that might be a good idea. But I will need to talk to her tomorrow. Tell her we're all sorry."

"I will."

* * *

Tom was just getting into his car when Jack rushed out after him. "Hey Tom, hold up."

He stopped and turned.

"It may not mean anything, but Andy was in the bar last night."

"So?"

"He was saying some things that were a little strange."

"Get in. It's too cold to stand out here."

They both got into the cruiser. Tom looked at him. "What's this about Andy?"

"Last night I was at Ben's when he came in. The place was beginning to empty out and he looked around, then he came over and sat next to me."

"So? No crime in that."

"True, but you know there isn't a lot of goodwill between us."

"True."

"You should have seen the look on Max's face when she turned and saw him. She was busy and didn't see him at first, but when she did … let's just say that the look she gave him could have frozen hell. Scared me."

"I can only imagine. So is it finally over between those two?"

"I think so, based on last week and judging from the look she gave him last night."

"So aside from this being some juicy gossip, why are you telling me this?"

"As we sat there, Andy had a few beers and then he began asking me questions about what was new around the harbor. The way he asked just seemed odd. It was as if he already knew the answers. He seemed to be trying too hard to give the impression that he was hearing everything for the first time. It was weird. When I told him about the body in the ice, he became much more animated. Like we were old buddies. He asked a lot of questions. You know, who she was, how she was killed. … He didn't ask how she died, but rather how she was killed. Struck me as odd."

"Really? … I may have to have a talk with our friend Andy," said Tom.

"Then when it was time to close up he gave Max a bit of a hard time, but not like last Friday. He kept saying that he wanted to talk to her. He kept insisting but finally got the message that she had no intention of talking with him, and he finally left. As he was leaving, he accused Max of sleeping with me and said he wasn't finished with us just yet."

"Jack, back it up a bit. Say that again? I hadn't heard anything about that."

"I didn't tell you that story?"

"I don't think so, at least it's not ringing a bell. Tell me."

"Let's see. It was the Friday before the body was found. I had gone over to Ben's to hang out. The place was really busy, so I sat at a table in the corner. Max was really busy when Andy came in, and he sat at the last open seat at the bar. She didn't see him at first, but when she turned and saw him, she froze. You could tell she wanted to kill him. I mean she was pissed. At first Andy was all nice and acting like he hadn't been gone for nearly a month. He sat there all night, and all she could do was try to ignore him. I felt bad for her. Anyway, as the night went on, he became more and more of a jerk. He was loud and kept talking at her until she finally told him he would have to leave. That's when he became a real asshole. I was just getting up to see if I couldn't ease him out when Scotch and Soda Man, who had been sitting at the end of the bar, stood up, went over to Andy, and whispered something in his ear. Andy left. Before anyone could say anything, he threw some money on the bar and left also."

"Really," said Tom. "Why didn't you tell me this before?"

"I thought you knew. Probably it just got lost in all of the excitement when the body was found?"

"Interesting," Tom said softly, more to himself than to Jack.

"He's such an ass."

"Jack, we all know he's a jerk, but he hasn't done anything illegal that I can see. All I can suggest is that you keep your head up and be careful. Same goes for Max."

"Yeah, I know. I just thought you might want to know."

Jack climbed out of the cruiser, and Tom drove off.

CHAPTER NINETEEN

A FUGITIVE'S FINGERPRINTS

JACK FINISHED THE PAPER and his coffee, and went back to his shop. How was he going to tell Max? The question kept reverberating in his head as he began working on the bookcase he was building for her. The news about her aunt was disturbing. Maybe Max didn't know her very well, but she was all Max had.

His thoughts were interrupted when he heard the phone upstairs in his apartment begin to ring. It stopped when his machine picked up, and almost immediately the phone in the shop began to ring.

"This can't be good," he thought as he picked up the phone. "Hello."

He recognized Tom's voice. "Jack."

"Tom. What's up?"

"You gonna be there for a bit?"

"Yeah. Why?"

"Stay there." Then he hung up before Jack could ask anything else.

"What the hell?"

It wasn't even ten minutes before Tom walked into the shop, but to Jack, it had felt more like hours. As he waited, his imagination was beginning to run wild. None of the scenarios was good. He looked up when the door opened.

"Hey Tom. What's up?"

Tom got right to the point. "It's Max."

"What about Max?" Jack's voice tinged with panic. "Was she in an accident? Is she all right?"

"She's okay," Tom reassured him.

Jack stared at him with questioning eyes.

"I just heard back from the coroner's office." He pulled a piece of folded paper out of his pocket. "It doesn't seem that Meredith's death was an accident."

"No?"

"The final cause of death was drowning, but there were bruises on her body that were consistent with a struggle. Definitely defensive. But here's what's interesting; there were other bruises and scratches that could not be so easily explained. Subtle, almost healed. Ones that she got some time before she ended up here in Rye."

"Are you saying she was murdered?"

"Most likely. I considered suicide, but it just doesn't seem likely. People may try to kill themselves by jumping off the high bridge on Route 95, but not by jumping over a guardrail and falling into a small tidal creek."

"Murdered? Why?"

"Don't know yet." Tom watched Jack pick up a scrap of wood and a pencil, and draw a line on it. Then he made several more marks on the board. The first one he labeled "today," then he labeled the other marks "body discovered," "car found," and now the last mark, "her aunt's death." He studied the piece of wood. Tom walked around the workbench, took it from Jack, and looked at it.

Jack said, "So do you think Meredith could have killed Lillian and was out here after Max?"

"I didn't say that."

"But you think that."

"We have to consider every possibility."

Jack was stunned.

"That makes no sense. If she killed Lillian, who would have killed her?"

"I have no idea."

"What else did the coroner's report say?"

"Well, her hands were rough, like someone who worked outdoors a lot, and she had several broken fingernails. We found what looked like skin under several of her nails. My guess is that she put up a good fight. We're still waiting for the DNA results from the state police crime lab. We lifted several fingerprints off the car as well. Some were our victim's and others, well, we don't know who they belong to, but at least we now know who she was."

"But you knew that without the fingerprints. Max ID'd her."

"True, but the fingerprints told a different story.

Jack looked back at him and said, "I'm not so sure I'm following you."

Tom began. "Her real name was Caroline Fitzwilliam. She was a fugitive."

"What? A fugitive? A fugitive from what?"

"Back in the early '60s, she was a civil-rights activist and had been arrested for some civil-disobedience actions. She escaped and until now had completely disappeared. The IDs found in the car matched one of the aliases she had used back then."

Jack interrupted, "That's all very nice, but what does this have to do with Max?"

"I don't know, but it worries me."

"Tom, this doesn't make much sense."

"I know, but listen to me. What if Lillian didn't know about Meredith's past? What if Lillian found out, they fought, and Lillian was killed, maybe by accident, maybe not. Meredith panics and flees. Maybe she …" His voice trailed off momentarily, then he continued, "Jack, in any event, we have two dead women: both deaths suspicious, and both seem to have some relationship to Max. That's enough to cause me concern for Max's safety, and I'd like you to help by watching over her. Can you do that?"

"Of course. You know she's gonna freak out."

"I know. That's why you will be the best person to break the news to her."

"First Aunt Lillian, and now this about Meredith," Jack thought.

"Will you let me know when she gets home?" asked Tom as he moved toward the door to leave.

Jack, still stunned, stammered, "Yeah, sure."

Tom was about to open the door, when he stopped, walked back to the bench, picked up the piece of wood Jack had scribbled on, and asked, "Can I keep this?"

"Sure."

"Thanks."

Tom opened the door, cold air rushed in, but before he stepped out, he turned toward Jack and said, "Remember, this conversation was between the two of us, and it stays that way."

Jack's response was lost as the door was pulled shut. "No problem Tom. Just between us."

This was a lot for Jack to process, so he did what came naturally when he needed time to think. He went for a run.

CHAPTER TWENTY

NEAR MISS

THE SUN WAS STILL OUT, although soon it would set. The roads were clear, there wasn't much breeze, and the temperature was in the high twenties, perfect for running. As Jack laced up his shoes, all his thoughts were on the run. Knit hat, gloves, tights, a technical shirt, turtleneck jersey, and his club's running jacket. He was ready. Most people would look at him and think he was crazy to go out so underdressed for the cold, but he knew the clothes would be perfect once he got going and warmed up. He felt the chill for the first few minutes; however, by the time he reached Route 1A he was toasty warm.

Jack didn't know exactly how far he would run. That would depend on how he felt after he got going. He headed north on Route 1A past the harbor at an easy pace. As he began to warm up and settle into a comfortable rhythm, his thoughts drifted to what Tom had said. Max's only remaining family member had been found dead in the desert. And Meredith's past, did Lillian know? Max was going to be devastated. Jack had a flashback to when he lost Marie and how totally alone and small he felt at that moment. Tom had been there for him, and now he would be there for Max. What was Meredith doing here? Did she know what had happened to Lillian? Had she been in the accident that killed Lillian? Why did she run? What about that ring that Max kept harping about? And Andy? What's with him?

The ocean to his right was flat and calm; the light was changing as the sun began to set in the west. Jack was tempted to stop and inhale the serenity and beauty, but he knew he wouldn't. Random thoughts came and went in his head. He felt a clarity, an understanding of what had happened and what he had to do. As soon as he tried to focus those feelings into the present, they vaporized and things seemed as disjointed as ever. When he reached the state park, he turned toward the sun and began to loop back toward home on a parallel road.

This road was wooded, and there was little traffic. In the tree-lined stretches, the shadows made it seem much closer to nightfall than it really was, creating a feeling of foreboding and gloom. Between these dark patches, there were areas of intense brightness where the setting sun flooded the road as if it were under a spotlight. At one point, where the road took a sharp turn toward the sun, Jack was emerging from the shadows and, for a moment, he was nearly blinded by the sun's brilliance. He didn't see the car until it was almost too late. "Fuckin' asshole!" he shouted as he dove off the side of the road, landing in a snowbank. The car missed, but it didn't slow down. "Son of a bitch," Jack swore as he stood up and began to take stock. He looked in the direction that the car was going—it was long gone. He didn't see any obvious damage from his dive off the road, but his heart was still pounding as he began to run again.

As the adrenaline rush began to wear off, he began to feel a soreness in his leg. It wasn't long before he was back on the main road, running along the water, albeit at a much slower pace. Every time a car passed him, the image of that car coming around that corner straight at him kept flashing through his mind. Over and over, he saw the car coming around the corner, never slowing nor swerving, straight at him. It was a dark red, nondescript car, a sedan. He didn't recognize it. The driver was silhouetted in the sunlight so he couldn't see who it was. Nonetheless something about it seemed familiar. By the time he reached the harbor, his pace slowed even more and he was convinced it hadn't been an accident.

He stopped running when he reached Ben's parking lot. His breathing returned to normal quickly; then a gust of wind hit him, and he shivered. "Tom was right. I do care for Max even more than I have been willing to admit."

As he walked the rest of the way home, more memories flashed in and out of his head. The car, Marie, Max. The sun had nearly finished setting as he opened the door to his apartment. The blast of warm air that hit him triggered more memories. He could almost smell the frangipani as he remembered the first time Marie walked toward him, only now, he saw Max looking at him. He jumped when Cat raced in, nearly tripping him. "Jesus, Cat! You scared the shit out of me." Jack grinned as he climbed the stairs, saying to himself, "What is your problem? It's not like you hit your head or anything. Max will be home soon enough."

* * *

"Jack. I thought you might be here." Tom's voice startled him.

"Are you stalking me or something?" Jack hadn't seen Tom come in. He was sitting alone at his favorite corner table at Ben's, sipping a beer, feeling the aches of his near accident slowly develop and trying to figure out how he was going to tell Max about her aunt.

"No, but I just talked to Martinez again."

"Martinez?"

"Dry Gulch PD. Officer Ruben Martinez."

"Oh yeah."

"Well anyway, I had sent him all of the fingerprints we had as well as what we had on Meredith."

"Yes?"

"As expected, Meredith's prints were in the car and their house. Now here's what is interesting. They had some prints from in the car and the house that they couldn't match up, and those matched some of the mystery prints I sent to them that we couldn't identify. It's still unclear whether these mystery prints belong to one individual or to several, but they do match."

Jack didn't move or say anything for a few moments as he processed what Tom had just told him.

"Tom, what if Meredith didn't kill Lillian? What if both women were killed by the same person and that person is here?" Jack spoke quietly and slowly, trying hard to mask the fear that began to grip him.

"I've thought of that, and it's a possibility. Other than Meredith's secret about her past, their lives seemed pretty quiet and off the radar screen. Right now we don't know who or, more importantly, why anyone would want them dead."

There was another long pause as neither man would give voice to the same thought: What about Max?

Jack exhaled slowly. "Son of a bitch," he said under his breath.

"I know," said Tom. "Do you know what you're going to say to her?"

"Not yet."

"Jack, I've got to get going. Call me in the morning. Tell Max that I'm sorry. Oh and don't forget, I will need to talk to her in the morning."

"I will. Good night."

As Tom walked out of the bar, Jack was hit with a feeling that things were going to get a lot worse before they would get better.

* * *

It was late, and other than Jack, the bar was empty save for the staff. Max hadn't called yet, so he would have to wait for her call at home. He paid his tab and was about to leave when the phone rang. Immediately his pulse quickened as he stopped to watch Peggy answer the phone. After a brief conversation, she looked in his direction and signaled that the phone was for him. As she handed the phone to him, she mouthed the words, "It's Max."

Before speaking, he took a deep breath to calm himself. "Hey Max, how was the trip? Did you just get home?"

"It was great, and yes we did. Patti is about to leave. We had such a good time. We shopped until we dropped, we played tourist and had dinner in this quaint little restaurant. You'd love it, we'll have to go sometime."

"That's great. You needed the break." He tried to sound as if nothing was wrong.

He may have failed because then she asked, "Jack, what are you doing at Ben's so late? I mean if I were there, it would make perfect sense," she said with a bratty, teasing tone of voice … then more seriously, "Is there something going on I should know about?"

Jack paused before answering. "Well, yes, there is something I need to talk to you about."

Max interrupted, "You better not have a new girlfriend."

"No, Max. There is no new girlfriend."

"Good. Then, what?"

"Listen. Can I come over? I need to talk to you in person."

Jack only heard silence on the other end of the line. Finally he asked, "Max, are you still there? … Can I come over?"

"Jack, you're scaring me. What is so important that you can't tell me now, over the phone?"

"I'm sorry… . I just need to talk to you." He tried to sound as soothing as he could.

"Fine. Come on over," she finally answered.

"Thanks. I'll see you in a few minutes.

He heard the click as she hung up. He could only imagine what was going through her mind. He didn't like deceiving her, but he had to tell her in person.

As Jack drove over to her house, he wondered if Patti was still there. He hadn't thought to ask, but it would probably be good if she were. As he pulled into Max's drive, he saw Patti's car. "Good," he thought. He turned off his engine, and before getting out of his truck, he began going over in his mind one more time how he was going to tell Max. The truth was, he was stalling. He really didn't know what he was going to say. He had never had to break this kind of news to someone before. Then, before he could completely gather his thoughts, the door opened and the light from inside flooded out onto the drive. Max was in the doorway looking out, so he jumped out of the truck and headed for the open door.

"Hi Max. Welcome home," he said.

"Hi Jack. Thanks. Come in. It's freezing."

All the lights were on, shopping bags were on the floor, and he could hear Patti moving around in the kitchen.

"So, what's so important that you had to see me tonight?" Max asked as she shut the door.

"Max," he paused, trying to compose his thoughts. Then before he could say anything else, Patti came out of the kitchen with a bowl of ice cream. "Jack. I didn't hear you come in. What's going on?" she asked.

"That's just what Jack was about to tell me," said Max.

The two women stared at Jack.

Without thinking, he blurted out, "Max, Tom got word this morning that your Aunt Lillian was found dead in the desert. Apparently she was in a car accident."

Patti's eyes widened, and she spoke first. "What?"

Max didn't react.

As soon as he said it, he wished that he could take back his words. Jack looked at Max and stepped toward her, wrapping his arms around her. Softly he said, "Max ..." He felt her shudder and take a deep breath followed by a muffled sob. She held onto him, and he held her.

They stayed like that for a few moments; then he relaxed his grip and leaned back away from her. She looked up at him, her eyes beginning to tear up. "Max, I'm so sorry," Jack said. "I didn't mean for it to come out that way."

"It's okay," she murmured as she slowly sat down on the couch. "Aunt Lillian is dead?" she asked in a small subdued voice, then she lowered her face into her hands, sobbing softly.

Jack didn't know what to do next, "Max, are you okay?" As soon as he said it, he realized it was a stupid thing to say.

Patti moved first. She sat down next to Max and put an arm around Max's shoulder, and Max leaned into her. They sat there until Max finally said, "Yes. I'm fine," as she wiped the tears from her face with her hand.

Patti looked up at Jack and said, "I'll stay with her tonight. She'll be fine."

Jack knew otherwise. He knew Max well enough to know she wasn't fine, but he also knew there wasn't much he could do at this moment. She had her own way of dealing with bad news, and he had to let it play out on its own. Patti was there, and Max didn't need two people hovering over her.

"I'll come by in the morning, and we'll go see Tom," he said gently.

"Sure … Jack … thanks," she said with an audible sniffle. "Good night."

"Good night Max. I'll see you in the morning."

CHAPTER TWENTY-ONE

MORE QUESTIONS

GAZING OUT OVER THE SALT MARSHES, Jack's mood was reflected in the weather. Gloomy. Low, thick clouds filtered out the sun, and snow was predicted. As he finished his coffee, he could see the first flakes beginning to fall. "Well Cat, do you think I should put the plow on now, before I go pick up Max?"

Cat was curled up on the couch and opened one eye, then closed it again without even lifting her head.

Jack noted her response of complete indifference, put on his coat and headed out. He looked up at the sky. His concern for Max overshadowed common sense. He decided to deal with the plow later, even though he knew that probably was the wrong decision.

By the time he got to Max's, snow had begun to cover the roads. Patti answered the door and invited him in. She closed the door behind him and he stood there, snow melting off the shoulders of his coat as he looked at Max. Not a word was said. Then, he held his arms out toward Max and she went to him. He wrapped his arms around her, and they stood there holding each other tightly. No crying, no words, just the reassurance that everything would be all right in this simple gesture.

Patti broke the silence. "Coffee, anyone?"

"Sure," said Jack, and Max nodded.

As they sipped their coffees, Jack noted how drawn and tired both girls looked. He could tell they hadn't slept much last night. He tried to keep things upbeat, but it was almost impossible. This morning's conversation skirted the news that Jack had given Max last night. They made small talk about the trip, but it was without enthusiasm. It was as if they were all avoiding the eight-hundred-pound gorilla in the room.

Coffee finished, Patti said goodbye. The snow was coming down hard as Max and Jack walked out to his truck. Neither said much on the ride to the police station to meet with Tom. Max didn't like driving in the snow, so she was glad Jack was driving; Jack was glad his truck had four-wheel drive, which was now a necessity, not a luxury. He wished he had put the plow on earlier.

When they arrived at the station, Tom was waiting. He guided them into a small, cold, impersonal room, with plain walls, a table, some chairs, and not much else.

Tom offered coffee or hot chocolate while they took their coats off. Jack and Max declined. "Sorry about the room. It's the only space I had available this morning," said Tom.

"That's okay," said Jack. Max remained silent.

"Please sit down," said Tom, motioning to the steel frame chairs.

As soon as they were all seated, Tom got right to the point. "Max," he said, "I'm sorry for your loss, but I must ask you a few questions."

Jack thought this was a little on the cold side. Yesterday he was lecturing Jack on feelings and other touchy feely stuff, and this morning when it seemed that's what Max needed, Tom was all business. Jack watched Tom closely as he addressed Max and realized this seemingly dispassionate disconnect might be the best way to handle this situation. Tom had a job to do, and even though they were all friends, he had to keep it professional. There would be time later to be a friend. This morning, he was a cop.

Max nodded her assent, and Tom paused before going on. Max sat there stone-faced.

Tom's demeanor softened as he began. "Max, as you know, your aunt was found in a car wreck on the side of the road."

"I know, Jack told me last night."

"At first the police in Dry Gulch assumed it was a simple accident. It's not uncommon for people to fall asleep at the wheel and to go off the road, but now they're not so sure."

"Why? What do you mean?"

"Well, even though the exact cause of death hasn't been determined because of the condition of the body, there is enough evidence, even though circumstantial, to make it probable that her death was not an accident."

"Not an accident?" asked Max while fighting to stay in control. She inhaled, and Jack could see her stiffen, trying to hold it together. He pulled his chair closer to hers and took her hand. She was trembling slightly. She looked at him. Her look pleading a thousand questions. In a soft voice, Jack said, "Everything will be all right. Let's see what Tom has to say."

Tom continued. "After finding her, they went to her house looking for her companion, Meredith. She wasn't there, and the house had been torn apart. As we know now, Meredith was the woman Patti found in the ice, and your aunt's death occurred about two weeks prior." Tom continued to fill in details, but Max didn't hear what he was saying.

She looked up. "Both killed?"

"It seems so," Tom paused.

"But why? Who would have done that?"

"We don't know. Now, here's where it gets interesting. Meredith was a fugitive, and the FBI had been looking for her since the sixties." He paused.

Max looked as if she had been hit in the stomach and had the breath knocked out of her as she gasped in disbelief. She stared at Tom. Jack glanced at Tom, then he turned his attention to Max. Her grip on Jack's hand tightened. He noted she wasn't trembling any more. Tom remained silent.

Those few moments of silence seemed like an eternity. Max's voice was the first to break the silence. "A fugitive? What? ... How do?" she stammered. Then more firmly, "Do they think she killed my aunt?"

"There are some questions."

"No. She couldn't have done it," said Max with resolve.

"What did you know about Meredith?" Tom asked.

"Not much, and I hadn't seen my Aunt Lillian since my grandmother's funeral. A few sporadic Christmas cards, but nothing more. Certainly nothing to indicate any problems. I just can't believe that Meredith would have killed my aunt."

"Do you have any idea who might have wanted to hurt your aunt?"

"No. I just knew that she lived in New Mexico with Meredith."

"Do you know what she did in New Mexico?" Tom asked.

"Not really. Something to do with art I think. ... I really don't know."

"Max, I know this is difficult."

She looked up at him. "Tom, I know that I know little about my aunt and even less about Meredith, but I also know that she couldn't have killed my aunt."

"Why?"

"I don't know. I just do. Didn't you just tell me that Meredith was also killed?" Max was beginning to get impatient.

"Yes. Everything points to both deaths being deliberate and not accidents."

"Then it makes no sense that Meredith killed my aunt and that she would have come out here. Wouldn't she have just disappeared again? I mean you just told me she had been a fugitive from the FBI. Sounds like she was pretty good at it."

Max's voice was becoming stronger as her impatience turned to anger. Jack watched her. She took her hand from his, and he could tell she was not going to just take this news. She was going to fight it.

"Max, you're right about that," said Tom, a little surprised by her outburst. "It doesn't make a lot of sense, but we have to consider every possibility."

Her voice softened. "I know you do Tom, but I just can't believe it. And what about the ring?"

"The ring?"

"Yes, my aunt's ring. Meredith had my aunt's ring on her finger, and now the ring is gone. Isn't it possible that whoever did this wanted the ring? Remember how it was in the pictures that Patti took when Meredith was found? It was on her hand, out on the ice, but it was gone by the time she was brought up into the parking lot."

"I'm sorry Max. There has been no sign of the ring. We're considering that possibility."

Through it all, Jack sat there next to Max. Occasionally he held her hand or stroked her hair for comfort. Tissues were at the ready, but were never needed. Max was tough, and he knew she would grieve in her own way, in her own time. Several hours had passed by the time all questions had been asked and they all stood to leave.

"Thanks Tom," said Jack.

"Max, we'll find her killer."

"I know you will. Let me know if you find the ring. I'd really like to get it back."

"Of course."

CHAPTER TWENTY-TWO

SNOWFALL

AS JACK AND MAX WALKED OUTSIDE, the snow was still coming down hard and the plows were out, making Jack again wish he had put the plow on his truck earlier. Then he looked at Max. The plow can wait, he thought.

Even though the walk to the truck was short, by the time he opened the door for her, snow was beginning to cover her hair. Before she climbed in, she ruffled her hair so it wouldn't be too wet as the snow melted. He watched her do this in silence. As Jack pushed her door shut, he could feel her emptiness, and as he walked around to his side of the truck, he was concerned. She needed company and support, and that had always been his job. "Hey Max, you hungry?" he asked as he closed his door and started the truck.

"I guess," was her unenthusiastic answer.

He knew she didn't have to be at work until four. He was hungry and knew that she would be as well, so he turned and drove toward Portsmouth.

During the ride into town there wasn't much conversation as they were both lost in their thoughts. The Rusty Hammer always had a bustling lunch crowd, and despite the snow, today was no different. Jack and Max found a table by one of the front windows. This gave them a view of the street as well as what little privacy could be had. They talked about the road trip she and Patti had taken. They ordered lunch and talked about this morning's events. Max was still bothered about the ring. She had just taken a bite of her sandwich and was looking out the window when she reached across the table and rapidly tapped

Jack's arm. "Wrook," she said, her mouth full of sandwich. Jack turned and looked out the window, not knowing what he was "wrooking" for. "What?"

"Across the street. On the corner," she said as she chewed and swallowed.

Jack turned and found the spot Max was pointing to. Through the falling snow, he saw only an empty street corner.

"I don't see anything."

"Did you see him?"

Jack shook his head "No. Who?"

"I just saw Scotch and Soda Man."

"Max, what are you talking about?"

"He was on that corner watching us," she insisted.

"Well, there is no one there now."

She was beginning to become quite animated. "That proves he was there."

"What?"

"As soon as he knew I had spotted him, he left."

"Max, you are being silly."

"Am not."

"Okay, for the sake of argument. He was over there, in the snow, watching us. Why would he do that?"

"I don't know."

"You probably just saw someone who was waiting to cross the street, and you thought it was him."

"No Jack. It was him. He was watching us, and when he saw that I had seen him, he disappeared."

"That makes no sense at all."

"No. Yes, it does."

"How?"

"Remember, when Meredith's body was found? He was down on

the ice helping get her body up over the rocks, but when Tom showed me the body, I don't remember seeing him anywhere around. And don't forget, the ring was gone too. Do you suppose?"

Jack cut her off. "Max, stop. You're getting carried away."

"I am not."

"I'm sure there's a very good explanation for why he hasn't been around. I mean, it's not like he lives here. Wasn't he just here on a business trip or something?"

"Well, yeah, but I still know that I just saw him outside watching us."

Jack smiled. Lunch seemed to have been just the ticket to take her mind off of her aunt's death. She was back to being her old self, imagination running wild, creating conspiracies out of nothing.

Lunch was finished and the check paid, but neither one of them made a move to leave. Then Jack said, "Come on. We've got to go. The snow is really beginning to pile up, and I have to go plow over at Ben's before dinner, and you need to get to work."

They stepped out into the storm, and when they were about halfway to the car, Max tugged on Jack's arm and stopped. "I know what I saw, and it was him. Maybe he thinks we know something. Maybe he took the ring. Maybe ..."

"Shhh," Jack said as he gently touched her lips with his finger. "Max, you're getting carried away. He was just visiting the area, and now he's gone. That's all. Now come on."

"Race you to the truck," said Max as she began to run.

She already had a good lead by the time Jack reacted. He didn't try very hard to catch her; the chase was more fun. She made it to the truck first and was leaning against the door, her breath forming a halo about her head as she gasped for breath. Jack walked the last few steps, stopped right in front of her, and gazed into her sparkling eyes. Her cheeks glowed pink from the cold, and snowflakes were sticking to her hair. He wanted to kiss her, but instead he pulled the keys out of his pocket, dangled them in front of her, and said, "Nice race, but I win." Then he reached around her to unlock the door.

She looked up at him, and as soon as she heard the lock click open, she stretched up, gave him a kiss on the cheek, opened the door, and jumped in.

"No. I win," she said triumphantly.

* * *

It was a slow ride back to Max's. While the plows had managed to keep the main roads somewhat clear, the side roads were still untouched. Jack knew how Max hated to drive in the snow, so he offered to chauffeur her to and from work, an offer that was readily accepted.

After dropping her off at Ben's, Jack went home, fed Cat, changed into his snow gear, attached the plow to his truck, and returned to Ben's. The parking lot was empty, so it didn't take long to clear, and by the time he finished, the first customers of the evening were beginning to arrive.

The snow wasn't letting up, and Jack had the time, so he decided to go plow Max's driveway. Just as he was about to turn onto the boulevard, he saw the headlights of an approaching car. He waited, expecting the car to pass, then at the last second, it turned and began sliding toward him. To avoid being hit, Jack stomped on the accelerator and his truck leapt forward out onto the boulevard. The car just missed him, barely staying on the road as it completed the turn. "Asshole," Jack shouted as he glanced back and saw the car's taillights disappearing down the road toward Ben's.

The rest of the ride to Max's was slow and uneventful. As he drove, he kept thinking there was something familiar about that car. It wasn't until he had nearly finished plowing her driveway that it came to him.

It was a red car. A chill went down his spine. Could it have been the same car and if it was—why? He could think of no reasonable explanation, but to have been nearly hit twice in as many days seemed too much of a coincidence.

His imagination was in overdrive, and his heart began to pound as he convinced himself that the car had been on the way to Ben's and that somehow Max was in trouble. He drove as fast as the snow would allow back to Ben's, and the closer he got, the more panicked he became. When he made the final turn into the parking lot, his panic turned to confusion as he looked about and saw the nearly empty lot. Only a couple cars were there and none of them red. That momentary confusion quickly turned into embarrassment. "I am such a fool," Jack said to himself, his voice breaking the silence of his thoughts. He parked and went in.

Patti and Max were the only staff still working, and the last customers were just paying their tabs. As Jack walked in and shook the snow off, he could hear Patti and Max talking.

"Isn't it just the way? Courtney goes on vacation, and everything happens. First the deep freeze, then the dead body, and now this blizzard. How does she do it?" asked Patti.

Max replied, "I know what you mean. She seems to do this every year. It's as if she plans it. Last winter we had those pipes freeze when we lost the heat. Good thing Jack was around."

Just as he heard his name, Jack entered the room, "Jack Beale, superhero here, how can I help you ladies?"

The girls hadn't heard him come in, and he startled them. "You weren't supposed to hear that. We were just talking about how whenever Courtney goes away on vacation, things happen around here," said Max.

The girls were engaging in the time-honored tradition at Ben's of trashing everyone who wasn't there to defend themselves. It's how they showed the love.

"Speaking of Courtney, has any one heard from her lately?" asked Jack.

Max and Patti both gave Jack the same look that spoke volumes. It was a little bit of "Get real," a little of "You've got to be kidding," and a smattering of "Wake up and smell the coffee." Almost in unison, they said, "No …, you know when she goes away, there is no way to contact her. She always says that she'll be too far away to be able to do anything so she'll find out when she returns. She thinks that when you vacation, you should just erase that time from your everyday life. No newspapers, television, radio, or any outside influences. It must be nice."

"When is she due back?"

"Maybe in the next few weeks; she was a little vague about that this year. We think she's having a steamy affair in some tropical paradise," answered Max.

"Yeah right," chuckled Jack.

Patti chimed in. "It's possible."

"Can this tired, old superhero have a beer?" asked Jack as he sat down at the bar. Max drew him a beer, and before Jack could ask her how her night had been, the phone rang. Other than the initial greeting, Max just listened and slowly a strange look came over her face. She trembled a little as she hung up the phone.

"Who was that?" asked Jack. She paused before answering him and then said, "I don't know. He said I should remember what happened to Aunt Lillian." The bar immediately became colder. Patti, Max, and Jack all looked at each other.

Jack said, "Max, you are not going home alone tonight. You can stay at my place, and we'll go talk to Tom first thing in the morning."

"No Jack, I'm not staying at your place. I'm going home. My clothes are at home. I don't have my toothbrush. I'll be okay."

Jack knew there would be no changing her mind so he didn't try very hard. He looked over at Patti and said, "Well at least have Patti stay with you."

Patti said, without hesitation while returning Jack's look, "Of course I'll stay with Max tonight. I just have to go home first to get some stuff. I'll meet you there. I have a key, and I'll let myself in if you aren't there yet."

As Patti got up to leave, Jack caught her and said, "Hold on. … If you get there before us, don't go in. Wait for us, so that I can go in first and make sure everything is okay."

The notion that the house needed checking hadn't occurred to either of the girls, and they both turned and looked at Jack. He said, "Listen, it doesn't hurt to be careful. Humor me, will ya?"

Grudgingly, Patti agreed. She left, and Jack helped Max close up Ben's. It was a slow, silent ride to Max's. Jack hadn't told her about his two recent brushes with the red car for it would only upset her more. When they arrived, Patti's car was already in the drive, parked next to Max's. Snow was rapidly covering Patti's car and the only clue that she was inside was the running engine.

Jack checked the house and made them promise to lock the door as soon as he left. As he was leaving, he turned and said to Max, "I'll pick you up at eight, and we'll go out to breakfast, then go see Tom and tell him about the call."

She was still resisting his need to watch over her and replied, "Jack, you don't have to."

"No. I'll pick you up at eight. There will be no more discussion. Now be sure to lock the door after I leave."

"Good night Jack," he heard in harmony as he went out the door.

As the door shut, he turned and said again, this time to a closed door, "I'll see you at eight." Then he heard the lock click.

CHAPTER TWENTY-THREE

ANOTHER MESSAGE

THE STORM HAD ENDED before sunrise, and Jack was up early. He hadn't slept well. The red car and the call Max received last night kept reverberating in his head. He went to plow Ben's again. It would take his mind off of last night's events, at least temporarily. By the time he finished, it was nearly eight, so he headed over to Max's. The roads were still snow-covered but passable and in a couple hours, they would be completely clear thanks to the plows and sun.

The girls were up, and while Max finished getting ready, Jack began brushing the snow off their cars. He did Patti's first and then started on Max's. Windows first, then he began on the doors. As the snow fell off the driver's side door, he saw there was a scratch in the paint. His first assumption was that Max had sideswiped something. This was not out of the question because she wasn't always the most careful driver. However, as more snow fell away, he realized it wasn't an accidental scratch. Carved into the paint were the words: "It will be mine." Jack froze, not believing what he was seeing. That's when he heard the door shut. He looked up and saw Max coming toward him.

"Max …" he said and moved to step in front of the door. He wanted to protect her, but it was too late. Before he could finish what he was about to say, she saw what had been etched into her car's door. She stopped and stared, then her scream shattered the silence.

"Jack! Oh, my god!" She began pacing back and forth. Her scream brought Patti out of the house. She was still in her flannel PJs and slippers.

"What's going on?"

Max continued to pace around like a confused and frightened animal. "My car." That was all she could say as she pointed at the door.

Patti came over and looked at the door. She didn't move. She just stared.

Random thoughts were flashing through Jack's head, none good. He went to put his arm around Max for comfort and support. "Max ..." She pulled away from him, still pacing. She was pissed, and all he could do was follow her around the car as she brushed more snow off. "Max, slow down. Do you have any idea when this may have happened?"

She flashed him a look that stopped him in his tracks. Then she nearly shouted, "I don't know. It had to be last night, and it sure as hell wasn't there yesterday." She had nearly made it all the way around the car when she froze and pointed, this time silently and began quivering.

"What is it, Max?"

She stood there, pointing down at the rear of the car. A tear slid down her cheek, then in a small voice that was just barely audible she said, "My tire ... knife ..."

Patti rushed around the front of the car, prancing like a show horse in an effort to keep the snow out of her slippers. She stopped when she could see what Max was pointing at, and she hugged herself in an attempt at staying warm while she stared.

Jack rushed around the back of the car to Max's side. He looked down and saw what appeared to be a knife handle sticking out of the side of her tire.

"I've seen enough, and I'm freezing. I'm going in," said Patti, then she added, "I'll call Tom."

A knot formed in Jack's stomach. He turned toward Max. She was still staring at the tire and beginning to shiver. He reached out and touched her shoulder. "Let's go inside."

The shock must have begun to wear off because she pulled away from him and screamed, "What the hell! Why? What is going on?" She began pacing back and forth.

"Max, let's go in. There's nothing else we can do out here. C'mon."

She turned and stormed toward the house. As she did, Jack knelt down and looked more closely at the tire. The knife's handle was faded black plastic and appeared to be the kind commonly used by the fishermen around the harbor. Knives like these were a dime a dozen. Jack stood and headed toward the house.

As he closed the door, Patti announced that she had called Tom. He wasn't in yet, but they were sending a cruiser over.

"Where's Max?"

"In the kitchen, I think," replied Patti.

Jack heard water running and a clanking sound. He went in and found Max, hands on the counter, her coat still on, snow melting off her boots, just standing there. Next to her a teakettle was on the stove.

"You okay?"

She sniffled, "Yeah. I'm okay."

"Why don't I believe you?"

"Because I'm not." Then spinning around, her eyes flashing a combination of anger, fear, and pleading, she faced him and demanded, "Why? What is going on? What do I have that someone wants?"

Before Jack could answer, Patti stuck her head in. She was dressed and had her camera in her hand. "I'm going out to get some pictures. The police may want them, and I know the insurance company will."

"Thanks Patti," said Jack. Then he turned back toward Max. Before he could do anything, she brushed past him and followed Patti into the living room. He followed and felt the current of cold air that remained from Patti's exit. Max was standing by the window, looking out. Her arms were crossed in front as she watched Patti do her thing. Jack joined Max and put his arm around her shoulder, and gave it a small squeeze. She didn't move.

"Water's boiling. Get you a cup of tea?"

"Thanks."

He gave her shoulder another reassuring squeeze, then he went into the kitchen, took a cup out of the cupboard, opened a package of Earl Grey, dropped a bag into the cup, and filled it with boiling water. Just as he was about to return to Max, he heard the door open and Patti's voice. He yelled out, "Patti, you want a cup of tea?"

"Sure," came back the reply.

He made a second cup and carried them out to the girls. While they sipped their tea, Jack said, "I didn't notice any footprints in the snow when we arrived last night. Did you hear anything last night?"

Together they said, "No."

"The snow didn't stop until about six this morning, and I didn't see any footprints when I got here this morning," Jack continued. "So I'm guessing it must have been in the middle of the night, not too long after I brought you home."

As Max stood there, the full impact of what happened began to sink in. "He was here. Whoever called me at the bar last night was here."

"Now Max, we don't know it was the same person."

"No! It was him. I know it."

* * *

When they finished their tea, the cruiser still hadn't arrived. Jack couldn't sit still; he had to do something. "Come on Max, let's go look for Tom. He has to be down at the station by now. Patti, will you stay here until the cruiser arrives and show them the damages?"

"Sure. You guys go on."

Max got into Jack's truck, and they headed to the station.

Tom must have arrived moments before they did. He still had his coat on, and his boots were leaving wet footprints on the floor.

"Hi Jack ... Max. To what do I owe the honor of such an early visit?"

"Hi Tom," replied Jack. "Didn't anyone tell you?"

"No. Tell me what?"

"Someone scratched a message into Max's car door and slashed one of her tires."

"Did you report it?"

"Yeah, we called it in, and they're sending a cruiser over. Patti stayed there to show them the damages while we came over here."

"Why didn't you stay?"

"Because there's something else. Last night, Max got a call at Ben's just as she was closing up that I think you should know about."

Tom looked surprised and, turning to Max, said, "What's this about a call?"

Max said nothing for a moment. Tom could see her discomfort. "Come on. Let's go in here where we can talk."

Tom took off his coat and hung it up. He motioned for Max's and Jack's coat, but they both declined, so he pointed at the two chairs at the table. "Sit. Coffee anyone? It smells like a fresh pot. I'm going to have some."

Jack said yes, and Max shook her head no to the coffee. Tom poured two cups, handing Jack his, then he began. "Max, again, accept my condolences over the loss of your aunt. Now, what happened last night?"

"Last night just as I was about to lock up, the phone rang and there was this man on the phone. He didn't say who he was or ask for anyone. All he said was that I was to remember what happened to my Aunt Lillian. So he must have known my voice or that I was the one who would answer the phone."

"Did you recognize the voice?" asked Tom.

"No I didn't. It was muffled."

"Why didn't you call me?"

"It was late. I didn't want to bother you."

Jack interjected. "I offered to have her stay at my place …"

Tom looked up, but before he could say anything, Jack continued, "She didn't want to do that, so I drove her home and Patti stayed with her. I checked the house before they went in and made sure they had locked the door before I left. This morning, we intended to go have breakfast first, then come over and tell you about the call. I was out brushing the snow off her car when I discovered the message. Max came out and found the slashed tire so we came over here first."

"It was him. The guy who called last night," Max suddenly blurted out, startling both Jack and Tom.

"What makes you think that Max?"

"I don't know. I just know that it was."

Tom looked toward Jack. "Did you see any footprints or anything around the car when you got there?"

"No. The snow was untouched."

"And there was no sign of anything wrong when you got there last night?"

"Nothing."

"Sounds like whoever did it must have done so shortly after you left."

"That'd be my guess," said Jack.

Suddenly Max chimed in again. "What about seeing Scotch and Soda Man in town yesterday when we were having lunch?"

"Who? What?" asked Tom, looking at Max.

Now it was Jack's turn to butt in. "Yesterday, Max and I went into town for some lunch. We were at The Rusty Hammer in that little table by the front window. Max looked out and thought she saw Scotch and Soda Man standing on the opposite corner, and before I could look, he was gone. I never saw him."

Tom continued to look at Max. "Okay Max. What's this all about?"

"He was standing on the corner across the street watching us."

"He was watching you?"

"Yes. I'm sure of it."

"But why?"

"I don't know."

"You're sure."

"Yes."

Tom looked back and forth between them. "I don't know what to say. Max, I'll get the state police crime lab guys over to see if they can find anything, but I wouldn't expect too much. Same with the phone call. You did all the right things, but unless something else happens, we're out of luck."

"It's the ring," insisted Max.

"The ring?" asked Tom.

"You know, my aunt's ring. The one that Meredith was wearing when we found her, and then it disappeared. That's the only thing I can think of that someone could possibly want from me, and I don't even have it. I think that whoever it is thinks I have it and is trying to scare the shit out of me. Which, by the way, he is doing."

"Max. I'm not sure what to say. We have no evidence to support any of this."

"I know what I know, and if you want to help me, great. If not well ..." she paused.

"Max, it's not that we don't believe you. We just have no proof," Tom said while trying to not sound condescending.

Jack's stomach rumbled. He needed food. Jack knew there wasn't much more that could be accomplished, and it was nearly lunchtime.

"Max, let's let Tom see what he can do about your car. For now that seems to be the best course of action. Tom, you'll think about what Max has said?"

"Of course. Just don't expect miracles."

"Max?" Jack asked.

"Fine. Thanks Tom. I'm sorry for being such a bitch."

"You're forgiven."

With that, Max and Jack left.

CHAPTER TWENTY-FOUR

What's Missing?

AS THEY WALKED OUT of the police station, Max spoke first. "Jack, what the hell is going on?"

"I wish I knew. It doesn't make any sense."

"Thank you for being here for me."

"Not a problem. What do you think of the idea of asking Patti to stay with you for a while? I'd stay with you, but what would people say?"

"You have that right. Patti yes, you no," agreed Max with a hint of a smile coming over her face. "I'll ask her when we get back."

Again, Jack had said just the right thing to break the tension.

It was too late for breakfast so they got into the truck and headed back to Max's, each lost in their own thoughts. Max sat silently looking out the window as images spun though her mind. "Meredith, my aunt, the missing ring, the phone call, my tire slashed. Andy, Scotch and Soda Man, and Jack. Jack … he's always there, he never asks for anything. Why is he such a good friend?" She smiled to herself and glanced over at Jack. She felt safe with him, comfortable.

"We're here." Jack's voice brought her back to the present.

Patti was still there, waiting, and she wanted to hear everything. While the two girls talked, Jack volunteered to make lunch. He knew that Max would have all the fixings for what he had in mind. She did.

While he worked on lunch, Max told Patti about their conversation with Tom; then Patti began filling Max in on what happened when the police came and looked at her car. As Jack walked in and announced that lunch was ready he heard Max say, "Oh Patti, you are so sweet. Thank you."

"What did I miss?"

"As soon as the police left, Patti called AAA and had my tire changed. What's for lunch?"

Then they both cried out with surprise and glee when they saw what he had prepared. "Jack, you are the best." He grinned while they sat down to a gourmet meal of mac 'n cheese with cut-up hot dogs.

"Thanks, Jack," Max said as she finished the last of her mac 'n cheese.

"Delish," added Patti. "Listen, I've got to get going. Max, you gonna be okay?"

"Yeah, I'm fine. I'll see you later at work."

While Max walked Patti out to her car, Jack began cleaning up lunch. He didn't know Max had returned until she said his name.

"Jack?"

"Yeah, Max."

"What happens now?"

"What do you mean?"

"Well, what happens to my aunt and Meredith? I mean shouldn't there be some sort of a service? I'm Lillian's last remaining relative, shouldn't I be doing something? And what about Meredith? I don't know if she has any family."

Jack turned and faced Max. She looked so small and helpless. Holding out his arms, she came to him and leaned against him, her face pressed into his chest. She wrapped her arms around him, he wrapped his around her and felt her shudder, then she began to cry softly.

Nothing was said. Jack held her, occasionally stroking her hair and let her cry. "It's going to be okay," he whispered. After a bit, her crying stopped, she released her hold on him and leaned back, looking up at him. Gently, he took her face in his hands and brushed the tears from her cheeks with his thumbs.

She sniffled, then said, "Thank you."

"For what?"

"For being you."

The urge to kiss her was almost overwhelming, but he didn't. Somehow it didn't seem to be the right time.

"You're right. ... I'll call Tom and ask him what's next."

"Could you call him now while I get changed? I have to get to work," she said while wiping her nose.

"Sure."

* * *

As soon as Max and Jack had left, Tom went to his office, closed the door, and sat at his desk. He sat back, put his hands behind his neck, and closed his eyes. In the silence he thought about all that he had just learned. "What am I missing? Scotch and Soda Man. The ring. Max's car, the phone call she got last night. Two deaths, both related to Max. Too many coincidences, but how do they all fit together? Do they fit together? What's missing?"

After a few minutes, he sat up and reached for the files he had started for each of the incidents. As he reached for the first folder, his arm knocked another onto the floor, spilling the contents. The photos Patti had taken splayed across the floor. "Damn it." He chided himself for being so clumsy, and he began picking them up. "I guess this is as good a place as any to start."

He looked at each picture as he sorted them into the correct sequence. He thought about what was going on at each of those moments. That's when he noticed it. Scotch and Soda Man—Franz—was in the early pictures. He was there on the deck when Patti first went down onto the ice. He was there helping to move the body up and over the rocks into the parking lot. That was the last time he showed up in a picture. Tom looked through the rest of the pictures a second time. Franz wasn't there.

Tom picked up the piece of wood on which Jack had scribbled that crude time line. Tom turned the piece of wood in his hands. Then he stopped and said to himself, "Of course ..." It was at this moment that Tom realized with more clarity and understanding that the one common thread through all of this was Max.

It was her aunt who had been killed, then her aunt's companion. Max recognized the ring that was now missing. Andy was back and had been his usual self, but this time she had made it clear she didn't want to have anything to do with him. And Scotch and Soda Man? Was he involved? He was the one who spoke to Andy and got him to leave the bar. Did they know each other? There was no indication that they did, but it was another thread to Max. The why and the how eluded Tom, but he knew that he was right. His train of thought was broken by the phone ringing. It was Jack.

"Hey Tom. There's something Max forgot to ask you when we saw you earlier. What about her aunt's body? Max would like to make some arrangements."

"Let me make a call for you."

"Thanks. And Meredith?"

"Let me get back to you."

"Thanks again."

The line went dead, and Tom slowly hung up his phone. He would call Martinez in New Mexico shortly, but first he had some things to do. Andy and Franz—Tom needed to talk to both of them. Since neither had permanent addresses, he would have to canvass the area for them. He looked through the photos again, pulled out the best one of Scotch and Soda Man, called Melanie, the department secretary, and asked her to get it copied and distributed around the area. The more sets of eyes looking for Franz, the better. He didn't have a picture of Andy, but he was well known in the seacoast, so Tom was sure he wouldn't have any trouble finding him.

Tom was about to place the call to New Mexico when Melanie buzzed him on the intercom. It was the crime lab. He picked up the phone and listened intently as he was told the highlights of the report. They had the DNA results from the scrapings that were found under Meredith's fingernails. It was human tissue. There was some skin, blood, and a small bit of hair. They all came from the same source, and it was male. The results had been fed through CODIS, the Combined DNA Information System, but no match was found. Tom thanked the technician for the call and was told that the full report would be sent over in a few hours.

After he hung up the phone, he sat there thinking about what he had just been told. The information told him as much as it told him— nothing. "Shit," he said aloud. Tom looked at the photo of Franz again, then made a list of all the motels and guesthouses in town. The list was longer than you would expect for such a small town. As Tom looked over the list, he was able to eliminate more than two-thirds of it because they were only open in the summer. This was the tedious part of detective work that people didn't see and was the least fun. He began dialing, knowing that he was going to need help and luck, not necessarily in that order. After an hour he had neither.

There was one more call to make. He had decided to save it for last because of the time difference. It was to Officer Martinez of the Dry Gulch Police Department. Tom dialed and waited while the phone rang. He hoped he'd have better luck with this call. Tom began reviewing what he knew when his thoughts were interrupted by the voice on the other end of the line, "Dry Gulch Police Department, Ruben Martinez speaking."

Officer Martinez didn't have much new information about Lillian's death. They talked about Meredith's quick departure and the house's ransacking. Tom filled him in on his latest findings, the phone call, the missing ring, and the DNA report. Other than the two victims' relationship, there didn't seem to be any hard evidence in common, although each had unexplained bits.

As they talked, Tom kept looking at the pictures on his desk. Then on a whim, he asked. "Listen, I have some pictures here of a guy we are looking for. I'm not even sure he's involved, but he seems to have disappeared. Could I send them to you on the off chance that he had been out your way? I can't think of any reason why, but what the hell."

"Sure. Send them over. I'll get back to you with what I find."

"Thanks. Oh, one more thing. Max, Lillian's niece, would like to plan some kind of a service for her aunt. How would she go about that?"

"She doesn't have to come out here if that's what you are asking. The medical investigator's office in Albuquerque still has the body. If they are finished with it, they can release it to a funeral home. I'll get you some names. They can then make all the arrangements and have the body shipped back east, although I would suggest having her cremated. There wasn't a lot left and what there was, was pretty nasty after two weeks in the desert."

"Thanks again. I'll let Max know." They talked for a few more minutes then hung up. Tom sent the pictures, then he sat and looked at them one more time before calling it a day. He was tired and needed some time to let all of today's new information sink in. He decided he could use a beer and wanted to check on Max, so he figured he'd head down to Ben's.

* * *

Jack was just hanging up the phone as Max returned, ready for work. "Did you call?"

"I did."

"And?"

"Tom will find out and let us know."

The roads were now clear, and Max wanted to take her own car to work. Jack tried to dissuade her, with no success, so after many words of caution, he gave in and they left her house with him following. After she made the final turn into Ben's, Jack continued on. He had some things to take care of, and after he was finished, he would go back to Ben's to wait for her to finish so he could make sure she got home safely.

* * *

Jack drove down to the harbor. He thought he'd go see who was around and if anyone had seen Scotch and Soda Man. Fred was there. He had just come in from his boat. Even though he was cold, it had been good to be out fishing again and he was in good spirits. They talked about the weather, the boat, winter fishing, Andy, and Scotch and Soda Man. Fred hadn't seen either of them recently, although he had thought he had seen Andy driving around.

"What kind of car?" asked Jack.

"Don't really know. Just one of those little shitboxes; they all look alike. I do remember that it was a dark color."

That got Jack's attention. "Really." A chill went down his spine. "Any chance it was red?"

"Can't say. I just recall that it was dark."

"If you happen to see either of them, could you let me know? The car also."

"Sure."

"Good talkin' to you Fred. See you later."

Fred nodded goodbye. Jack turned and headed back to his truck.

As he walked, his mind was racing with this new information. Jack was just pulling his door shut when Fred called out. Jack climbed out and waited while Fred walked over. "You know, it's strange. I heard that Andy was lookin' round for that other feller. You know, the quiet guy who has been down at Ben's most nights."

"When was that?"

"Not sure." He paused and tapped his forehead with his head slightly bowed. "Don't remember exactly, but it was after they had words in the bar that night."

"You knew about that?"

"It was all over the harbor. No one likes that Andy, he's so full of himself, thinks he's God's gift. Besides, he's such a shit to Max. Don't think anyone really likes him. Of course, we heard about it."

Jack was stunned by this revelation. He thanked Fred and good-byes were repeated. Jack needed to think and that meant a run.

CHAPTER TWENTY-FIVE

DRY GULCH

THE PICTURES TOM SENT arrived in Dry Gulch soon after the call was completed. Officer Martinez looked at them, made several copies, and forwarded them to the state police and the other nearby departments. He saved one copy for the the other member of the Dry Gulch Police Department, then he headed out to see if anyone had seen this man. Dry Gulch was a very small community, not much of a town, with most of the residents scattered around the countryside. Not much ever happened here. Ruben's first stop would be the gas station. Nearly everyone who comes to Dry Gulch ends up stopping there because no one wants to run out of gas in the desert.

On his way to the gas station, he thought about the two dead women. Even though he knew everyone in Dry Gulch, he hadn't known Lillian or Meredith very well. They pretty much kept to themselves out at the old commune on the edge of town. It had started back in the '60s. He had heard that they had been original members of that group, but that was long before he had come to Dry Gulch in the early '80s. The two women were the only ones left. The house they lived in was simple but comfortable. He wasn't exactly sure what the two women did to make a living, but he had heard they were artists of some sort.

Pulling up to the single pump, Ruben got out of his car. Roddy— the station's owner and an old friend—sauntered out, his boots kicking up dust while he wiped his brow with an old red bandana. "Hey amigo, what brings you out here today? I know you don't need gas."

"You're right Roddy, I don't." Martinez said. "This is business."

"What's up?"

Officer Martinez pulled out the pictures he brought, handed them to Roddy, and said, "Do you recognize this man?"

Roddy looked through all of them, looked again at several, and finally said, "Maybe."

He stood watching, as Roddy went through the process of remembering.

After a few moments, he looked up, mopped his brow again, and said, "Only snakes and horned toads should be out in this heat. Why don't we go inside the office?" There was no argument from Officer Martinez.

The office was small, cramped, and dark. There were only two windows in the room. A dim diffused light made it through the many layers of dust, dirt, and grime on the front window that overlooked the lonely gas pump outside. The second window was filled with an ancient air conditioner that provided minimal relief. The door was quickly shut to preserve what coolness there was. Roddy turned on the room's only light so he could see the pictures. He finally said, "Yeah, I'm pretty sure I saw him."

"When?"

"It was a coupla' weeks ago, nearly closing time, and he came in to get some gas."

"You sure?"

"Yeah, pretty sure. Paid cash."

Officer Martinez cursed silently to himself. "Damn. If he had paid with plastic, that would have made things so much easier. It would have been a quick confirmation."

"I remember because he asked for directions to the old commune." Roddy paused, looking at the photo. "Say, wasn't one of the ladies that lived out there just found out in the desert dead and her friend missing?"

"Yeah. Coupla' weeks ago."

"Too bad. Really makes you wonder, don't it?"

"It does. It really does."

"So did this feller have anything to do with it?"

"Don't know."

Officer Martinez took the picture back and said, "I've got to get going. Thanks Roddy." He turned and opened the door to leave. The heat slapped him in the face, stopping him in his tracks. He turned back to Roddy and said, "You know, we should get together sometime and go fishing like we used to."

"Yeah. Sounds like a good idea. It has been a while."

Officer Martinez put his sunglasses back on as he stepped out fully into the heat and the brightness. The gravel crunched under his feet as he walked to his car, and even though he had left the windows open, the inside of the car was even hotter than outside. He threw the picture on the seat and turned the key. Immediately hot air blew in his face from the not-yet-cooling air conditioning. When he stepped on the gas, the tires spun slightly in the loose gravel, shooting out a spray of small stones and dust. By the time he was on the pavement, cool air began to wash over him, and he rolled up the windows and drove down the road.

He didn't see Roddy come out of the office and give a halfhearted wave as if signaling that he had more to tell.

Roddy watched him drive off, shrugged his shoulders, and turned back to the office. "Fuck it." Roddy had remembered that the guy in the picture had some kind of an accent, definitely not from around here. "Next time I see him, I'll tell him." With that, he went back into the dark and slightly cool office.

* * *

Sadie's Emporium was the center of Dry Gulch. It was the post office, hardware store, and place to get groceries and just about any other sundry item you might need—and it was Martinez's next stop. There was a small lunch counter, and the whole enterprise was presided over by Mabel. She had been there for as long as he could remember. She was helping someone get some nails, waved hello, and said she'd be right with him. He went over to the cooler and got himself a bottle of lemonade.

Mabel finally finished with her customer and came over to where Officer Martinez was looking at some fishing gear. "So what do I owe the honor of this visit today?" she asked cheerfully.

"Mabel, today it's official business, although this fishing gear looks mighty good," he said, admiring a rod-and-reel combination. He held the picture out to her. She took it and looked at it.

"So?"

"Have you ever seen him before?"

She looked at it again, "No. Can't say as I have. Why?"

"You're sure?"

She studied it this time before handing it back. "No. I don't recognize him."

He took the picture, and said, "Thanks. I've got to get going," and he turned to leave.

"Hold on a minute Ruben. You're not getting away that easy." Mabel was one of those naturally curious people, and there wasn't much that went on in town that she didn't know about. "Why are you looking for this guy?"

He stopped and looked at her. "He's wanted for questioning in an investigation back East. They sent me the picture because they thought he might have been around here."

As Mabel listened to his explanation, he could see she was thinking hard about what he was saying.

The bell on the store's door jingled as some new customers came in so she excused herself to go tend to them. "I'll be right back. Don't go away," she said. While she was helping them, Martinez returned to looking at the fishing poles. He was feeling a little trapped. He really didn't know much himself, and he knew that Mabel would spin whatever he told her into a complete story, to be told to everyone, and before long, it would become fact. He also knew she could be very helpful.

"Does this have anything to do with those gals over at the old commune?" she asked when she returned.

"She's doing it," he thought. He answered, "What makes you think that?"

"Well, one of those gals just turned up dead and the other disappeared. I know Lillian had ties back East, and that's the only excitement that has gone on around here, so it just seems logical to me."

"Mabel," he began, "you're right. I don't really know many details, but Lillian, who we found out in the desert does have a niece back East. Her friend Meredith turned up dead in the town where her niece lives."

"So who's the guy?"

"His name's Franz. They want to ask him some questions, but they can't find him. For some reason, they think he may have been out here."

Mabel was all ears. This was news. "Thinking back, and I'm sure that it may not mean anything but, at about the same time Lillian was killed, there was another fella who came in also."

"Another guy?"

"Yeah."

"Why didn't you tell me this before?" he asked, as she now had his full attention.

"You didn't ask, and besides I never saw any possible connection until now. It was a coupla' of weeks ago. Normally I don't pay a lot of attention to tourists, but there was something about him. He seemed nervous ... no not nervous, more agitated ... and a little distracted. Like when things just aren't going right, and you're trying to figure out why."

"Did you talk to him or anything?"

She paused, "Briefly at the register. I think he bought himself a sandwich, a map, and a flashlight. I'm pretty sure that was all. ... Yeah, that was all."

"What did he look like?"

"I don't really remember, ordinary, a little younger than the guy in the picture. I'll try to remember more. I did notice that as he was leaving, he was talking to another couple who had just come into the store. It looked like he was asking them for directions. By the time I got over to see if I could help, he was gone. They told me he was asking about the old commune. I just put him out of my mind until now. Do you think he's also involved?"

"Probably not. Thanks Mabel, you've been a real help."

"Sure, anytime. Let me know what happens."

Walking out to his car, Ruben thought that she should have been a cop.

The sun was now well on its way to setting. Even though the heat of the sun wasn't as intense, it was still stifling hot. It was several minutes before his car's air conditioning began winning the battle against the heat. His next stop would be the Double-Bar-R Motel. Located on the old main road to Taos, it was the sole remaining place in the area where someone could stay. When the new highway went in and by-passed the town, places began closing as travelers no longer had reason to stop.

The dozen or so cabins were loosely arranged in a horseshoe shape around a single tired house that was waiting for a long overdue coat of paint. A sign for the office hung out front. A pay phone, soda machine, and ice machine were around the corner, sharing the small patch of shade created by the building. Near the cabins, an old shuffleboard court—paint flaked off and cracks decorating its surface—was a reminder of a different time. The tires of Ruben's cruiser scratched on the gravel as he slowed to a stop. A vacancy sign in the office window clashed with the sign on the door: "Closed today, back tomorrow."

Ruben Martinez sat in the coolness of his car, almost relieved he didn't have to get out. He would return in the morning.

CHAPTER TWENTY-SIX

ANDY, AGAIN

WHILE OFFICER MARTINEZ was visiting Mabel at Sadie's Emporium, it was already evening in New Hampshire. Showered and refreshed from his run, Jack drove over to Ben's. The parking lot was beginning to fill. "Max'll be busy," he thought. "That's good. It'll take her mind off all this stuff going on." He didn't see Tom's car parked on the far side of the lot. Jack wanted to talk to Tom about the news from the harbor but decided to see Tom in the morning. Tonight Jack's concerns were for Max. He hurried in.

As Jack stood in the doorway to the bar, scanning the crowd, he saw Tom sitting at the small corner table by the woodstove staring out the window. Realizing that Max was too busy to talk, Jack stopped at the bar only long enough for a quick hello. She handed him a beer, and he headed over to join Tom. Jack couldn't imagine what Tom was looking at; it was dark out, and other than his own reflection on the glass, there couldn't be much to see.

"Mind if I join you?" asked Jack as he pulled out the empty chair and sat down. Tom didn't say a thing. Just a quick glance over, then he returned to staring out the window. "Hey, you okay?"

Without turning his head away, Tom replied, "Yeah. I was just thinking."

Jack watched his friend sit there, then he asked, "Any luck finding Scotch and Soda Man yet?"

"Not yet." Tom continued looking out the window into the darkness of the harbor. Jack looked out the window and saw the only lights outside were at the commercial dock across the harbor. Without any boats tied up or trucks on the dock, the harbor appeared deserted. Tom finally turned and said, "I'm waiting to hear back from New Mexico."

"Max's aunt?"

"That too."

"What else?"

"I sent them a picture of Scotch and Soda Man on the off chance he had been out there. There's been no sign of him, and other than the picture and the fact that his name is Franz, we really don't know who he is. Might as well cover all the bases. I've already circulated his picture to all the other departments here, but unless I can come up with something more concrete than what we've got, I won't be able to put much pressure on them to make finding him a top priority. If not, we won't be getting much help …"

Tom stopped mid-sentence and pointed at the bar. "Son of a bitch. Look, over there, at the bar." Jack twisted around and looked toward the bar just as Andy was taking a seat. Max saw him in that same moment. Jack saw her face tighten as her eyes met Andy's. This was Andy's second time in the bar since the incident with Scotch and Soda Man, and now Jack, Tom, and Max watched Andy, each for a different reason.

Andy said hello and ordered a beer. Without saying anything, Max put the beer in front of him then turned away. Jack angled his chair so he didn't have to turn quite so obviously to see and stared. Jack had a special interest in Andy that Tom was as yet unaware of, and Jack decided to keep it that way, at least for the time being. He watched a moment longer as Max turned away and went back to work after putting the beer in front of Andy.

Tom had been looking for Andy, and since he was sitting quietly, Tom decided to wait a bit before going over to talk. Jack continued to stare for a few more moments, then he turned back toward Tom. "You were talking about finding Scotch and Soda Man."

Tom refocused and went on about how they would have to find

him on their own.

"Do you think he could still be in the area?" asked Jack.

"I have no reason to expect that he is, but anything is possible."

Jack was thinking that without a good dose of dumb luck, they would just have to be patient and keep an eye out for Scotch and Soda Man. It was at that moment Andy's voice rose and became audible above the normal background noise of a busy bar.

"Bartender." Andy was trying to get Max's attention, and she was doing a good job of ignoring him.

"Hey bartender! … C'mon Max talk to me!" There was a slight whine to Andy's voice as it gradually became louder and persistent. Jack and Tom focused on Andy, wondering if they would need to intervene. Then it happened. Andy said in a voice loud enough for everyone to hear, "I know about the call you got the other night and what happened to your car."

Max stopped dead in her tracks. Jack and Tom looked at each other and stood up at the same moment. Together they went over to the bar. Jack stood behind Andy while Tom took the empty seat next to him. Andy didn't notice them until Tom said quietly to him, "Andy, I couldn't help but hear what you just said to Max. You and I should talk."

Andy turned, surprised, and looked at Tom while flashing a more menacing look at Jack. "Sure, but not with him there,"Andy said with an edge in his voice as he jerked his head toward Jack.

Tom said, "OK, let's go over there," nodding toward the table he had just left. Andy got up and moved toward the table, but not without first getting another beer from Max and giving Jack another look. It said, "I know who you are, and I'll be watching you." Jack took the seat that had just been vacated.

Max came over to Jack. She didn't have to say anything. Jack knew what she was feeling and said to her, "Max, it's okay." He handed her a

Hershey's Kiss. "Here, you need to eat some chocolate and buck up."

A slight smile came over her face, her eyes softened, and Jack could see the tension leaving her. She slowly unwrapped the kiss and put it in her mouth, thinking this was exactly why Jack was such a good friend. He always found a way to keep her grounded.

"The guy's a jerk. He can't do anything to you. We are all looking out for you. Nothing is going to happen."

She looked at him. "Thanks, Jack."

Before he could say anything else, an order came into the bar, and she turned and went back to work. The moment passed and he was left wondering. He had seen something in her eyes, or at least he convinced himself he did, and wondered what it meant. Tom was still talking to Andy. Jack glanced over from time to time. He couldn't wait to find out what Andy had to say.

By the time Andy left, the bar was beginning to empty out as the night wound down. Tom returned to the bar, pulled up a seat, and faced the questioning glares from Max and Jack. Together and as if on cue, they asked, "Well, what did he have to say?"

Tom sat there silently as Max and Jack looked at him expectantly. It was obvious that Tom had learned something from Andy. Max broke the silence. "Come on Tom, what did he say?"

"He claims that he knows who made the call to you and also damaged your car. He also claims to have information about the body that was found in the ice."

"So you just let him go?" Jack and Max said in astonished two-part harmony.

"Yes, for the time being."

"Why?" they asked.

"He also gave me some information about your aunt's death that I need to check out."

"What?" Max blurted out.

"Listen, most of what he said was pretty general. I had no reason to hold him, and until I check out what he said … ."

Jack cut him off. "He has information about two deaths, and you let him walk out of here?"

"Jack. I had to. You have to trust me. He's not going anywhere, and I need to check out some things."

"What things?"

"Not tonight." With that, Tom got up, put some money on the bar, and walked out before either Jack or Max could protest further.

They watched him leave in silent disbelief. Max turned to Jack, her frustration evident. "What the hell just happened?"

Before Jack could answer, she continued, "Assholes. I'm not sure who's the bigger shit: Tom or Andy. Andy is such a manipulative creep. He just told Tom something, which was probably pure bullshit, and Tom acted like he believed him. Tom should have arrested Andy or something, but he just lets him walk away!"

Before she got any more agitated, Jack said, "Max, settle down. I'm sure Tom knows what he's doing. Cut him some slack."

"Slack my ass. It was my car. I got the phone call. Both my aunt and Meredith were killed. I should be told what is going on."

"That's precisely why you shouldn't be told anything."

She turned away from Jack, still fuming, and continued working on closing the bar all the while keeping up a running dialogue. Mostly she was talking with herself, but occasionally she would turn and address Jack. All Jack could do was sit there, nod his head, and finish his beer; because he couldn't get a word in even if he wanted to. "It's Scotch and Soda Man," she said.

"Max, what are you talking about?"

"Scotch and Soda Man. He did it. I told you before. He did it."

Jack let her go on for several minutes. Finally she paused, and he looked at her and asked, "Why?"

This stopped her cold. She stood for a moment, thought, and finally in a deflated voice said, "I don't know."

"Precisely. We don't know what Andy told Tom. Tom knows what he's doing. We will just have to trust him. Now, let's get out of here."

"Fine. But tomorrow, he'll have to talk to me."

With Jack's help, Max finished closing the bar. After the doors were locked, Jack walked her to her car.

"I'll follow you home," said Jack, as he pushed her car door shut.

Max rolled her window down. "You don't have to, I'll be fine."

Yes. I do," and he turned toward his truck.

Max could tell from his voice that there would be no discussion. As she began to roll up her window her last words were, "I know it's him. You'll see."

CHAPTER TWENTY-SEVEN

FINALLY, A SUSPECT

THE NEXT DAY WAS GRAY but mild. There was another storm brewing out over the ocean, and while the thermometer said it was in the mid-thirties, the breeze off the water, coupled with the grayness of the day made it feel much colder. Tom arrived at the station about 9 a.m., poured a coffee, and went into his office. There was a fax in the machine. It was from New Mexico and had all the information he had requested about shipping Lillian's remains back. He put it on his desk, deciding he would talk to Max later in person. Then he sat down and began planning his day. As he looked over his notes from last night, there was a knock on his door. He looked up and saw Jack standing there. "Come on in. Coffee?" he said.

Jack declined the coffee as he sat down in front of Tom's desk. "So Tom, are you going to tell me what Andy told you last night? I know you were holding back, and I have no problem with that because I have a hunch it was not in Max's best interest for you to tell us everything last night."

Tom nodded his head, "You're right. Andy told me an interesting story last night. I think it was just that, a story, but I will be checking it out."

"What did he tell you?"

"Before I tell you anything, you must remember that nothing has been confirmed."

"Understood."

"The long and the short of it, according to Andy, is that Scotch and Soda Man—Franz—is the guy we want. He killed both women, took the ring, and still is in the area, hiding out because Max has something else he wants."

"You're shitting me."

"No, I'm not. Andy was vague about the why for all of this, and it could all be just talk."

"Knowing Andy, it probably is bullshit."

"True. But why would he make up such a story?"

"I don't know. What can I do to help?"

"Help me find Scotch and Soda man."

"Haven't you already given his picture to all local departments? What can I do that they can't?"

"You can keep a close eye on Max in case he tries to contact her."

"No problem. You know Tom, she also thinks it's him."

"What?"

"Last night as we closed the bar, she began to weave a story based on circumstance and conjecture, and convinced herself that it was him. I'm sure she'll be by today to talk to you."

"Good. I need to see her. I have some information for her about how to bring her aunt's remains back here from New Mexico. I want to tell her in person."

"That's great. Thanks."

"You know Jack, you'd think that with all the resources available, it would be easy to find Scotch and Soda Man."

"You'd think."

"Maybe we'll get lucky."

The phone rang.

* * *

While Tom was having his conversation with Jack, Ruben Martinez was starting his day.

"Who are you, and what were you doing out here?" Officer Ruben Martinez said to himself as he lowered the grainy photo, took a sip of his morning coffee, and gazed out over the desert. This morning, as he did most mornings, he rose early, poured his coffee into a travel mug, drove out to a bluff that overlooked Dry Gulch, and watched the day begin. It gave him time to think without distraction.

The landscape came alive as the early light struck the rocks and scrub, creating a dance of shapes and shadows. Some days, it seemed as if the spirits of the night were running in terror from the light. On other days, they seemed joyful as they celebrated the start of a new day. Today it felt like the former. It had been quite cold overnight, and the sun had not yet begun to warm the land. He shivered and took another sip of his coffee.

Questions ran through his head. "Lillian. Meredith. Did Lillian know about Meredith's past? Did Meredith kill Lillian because she found out? If so, why tear up the house? To throw off suspicion? Maybe. If it wasn't her, then who tore up the house? Did they find what they were looking for? What about those prints we can't identify? What about this picture?"

Today he'd visit Jed at the motel, then he'd call the medical investigator's office and get the names of some funeral homes. Then he'd call New Hampshire. His day planned, he took the last sip of his coffee, started his car, and drove off.

Martinez arrived just after nine at the Double-Bar-R Motel. He noted there weren't any cars in front of any of the cabins. He didn't see anyone in the office even though the door was unlocked and the closed sign had been turned to open. The little desk bell binged loudly as he tapped it several times. "Jed? Anyone here?" Martinez called out. No response. He tried again, without any results, so he began to walk out toward the cabins. There wasn't anybody at the first cabin, but as he rounded the corner and headed for the second, he was nearly knocked over by Jed, who was on his way back to the office. They surprised each other equally and got a good laugh out of it. After hellos and small talk, Officer Martinez got right to the point. He handed the pictures of Scotch and Soda Man to Jed and asked, "Ever seen this man?"

Jed replied, "Yep," without any hesitation. "He stayed here a coupla' weeks ago."

That quick answer surprised Officer Martinez. "How long did he stay?"

Jed answered again without pause. "He only stayed one night and left the next day."

"Really?" Before Martinez could ask another question, Jed continued, "He checked in late Sunday night, I remember because he interrupted my show. I remember he had an accent, and he asked me if I knew where the old commune was. I thought this a bit strange, but almost anything to do with that place seemed to me to be a bit curious, and I wanted to get back to my show, so I just gave him directions and the key to his cabin. I always get up with the sun, and that next morning as I was pouring my coffee, I heard him driving off."

Martinez stopped Jed, "How do you know it was him? Did you see him?"

"Nope, didn't need to. He was the only person staying here that night, and when I got to the door, I saw his car was gone. Oh yeah, I'm sure it was him."

Martinez nodded to Jed to continue.

"Anyway, it weren't no more'n a coupla' hours when he returned, got his stuff, came into the office, paid his bill, and left real fast. Paid cash and just left. Didn't even get a chance to be sociable; he was in a real hurry and definitely agitated."

"Do you have his registration card?"

"Sure do, it's in the office." Jed led Martinez back to the office. As they walked along, Officer Martinez tried to learn more about this mystery man, but Jed had told him all he could.

"Here it is," said Jed as he looked at the card. "Franz Stokel. He had a rental car and his license was Swiss."

"Can I see that"

Jed handed Martinez the card, and he studied it. "Can I keep this to make a copy? I'll bring it back later."

"Sure." They shook hands, and Officer Martinez left and headed back to the station. He needed to call New Hampshire.

* * *

Tom answered on the second ring. As he listened to the voice on the other end, his face reflected what he was hearing. He said very little as he listened intently, nodding his head while interjecting "Yes," "okay" and "I see." It wasn't long before he was thanking the caller, and as he hung up the phone, he jotted something down on a piece of paper.

Jack stared at Tom, almost afraid to ask. He didn't have to, Tom spoke first. "That was Ruben Martinez from the Dry Gulch Police Department. It seems that our Scotch and Soda Man was out there about the time Lillian was killed, and according to a motel clerk, his name is Franz Stokel and he's from Switzerland."

As soon as Tom made this pronouncement, the room filled with silence and the two friends sat there staring at each other for a few moments while this news sank in. Jack spoke first. "Holy shit."

"This may be the break needed to get things moving."

"What can I do?" asked Jack.

"First, I don't think we should tell Max about this yet."

"Agreed."

"Second, I'd like for you to keep a close watch over her. We'll increase patrols by her house, but that may not be enough. Can you stay close to her without raising too much suspicion?"

"Don't worry. I'll take care of her." As Jack said that, he was surprised by the feeling that washed over him—a feeling he hadn't felt in many years, not since Marie—and it felt right.

"Great. I'm going to start by notifying all of the other seacoast departments that we now have a suspect in two murders."

In the few moments that passed between Tom telling Jack about Scotch and Soda Man having been in New Mexico and asking for help watching Max, Jack's thoughts shifted into overdrive. If Scotch and Soda Man were still in the area and was trying to be invisible, Jack thought it unlikely that he would stay at any local motel, but they all would have to be checked out in short order. Tom and the police would be doing that. Jack thought Scotch and Soda Man would stay somewhere a little bit more anonymous. What better place to disappear than Hampton Beach? Jack's running buddy, Dave, lived there and knew everyone, or at least seemed to. That's where Jack would begin his search, and he could do that while Max was at work. She wouldn't suspect anything because he and Dave ran together often. Jack needed to find Franz before the police did.

Once Scotch and Soda Man was in custody, Jack's chances to find out what was behind all of this would be very limited at best. He didn't trust Andy, but this new information from New Mexico seemed to corroborate his story. Despite Tom's friendship and request for help, and even though Jack had worked undercover for Tom a long time ago in Miami, the fact remained that he was not a cop and would be out of the loop as soon as Franz was caught.

"Okay, then," said Jack as he stood to leave. What he didn't say was that whenever he wasn't watching Max, he was going to be searching for Scotch and Soda Man. Jack knew what he had to do and he'd have to be careful because he was sure Max would sense that something was up before too long.

"Then it's agreed. You'll keep a close watch over Max, and I'll increase patrols by her house and intensify the search for Franz," Tom said.

"Sounds good. I'll talk to you later."

Jack left as Tom picked up his phone.

CHAPTER TWENTY-EIGHT

THE SEARCH BEGINS

AS JACK DROVE AWAY from the police station, his heart pounded in his chest. He wanted to do everything all at once, but he knew that time, luck, and patience were what were needed most. As he drove, the adrenaline rush began to subside and he began to think more clearly about what he needed to do. First he'd check on Max and make sure she was safe at work, then he'd call Dave to see about going for a run. While Thursday night runs with Dave were part of Jack's regular routine, getting together on other days should not raise suspicion and would be the perfect cover for searching the beach. Dave lived at the south end of the beach; knew everyone and like most runners Jack knew, enjoyed beer; and more importantly, he knew most of the bar owners in the beach area. A run with Dave would be the perfect starting point for Jack's search.

* * *

Tom now knew that Scotch and Soda Man had been in New Mexico. The pictures of Scotch and Soda Man had been positively identified by two people as having been in Dry Gulch around the time that Lillian had been found. According to the motel registration and driver's license information, his name was Franz Stokel from Bern, Switzerland. Since he wasn't American, there had to be a visa or passport record of his entry into the country. If he flew to and from New Mexico, there would be records of that with the airlines. Tom picked up the phone and began making calls. His first call was to U.S. Immigration and

Customs Enforcement. Busy. Next stop, Google. He began by searching the web for Franz Stokel in Bern, Switzerland. "What a wonderful thing," thought Tom. He could now do in minutes, even seconds, what only a few years earlier would have taken days at best and probably weeks.

Bingo! First try, he found a Franz Stokel III in Bern. He was listed as an attorney so that made it easier to narrow Tom's search. Sometimes a little luck is needed and today was Tom's lucky day. He found that Scotch and Soda Man was the managing partner of an old and respected law firm that had been founded by his grandfather, Franz Stokel. A quick visit to the firm's website, and Tom knew more, except there was not a picture. He could only hope the two men were one and the same, so he placed a call to attorney Stokel. Tom looked at the clock and calculated the six-hour time difference. He didn't know how late lawyers worked in Switzerland, but it seemed a reasonable assumption that his office would still be open. He dialed. The phone rang and, on the second ring, was picked up by an efficient sounding receptionist. Her greeting was in German, this caused Tom to pause for a second, and then he asked if she spoke English. "Of course," was the reply in perfect, although accented English.

Tom identified himself and asked if Attorney Stokel were available. There was a short pause on the other end of the line before that efficient voice returned and replied, "I'm sorry, Herr Stokel is not presently available. Would there be a message for him?" Tom asked when Herr Stockel would return, and she said she didn't know. He was away on holiday. Despite Tom's best efforts, no more information was forthcoming. Finally Tom gave her his number, asked that Herr Stokel call as soon as he returned, and said good-bye.

Tom hung up the phone and thought to himself, "So he's on holiday. Oh Franz, you're looking more and more guilty every time I find out something new." Nearly an hour had passed since his first call to customs and immigration, time to try again. This time the phone rang, but it still took several sessions on hold, countless times of pressing one for … , and several transfers before he was able to speak to a real person. After explaining who he was, and who and what he was looking for, Tom was told that it would take a few hours to get the information and that someone would get back to him. He hung up the phone and took a deep breath.

* * *

Jack stopped at his apartment and, before calling Dave, called Max. Patti answered the phone. "Hey Patti."

"Hi Jack. What's up?"

"I was just calling to see what the two of you were up to."

"Not much really. Just hanging out. We have to be at work in a coupla' hours. You want to talk to Max?"

"Sure, put her on."

"Hold on." There was a clunk as she put the phone down. He could hear her footsteps as she walked away and then muffled voices. What was said he couldn't understand, but he could hear giggling.

Max picked up the phone. "Hi, Jack?"

"Hi, Max. How are you holding up?"

"Good, thanks for asking."

"What are you doing?"

"Nothing. Why?"

"I just wanted to say 'Hi.' No reason."

"You're checking up on me aren't you? Tom put you up to it, didn't he?"

"No. He didn't."

"Well I'm fine. Patti's here, and we're going to work soon. Stop by later."

"I will."

Jack hung up and thought to himself how her life was becoming like one of those soaps she watched sometimes. Satisfied that she would be all right getting to work, he called Dave. No answer. A run with Dave would have killed two birds with one stone, a run and a chance to look for Franz. Since Dave wasn't around and Jack's real motivation was to find Franz, Jack decided to drive down and cruise the beach. Maybe he'd get lucky.

It would only take between fifteen and twenty minutes to drive the roughly eight miles to the beginning of the main beach area. Not too many years ago, there were still stretches of road that were undeveloped. Now it was either huge expensive homes or condo complexes. Smaller more modest homes were becoming extinct as they were sold at high prices and became tear-downs. There were still a few motels along the way, and Jack wondered how long they would remain before being cashed in and another super-home built on the property.

As he rounded the final curve at Boars Head and began the drive down the strip, his speed slowed and he found himself rubber-necking like a tourist. If this were a summer afternoon, his would be one in an endless stream of vehicles barely creeping along. Some of the cars would have been filled with families out to spend a day at the beach, looking for a place to park. There would be cars with impatient locals trying to get somewhere in a hurry. Rounding out the mix would be the delivery trucks, motorcycles, scooters, and cute girls on roller blades and bicycles. Together they would become a moving stream that is the life-force of a crowded beach resort. As night would fall and the air would cool, the flow of cars and people would change in tempo and makeup. On foot, there would be herds of families going in and out of the arcades, accented by young teens trying to look much older than their years but acting like a pack of puppies giggling and wiggling their way down the strip. Cars filled with slightly older boys and girls would cruise the strip hoping to get lucky. The nightclubs would open, shows would begin, and the cops would be out in full force refereeing the game that was a night at the beach.

It wasn't like that now as Jack drove down the strip. Many of the motels and hotels were closed for the winter, and those that were open were mostly vacant. Even McDonald's was boarded up for the winter. Snowbanks filled most of the parking places, and Jack's truck was the traffic flow, and so he drove on, keeping a hopeful eye out for Scotch and Soda Man.

Driving south through Hampton Beach, you pass through three distinct zones. The north beach area is mostly hotels and motels with a few restaurants mixed in. Most of these places are fairly well-cared for and have kept up with the times—the more affluent area of a working- class resort town. The Ballroom is the focal point of the central beach area. In the summer, it is the place to see big-name and not-such-big-name entertainers and groups. Arcades, souvenir shops, and carnival food add to the central beach area's honky-tonk atmosphere. At the south end—past the Casino, past the t-shirt shops, past the arcades—were more bars, dance clubs, and late-night action. The motels were not as fancy as those in the north beach area. The bars and restaurants a bit seedier. The crowds a bit more dangerous.

As he neared the end of the strip, he slowed and tried to visualize where Scotch and Soda Man might be staying. This south beach area was not anything like its more famous namesake in Miami. There wasn't any glitz or glamour, and more importantly, there was little money. This south beach seemed to be a notch below working class. It was an area of crowded, older summer homes that people lived in year-round. The houses and motels looked cold and drafty, and the gray skies and stiff breeze off the ocean added to the dreariness and gloom that Jack felt.

It was an area ripe for development. Distressed properties were being bought up, condos and townhouses built. In ten years, far fewer of the current year-round residents would still be living here. Jack's friend Dave lived in one such townhouse complex overlooking the marina. Jack drove by Dave's, hoping to see his truck. He didn't, so he continued his tour, seeing the area in a whole new light now that he was looking for someone who might be hiding out here.

Jack had reached the end and began the return trip north. He hadn't seen any sign of Scotch and Soda Man but didn't expect to either.

* * *

While Jack spent his afternoon cruising Hampton Beach, Tom was waiting to hear back from Immigration and Customs Enforcement. He was restless. His brain was cramping from an information overload, and the walls of his small office were too confining. He needed some fresh air, time to think, and something physical to do. There were a few motels in Rye that were open throughout the winter, so he gathered up his pictures of Scotch and Soda Man and headed out to visit them. On the way out, Tom grabbed the fax from New Mexico. He would visit Max as well. He had found that often just driving around would help him focus. The combination of no disturbances and the stimulation of fresh scenery would open his subconscious. Thoughts and ideas would come and go, sometimes leading to revelations and insights. Maybe today he would get lucky.

As Tom drove from place to place, he thought about all he had learned. He now knew who he was looking for. The evidence seemed to indicate that Stokel may have committed two murders, one here and the other in New Mexico. That would mean federal involvement. Tom intended to make sure there wouldn't be a third. So far everything was highly circumstantial, but it all seemed solid. The one thing that kept nagging at Tom was the motive. Why would a respected lawyer from Switzerland fly all the way to the United States, murder one woman in

New Mexico, another in New Hampshire, and threaten a third? It just didn't make a whole lot of sense. The question "Why?" kept reverberating in Tom's head.

As he drove past the harbor on his way south to yet another motel, his thoughts drifted back to the day when the body was found in the ice. The confusion, the crowds, and later Max's insistence that the ring—the missing ring, the ring that existed only in the picture Patti had taken—was her grandmother's. The ring. Max kept bringing it up. Had he made a big mistake by not taking Max more seriously? Could that be the key? If it was, why? Again that question. He needed to talk to Max. Glancing at his watch, he saw it was nearly five and guessed she would probably be at work by now. Having already driven past the turn to Ben's, he continued on to the last motel on his list. Then he'd return to Ben's to talk to Max.

Tom hadn't seen Jack pulling into Ben's behind him. Tom hadn't had any luck at the last motel. He parked and, before getting out, called the station on his radio. He was hoping that Immigration and Customs Enforcement had returned his call. After asking the same question several ways, the dispatcher finally convinced Tom there hadn't been a call. He thanked her and ended the call. He hit the steering wheel in frustration. "Damned bureaucrats. Now I'll have to wait until Monday," Tom thought to himself. As he sat in his car, trying to reorganize his thoughts, he didn't notice Jack approaching. A knock on the window brought Tom back to the present.

Tom looked up and was surprised to see Jack standing there. As Tom climbed out of the car, they both said in unison, "What are you doing here?" Tom answered first that he had a few things he wanted to ask Max and that he had some information for her about bringing her aunt's remains back from New Mexico. Jack didn't tell Tom about driving to Hampton Beach, only that he saw Tom pulling in and thought he'd see if Tom wanted to join him for a beer.

CHAPTER TWENTY-NINE

SPECULATION AND INFORMATION

IT WAS EARLY so Ben's wasn't yet busy. Peggy was at her station and greeted Jack and Tom; Patti waved hi as she went by on her way into the kitchen; and Max was at the bar. The regulars were already in place. Jack and Tom ordered two beers from Max and told her they'd be at a table.

When she brought the beers over, something told her this was more than a purely social visit. So Max, being Max, looked at Jack and Tom and said, "What's up? You're not here just for the beer; I can tell." Tom chuckled and said, "It's that obvious?"

She shot back, "Duh. So what's up?"

"You got a minute?" Tom asked Max.

"Sure, I just need to get someone to watch the bar for me."

Before she could turn to go, Jack said, "I'll watch it, you go ahead and sit here with Tom," and began to get up. She looked over at the bar, then down at Tom, and finally back at Jack, and said, "Okay."

She sat down, and Jack went to the bar. "So Tom, what's up?"

"I have a couple things to talk to you about. First, I have some information for you about your aunt's remains. The medical investigator's office has finished with her, and the body can be released. Here is a list of funeral homes in Albuquerque." As Tom handed her the fax he had grabbed on the way out of the office, she said "Albuquerque?"

"That's where the medical investigator's office is. You will need to contact one of these funeral homes, they can claim the body for you and make the arrangements. It can all be done over the phone and with faxes. Because of the way she was found, it might be a good idea to have her remains cremated and then sent here."

Max sat silently, staring at the paper while Tom filled her in on the procedure. In a soft voice she said, "Thanks. I'll call on Monday." Then looking up, she asked, "You said there were a couple things you wanted to talk to me about. What's the other?" She glanced over at the bar and saw Jack fully engaged in an animated discussion with the boys.

* * *

Déja vu. To Jack it felt like the night the body was found, and when Jack returned to the bar instead of Max, the boys at the bar gave lots of looks. Paulie was the first to speak up. "So Jack, what's up over there?" as he nodded his head in the direction of Max and Tom.

"Don't know. He wanted to talk to her."

"About what?"

Jack just shrugged, indicating that he had no idea.

"I bet it has something to do with that body that was found in the ice. You know there is a lot of talk going around about how she and Max knew each other."

This got Jack's attention, so he asked, "Says who?"

Paulie kind of shrugged in a way that said, "I know but I don't want to tell you." Instead, he said, "I dunno. There's been talk down at the harbor. I heard that Max and the dead woman had been lesbian lovers a long time ago and that she was back here to find Max and to ..."

He was cut off by Leo. "You are so full of shit. What would ever give you that idea? You know she's hot for me." This brought a laugh from everyone.

Jack shot them a look that said they were way out of line, then asked, "What makes you think that they knew each other?"

Paulie, embarrassed by what he had just said, grew silent and red-faced, and looked down at his beer. Ralph chimed in, "Because Andy told him so."

Paulie gave Ralph a quick elbow to silence him.

"Andy? What does Andy have to do with this?" Jack asked with more force.

Paulie was still maintaining silence, so Ralph chimed in again. "He was telling Paulie how that quiet guy ..."

Jack interrupted, "Who?"

"You know, that quiet guy who used to hang out here and disappeared just after the body was found. Shit, he gave me the creeps."

"You mean Scotch and Soda Man?"

"Yeah, that's him. Scotch and Soda Man." Ralph went on, "He, Andy that is, told Paulie about how he had met the quiet guy a while ago and that Scotch and Soda Man got real friendly when he found out that Max was his, Andy's, girl. He asked a lot of questions about where she lived and where she worked and stuff like that."

Jack looked at him and repeated what he thought he heard Ralph say. "So what you're telling me is that Andy and Scotch and Soda Man met some time ago, and after he found out that Andy was dating Max, Scotch and Soda Man tried too hard to become Andy's friend and was asking a lot of questions about Max."

"Yeah, that's right."

Jack stared at him.

Ralph took a contemplative sip of his beer, then put the bottle down, looked at Jack and said, "Yeah, that's what I'm saying."

Ralph's story was not making a lot of sense to Jack, especially this new revelation about Andy and Scotch and Soda Man knowing each other, and that worried him.

* * *

"Thanks, Jack," said Max as she gave him the "I'm glad you're my friend" look.

He rejoined Tom at the table. "So how did it go with Max?"

"Fine," was the reply. "And the boys? They seemed pretty animated."

"The boys are always interesting. Apparently Paulie had had a conversation with Andy."

"Paulie?"

"So Ralph said. With those three you can never be too sure what is fact and what is fiction. It could have been a simple hello that Paulie remembers as a full blown conversation. Who knows?"

"So what did he say?"

"As best I could understand, Andy knew Scotch and Soda Man sometime in his past and that he—Scotch and Soda Man—wanted something from Max. It didn't make a lot of sense, but not much of what those guys say makes a lot of sense."

Tom looked at Jack, shook his head, and said, "Really?"

"Yeah, I know. You never know with those guys."

Jack didn't want to discuss their speculations any further. "So, what did you want to talk to Max about?"

"This afternoon I was reviewing everything, trying to find a motive for all of this. All I could come up with was that maybe it had something to do with that ring Max keeps talking about. I just wanted to ask her a little bit more about it."

"And was she helpful?"

"Yes and no. She really believes it was her grandmother's ring. Apparently her great-grandfather had it made for her grandmother when she was born. While Max was growing up, her grandmother would tell her stories about the ring, how it was magical, how it had special powers, how it was the key to a great treasure. You know, fairy tale-kind of stories that a grandparent might tell to a child."

The power of beer must have been contagious because Jack's imagination began to kick in. "What if those stories were more than just stories? What if that ring really were the key to some kind of treasure. I remember Max told me her great-grandfather was a diamond merchant in Europe before World War II. Let's suppose that it was her grandmother's ring, the stories were true, and someone was after it. Lillian gives it to Meredith to protect it. Lillian was killed. The killer doesn't find the ring. Meredith bolts, and the killer follows her here, suspecting she may have it. She does, she ends up dead, and the ring disappears."

"If that were all true, then we'd certainly have a motive."

"We would, wouldn't we."

"Yes we would, but we don't have any hard evidence to support any of this."

"I know."

Jack and Tom sat there in silence for a few minutes before Jack changed the subject and asked, "Did you find out anything more about Scotch and Soda Man?"

"Sort of. I did locate a Franz Stokel in Switzerland. He's a lawyer, so I checked out his website. There wasn't a picture of him, but I did get contact information. I called his office and talked to his secretary. She told me he was on vacation and that she didn't know when he would return. Beyond that, she wasn't very helpful. I'm not sure yet that he's the correct Franz Stokel, but I'm hopeful. It seems possible. After all, we now know that a Franz Stokel was in New Mexico at about the time Lillian was killed and then he was here when her companion was killed. I've contacted all of the other seacoast towns and formally requested their aid, and I sent his picture to the state police. I'm waiting for some further confirmation from Immigration and Customs Enforcement. I even checked out the few motels in Rye that are still open on my way over tonight."

Jack took all of this in and then looked over at Max. She was so at ease behind the bar. He liked to watch her work, putting up with the boys, verbally sparring with them, unaware of just how much danger she might be in. "You're right. We need to find him."

The bar finally emptied out, and Max was starting to close up. Tom said his good-byes and left. Jack moved over to the bar and asked Max if she needed a ride home. She said no because she and Patti had come in together in Patti's car. Patti was still staying with Max, which made Jack feel a little better. Patti and Peggy finally finished closing the dining rooms and joined Max and Jack in the bar. Ben's was officially closed, good nights were exchanged, and they walked out together.

* * *

Even though Max and Patti were in the same car and Patti would be staying at Max's, Jack still worried about them. He had decided to follow them to make sure they got home safely. Not wanting them to know, he took his time starting his truck, letting it warm up before leaving. He fiddled with his radio, settling on an oldies station. "You Belong to Me" was playing. Jack loved these old doo-wop classics and began singing along. He found himself thinking of Max as he watched her and Patti drive off, followed by Peggy. When they reached Route 1A, Patti turned right, heading north toward Max's while Peggy turned south.

As Jack watched the taillights on Patti's car moving north on the boulevard, another set of lights came on over at the commercial wharf. Jack turned his radio down as if the silence would help him see better. Something didn't feel right. The warm glow he had been feeling from the music was gone. He watched intently as those lights began moving. As they passed under a streetlight, he saw it was a car, not a truck. While it was common for fishermen to be around the docks nearly twenty-four hours a day, most drove trucks. He watched as the car became a set of taillights and continued moving toward the boulevard.

When they turned north, his imagination took over. Slamming his truck into gear, Jack took off as fast as he could. Fear for Max's safety overtook reason as he sped after the car. It felt like an eternity before he had those taillights in sight.

Far ahead, he saw Patti's taillights brighten as she braked and made the left-hand turn that would take them to Max's street. The car following them slowed as well. It was about to take the same turn when Jack caught up, catching the car in his headlights. The driver looked into his mirror; jerked his wheel right, pulling out of the turn; and took off. As the car pulled away, Jack realized it was dark red. He went cold as the taillights grew smaller in the distance. His foot pressed hard on the gas, and his truck responded as he began to chase the red car.

Whoever was driving knew he was being pursued and, using a combination of traffic lights and quick turns, he lost Jack. Jack continued driving around, hoping to find the mystery car. He didn't. As discouraged as he was because he lost the car, he felt he had sent a message to the mystery man. It was now almost two in the morning, and Jack was tired. The rush of the chase had worn off so he headed back toward Max's. As he drove past, all was quiet. Jack was confident no one would bother Max and Patti for the rest of the night, so he went home to get some much needed sleep.

CHAPTER THIRTY

THE CHASE BEGINS

IT WAS NEARLY NINE when Jack awoke. Remembering the incident last night, he decided to call Max.

"I'm fine Jack. You don't have to keep checking up on me. I'm a big girl, and besides, Patti is here."

"I know, but I can't help but worry about you."

"Oh Jack, that's sweet. Will I see you later? I'm working at four."

"I'll stop by. I didn't catch Dave yesterday so I'm going to call him again. I really need a run."

There was no indication from Max that she thought she had been followed, and Jack didn't tell her about his escapade. He almost felt a little foolish now that he thought about it in the bright light of day. They said goodbye and that was that.

He went back to bed content that Max was okay. It was nearly noon when he finally started his day. He called Dave, and plans were made. Jack put on his running gear, packed some dry clothes in his gym bag, grabbed the pictures of Scotch and Soda Man, and headed out.

Dave was waiting for him. A few stretches and discussion about which route to take, and they were off. They settled into a comfortable pace that allowed for conversation. Dave asked Jack what he had been up to recently. "Not much," was the initial reply. "Well, actually I'm looking for someone who may be living down here in the beach area." Jack proceeded to tell Dave about Scotch and Soda Man. "Any chance you might be able to help me look for him? You seem to know every-one down here, and quite frankly I don't know where to begin."

Without hesitation Dave said, "Of course."

"I have a picture of him with me; I'll leave it with you when we get back."

For the rest of the run, they discussed how to proceed and formed a plan. Dave's place would be their starting point, and they would work their way around the beach in true pub-crawl fashion. It would be best to start later when the night was in full swing and most of the bartenders Dave knew would certainly be working. By the time Jack and Dave returned to Dave's, they had run about six miles. After changing into some dry clothes after drinking a quick beer with Dave, Jack left the picture and headed home. They would meet later that night at Dave's to start the search.

As Jack headed north on Route 1A, he kept thinking about last night: Max, the car, what Tom had told him, and what he learned from the boys at the bar. Was he just being paranoid or was that car really following Max? He decided it had to have been following her because of the reaction to his pursuit. As he drove past Ben's, he saw Patti's car and knew that the girls were at work. He'd stop by after a shower and a power nap.

A few hours later, a grumbling stomach woke Jack up so he headed to Ben's for some food and to check on Max and Patti before going back to Dave's. Jack ordered a Ben's Burger, medium rare, with fries—the classic American meal—and thoroughly enjoyed it. Patti was going to stay at Max's again so with his hunger and concerns satisfied, he paid the check and headed south.

* * *

Dave was looking out his kitchen window when Jack pulled into the parking lot. As Jack got out of his truck, Dave signaled for Jack to come on in. Dave greeted Jack with a beer that was gratefully accepted.

Franz's picture was on the table. As Dave and Jack drank their beers, they worked out a game plan. They'd take Dave's truck since their quarry probably would recognize Jack's. The starting point would be the farthest away so that as the night progressed they would be closer and closer to home in case walking became necessary. "You ready?" Dave asked.

"Yeah." They drained their beers, grabbed the picture, and headed out.

First stop, Wolf's, past the north beach area and located in condo alley. No luck. They headed back toward the beach. The Landing was next with the same result, followed by the Stewart's Hotel. On Saturday night, Stewart's was a place for dancing for the not-really-young-anymore crowd. Tonight it was empty so Dave and Jack moved on. By now it was after eleven, and they were getting deeper into the south beach area. Even in the dead of winter, the bars that were still open were busy, the crowds boisterous, and the atmosphere more charged. There was an edge that was not for the timid in this area of Hampton Beach. It really wasn't Jack's kind of place, but he felt right at home with Dave. Since Dave was a long-time resident, he knew all the key players, from bartenders and bouncers to some of the more colorful patrons. It was at Mary and Lou's that Dave and Jack's luck began to change.

* * *

Mary and Lou's was just down the street from Dave's, so they left the truck at his place and walked back over. For a midwinter Sunday-night, the place was hopping. Most of the pool tables were in use, the music was loud hard rock, and everyone was having a good time. As they walked in and headed for the bar, there were many shouted "Hello"s to Dave and even a few "Who's your cute friend?" comments as well. He made the rounds, introducing Jack to seemingly half the people there. Finally they were able to find a couple seats at the bar, and beers were ordered and quickly delivered.

Dave began a running commentary for Jack about all of the characters there. He nudged Jack to take a look over at the farthest pool table. A crowd had gathered to watch the match in progress, if you could call it that. The two competitors didn't quite fit the image Jack had of serious billiard players.

Two women—one with long auburn hair and the other with short blond hair—were circling the table with cues in hand to the delight of the gathering crowd. The girl with the long hair was exotic looking with slightly almond-shaped eyes, high cheek bones, and a complexion as smooth as a china vase. She was drop-dead gorgeous. The blonde looked more Scandinavian with fair, perfect skin, ice blue eyes, and a freshness that would take your breath away. They both had long, shapely legs that sprouted from high-heeled shoes and disappeared into equally short skirts. As the women bent over the pool table, bejeweled thongs could be seen creating sparkling whale's tails diving into the deep.

Ample, too-perfect breasts accentuated by tight, low-cut, brightly colored tops completed their ensembles. "They must be cold, dressed like that in the middle of winter," Jack mumbled to himself. He tried not to stare, but that was nearly impossible. There was a sensuous almost serpentine rhythm to the way the women moved around the table. They were clearly playing to the mostly male audience that had gathered to watch. Each shot was deliberately stroked, punctuated by the sharp clap of the balls hitting each other—much to the delight of the approving gallery. Dave had to give Jack an elbow to the ribs to regain his attention. "Those two, they're strippers." Jack could only reply with a breathy, "No shit."

Dave continued his who's-who narrative while Jack kept stealing glances at the two pool players. When Dave and Jack were about halfway through their beers, the bartender had a momentary lull so he came over. "Dave, bro, how are ya? What brings you out here tonight? Your friend seems to be enjoying Erin and Lori over at the pool table."

"Tony, this is one of my running buddies, Jack. Jack, Tony. Tony, Jack."

"Hey Jack, any friend of Dave's is a friend of mine. So what brings the two of you out tonight?"

"We're looking for someone," replied Dave.

"Oh yeah?"

Dave pulled out the picture of Scotch and Soda Man, passed it over to Tony, and said, "We're looking for this guy. He may be involved in some threats toward Jack's girlfriend."

Jack interrupted, "She's a close friend who happens to be a girl."

"Right," was the sarcastic reply from Dave as he looked at Jack. "Anyway, have you ever seen him in here?"

Tony looked at the picture. He started to hand it back when he looked at it again. Both Dave and Jack were watching Tony intently. He finally handed it back and said, "Yeah, I think he's been in here."

"Are you sure?"

Looking at the picture again, Tony said, "I'm sure. He's been in a few times over the last week or so. Comes in early when things are quiet. Never says much, just sits at the end of the bar, sips his scotch and soda, and then leaves. He's a little strange."

"Any idea where he might be staying?" asked Jack.

"Nah," replied Tony. "He just sits there, doesn't say much, although he does have some kind of an accent. I wish I could help you more. I'll be right back." Tony left to tend to some thirsty customers at the other end of the bar.

Jack was pumped. His mind was racing. "He's been here. He's still around. He's mine," he thought.

Dave was also psyched. "What's next?"

Jack enjoyed the moment before answering. "I'll just have to spend some more time down here," as he stole a glance at the pool table, "and see if I can't spot him."

Dave said, "Don't you mean we?" He hadn't had this much fun in a long time and had no intention of being left out.

"Sure," Jack answered. "I just didn't want to involve you if you didn't want to be."

"I'm in bro. Whatever you need."

Closing time was near, the last-call bell had been rung, and Jack was buzzed from the combination of many beers and the news that their quarry had been seen. The billiards match had finally ended, and he watched Erin and Lori leave with two very large guys. That's when he suddenly realized he had left Max and Patti alone. They didn't know that they were alone, or even that he had been watching over them. He had been so intent on finding Scotch and Soda Man that he had forgotten them.

He pulled out his cell phone and called Max. She answered after a couple of rings with a smoky, sexy, just barely awake voice. "Hello."

Jack paused a moment before saying anything. That voice stirred something primal in Jack. Maybe it was the beer, maybe not, but it stirred something. "Max, it's me, are you all right?"

She was awake now, a little pissed off, and that sexy timbre to her voice was gone. "Jack, what are you doing calling me at this hour? I was nearly asleep. What is all that noise in the background?"

The power of beer had struck again. "I'm sorry Max, I didn't mean to wake you. I lost track of time. What time is it? I'm down with Dave at a bar in Hampton Beach. The night kind of got away from me. I'm sorry."

"Jack, stop babbling. You sound drunk, I'll see you tomorrow. Drive carefully." The phone went dead as she hung up on him. He felt that he had bothered her, but at least she was all right.

The ride home was a blur, partly because of the beer and mostly because of his excitement. He knew they were going to find the bastard.

* * *

Jack found it hard to sleep. He was too wound up. Eventually sleep did come, and it was mid-morning when he finally rolled out of bed, showered and headed over to Paula's for coffee and breakfast. The weather reflected his upbeat mood. The sun was back out, and it wasn't too cold.

Paula's was jumping this morning. Everyone was in high spirits. For them it had to be the sun and the hint of spring in the air; for Jack, it was much more. As he settled in with his coffee and paper, he couldn't help but grin a little as he thought about last night's successes and excesses. Today he would go back down to Hampton Beach and continue his search in the daylight.

Ben's was just opening as Jack returned home. He saw both Patti's and Max's cars in the parking lot so he pulled in. As he headed for the bar, he said hi to Peggy; she gave him a look that said, "You are in deep shit" with her returned "Hello."

Max was behind the bar checking over everything because she knew today would be busy. She stopped when she saw him, put her hands on her hips, and stared at him with a look that said it all. Jack could feel her eyes boring deep into his soul. He felt the gazes of others watching and waiting for something to happen. "Oh shit," he thought. Then he did the guy thing and with the innocence of a baby said, "Good morning, Max," as if nothing had happened.

She continued to stare at him. He knew she was pissed at him. "What?" was all he could get out.

"What? You know what, Jack Beale. What were you doing calling me, waking me up at 2 a.m.? What were you doing down in Hampton Beach in some skanky bar? What?"

Being the perceptive guy that he was, he now knew she wasn't just pissed at him, she was really pissed. Jack couldn't tell her the truth, that he was down there looking for Scotch and Soda Man because he was the one who killed her aunt and her aunt's companion. He couldn't tell her that she might be next. He was in deep shit, and he did the only thing he could: He got pitiful and stretched the truth as he explained last night.

"Max, I'm sorry. It was insensitive of me to call you when I did. Dave and I went for a run yesterday afternoon, and we decided to get together for a few beers last night. There was a pool tournament going on at Mary and Lou's, and it was kind of cool to watch. I lost track of time, and before heading home, I just had to call you. I know it was stupid, but I just wanted to make sure you got home all right." As his mouth was saying this his brain was thinking, "You are so dead. Shut up. Don't say anything else. She's not buying it. Stop." He couldn't stop himself, and it was the sound of her voice that finally got through.

"Jack. Jack. Shut up. It was sweet of you to want to make sure that I got home all right, but you didn't have to." His brain was on overload so he finally shut up. He could hear the twitter of other voices behind him, but when he turned around, they were gone. It must have been his imagination.

Jack sat at the bar for a while, and they talked until it just got too busy, so he left. He wasn't sure exactly what had just happened, but it felt good, and by the time he left, he was pretty sure she had forgiven him. He went home, called Dave, and got ready to go back down to Hampton Beach.

* * *

Dave had the day off and had run earlier that morning, leaving his afternoon free. When Jack arrived, Dave was waiting for him. "What's up bro? How're you feeling today."

"I'm fine. How are you this morning?"

Dave answered, "I'm good. I went for a twelve-mile run this morning, and I feel great."

"Sick puppy," Jack muttered under his breath.

"So where are we going today?"

Jack thought a minute, and said maybe it would be a good idea to ask at some of the convenience stores and try some other bars and restaurants later. He also suggested they walk; it was a nice day and they could take a better look around this way. After last night, the fresh air would be good.

The first stop was the convenience store just down the street from Mary and Lou's. It was your typical beach store, crowded and packed with more stuff than you could imagine. The aisles were narrow and between the magazine racks—filled with newspapers, men's magazines, and gossip rags—and the stacks of soda specials, you could find some dusty staples at inflated prices. Jack wondered how long some of this stuff had been on the shelves. Across the back of the store were at least a dozen refrigerated cases filled almost entirely with beer. If you looked hard enough, you could find some milk, butter, yogurt, a package of bacon, and some pre-made sandwiches. There were leftover beach toys from last summer, and behind the cashier was a wall of cigarettes. Next to the register sat a lottery machine.

The clerk was behind the counter, almost hidden by the displays of nail files, flashlights, batteries, and other necessary and yet useless things. It was an impulse-shopper's paradise. Dave knew the clerk and did the talking. "Hey man, what's goin' on? How you been?"

"Good Dave. Yourself?"

"Good. Say have you ever seen this guy?" Dave handed the clerk the picture of Scotch and Soda Man to look at.

"Yeah, why?"

"My friend here is trying to find him. He owes him some money." It wasn't exactly true, but it was enough. The clerk handed the picture back and said that Scotch and Soda Man had come in occasionally to buy a paper.

"When was he in last?"

"Oh, I don't know, couple days ago. I don't remember exactly."

"You sure?"

"Yeah. This time of year it's mostly regulars, so new faces stand out."

"Thanks man," Dave said as he and Jack turned to leave. As they reached the door, Jack looked back and said, "If he comes in again, I'd appreciate it if you didn't tell him we were looking for him." The clerk said, "Sure, no problem," and went back to work.

Dave and Jack spent the afternoon going in and out of every store that was open within a mile radius with no further success. The sun was beginning to set as they returned to Dave's. On the way, their conversation went from running to their search for Scotch and Soda Man, with moments of silence. Dave suggested getting a bite to eat, but Jack, remembering last night's escapades, declined. Max would be getting off work soon, and he felt he really ought to be around when she did.

As he drove north, his thoughts drifted—the body in the ice, the phone call to Max in the bar that night, the news from New Mexico, summer nights at anchor on the boat and Max. Somehow it always came back to Max. What was going on? They were good friends, always had been. He felt like he was walking into a dark room not knowing what he would find there. Before he could turn on the lights in that room, he was turning into the parking lot at Ben's. It would be an early night. There were only a few cars remaining, and none looked familiar.

As Jack was parking his truck, he saw Andy leaving. He walked straight out, got into one of the cars, and left. Jack found this unsettling and hurried in, not too fast, but with purpose. Patti was sitting at the bar, and Max was not in sight. Jack went over and sat in the chair next to Patti. "Hey Patti. Where's Max?"

Patti looked at him and said, "She's out back. Andy was in here. Max didn't want to deal with him so she went out back and left it to me to get rid of him."

"I saw him leaving as I pulled in, and he didn't look happy at all. You must have done a good job. I know how slow he is to take a hint."

Patti looked over at Jack, and he could see she wasn't quite as calm as he first thought. Her hand was trembling slightly, and her voice quivered slightly. "Yeah, he's gone. He is such a creep. I told him Max didn't want to see him and he should just leave. He wouldn't hear of it. He kept saying he had to see her. I had a hard time convincing him it wasn't going to happen and that he should just leave. Finally he did, but not before being a complete jerk."

Before Jack could say anything else, Max came back into the bar. Her face told a complete story—anger, fear, relief. Patti got up and gave Max a hug. Jack looked at her and asked "You all right?"

"Yeah." This was followed by an awkward moment of silence as no one really knew what to say next.

Jack slipped into his soap-opera-announcer voice and said, "Stay tuned for another chapter in *As The Harbor Turns*." The tension broke, and they laughed. After locking up, drinks were made—Max had a halvsie; Patti a glass of merlot; and Jack, his usual draft ESB. They drank to friendship and spent the next few hours just enjoying each other's company.

Eventually the night had to end. It was time to leave. Max and Patti had come in separate cars. Patti was staying at Max's again. By now Jack had slipped back into his protector role, making them promise to drive safely, be sure to lock the doors when they get home, and call him when they get there. The reply in sarcastic two-part harmony was, "Yes Daddy."

It was early enough in the evening, and there was still traffic on the road. With some effort Jack convinced himself they would be fine driving to Max's without an escort. Besides, if he insisted on following them, either they would become completely spooked, or they would make fun of him and not be as careful. He watched their taillights disappear into the night, and then he climbed into his truck and drove home.

CHAPTER THIRTY-ONE

ANOTHER CALL

JACK HAD BEEN HOME for a while and had not heard from the girls. He was beginning to worry when the phone rang. The phone call only lasted a moment. Relief quickly turned to fear when he heard the voice on the other end of the line. It was Patti; her voice was slow and measured. She merely said, "Jack, you've got to get over here."

"Is Max all right?"

"Yes. Now get over here right away." She hung up.

Jack grabbed his coat, took the stairs two at a time going down, and rushed to Max's. He drove as fast as he dared, questions echoing in his head. Had someone broken in? Had Max's car been vandalized again? What could have happened for Patti to sound so desperate? She said Max was all right. What happened? It felt as if everything were moving in slow motion and he couldn't get to Max's fast enough, even though the reality was that he got there faster than would seem possible.

When Jack arrived, everything looked normal. The two cars were in the driveway. The porch light was on, shades were drawn, all was in order. He ran to the door, and before he could knock, Patti opened the door. "Jack, come in." As he entered the house, he didn't see anything out of place, except Max wasn't visible, which only increased his anxiety. "Where's Max?"

"She's in her room."

"What's going on? Is she all right?" He was still looking around and seeing nothing wrong.

Calmly Patti said, "Max is fine."

"Then what?"

"When we got home, the phone was ringing. She picked up the phone and never said anything. She just got this weird look on her face; hung up the phone; said, 'It was him'; and ran into her room. She's been there ever since. That's when I called you."

"Shit," Jack mumbled under his breath. The adrenaline rush that had fueled his drive over was beginning to subside. He took a deep breath and looked at Patti. "Thanks," was all he said before walking to her bedroom door. He paused for a moment before knocking. Trying to sound as calm as possible, he said through the door, "Max, it's me, Jack. Can I come in?" He could hear her snuffling and blowing her nose.

"Just a minute," was the muffled reply. The knob finally turned, and she opened the door. She had been crying. He opened his arms, she moved into them, and he hugged her. They stood there for several minutes, her head buried in his chest. He stroked her hair. "Jack, he called again. What does he want from me?" Max's voice was small and trembling with fear. All he could do was hold her and try to reassure her that everything would be all right.

He guided her out to the living room, and they sat on the couch. Patti had made some chamomile tea and gave them each a cup. Not Jack's drink of choice at a moment like this, but he held onto it anyway. Max sipped hers carefully, trying not to burn her tongue. Gently, Jack said, "Tell me what happened."

Max told him how she and Patti had come home, and as they went into the house, the phone started ringing. She answered it, and before she could even say hello, the voice on the other end said, "You have something I want. Remember what happened to your aunt."

"Max, are you sure it was the same voice?"

"Yes, I'm sure."

Jack was stunned. "I'm calling Tom." This time there was no consideration given to waiting to call him. Jack went to the phone and dialed. Tom answered on the second ring, his voice slurred by sleep.

"Tom, this is Jack. I'm over at Max's. She just got another phone call."

The sleep went out of Tom's voice immediately. "Give me a few minutes. I'll be right over."

Jack thanked him and hung up. "Tom's on the way over." Max started to protest, but Patti and Jack hushed her. It was more like half an hour before Tom arrived. Everyone's adrenaline had stopped pumping, and now fatigue was beginning to set in.

Max repeated her story for Tom. He asked her some more questions, took a look around the house, and within the hour was ready to leave. Before he left, he took Jack aside. "Look Jack, I don't know what's going on here, but I'm expecting to hear from Immigration and Customs Enforcement later this morning, and that may give us some more answers. We'll find this Franz Stokel and get to the bottom of this. In the meantime, will you stay here to keep an eye on the girls?"

Jack said he would and then added, "Tom, I think I know where we can find this guy." Tom looked up in surprise. "I was going to see you later this morning, but I might as well tell you now. I did some nosing around in Hampton Beach the last couple days. One of my running buddies lives down there, and he knows a lot of people. We found several places where Stokel had been seen recently. I know he's there."

Tom said, "Jack, that was a stupid thing to do. You should have at least called me. Before you do anything else, I want to see you in my office first thing." Jack agreed. "Now, go take care of the girls and all of you get some rest. I'll see you in a couple hours."

Tom left, and Jack announced he would be staying on the couch for the rest of the night. There weren't any arguments.

It wasn't the most comfortable couch. Sleep came in small doses as Jack's mind raced, continually going over all that had happened. It was at the end of one of those short periods of sleep that he smelled coffee brewing.

CHAPTER THIRTY-TWO

CONFIRMATION

JACK WALKED INTO Tom's office just before ten. "Hey Tom, sorry I'm so late."

"Mornin' Jack. How's everyone holding up?" Tom asked as he motioned for Jack to take a seat.

As Jack sat down he said, "The girls are okay, a little tired and frazzled. I think they are more scared than they'll admit, but they'll be all right."

"Good."

"Any news yet on Franz?"

"As a matter of fact, yes." Tom picked up a piece of paper from his desk. "This was waiting for me this morning in the fax machine." He held it up.

"What's that?"

"His fingerprints."

"And?"

"I'm about to send them to the crime lab to see if they match, and then I'll send them off to New Mexico.

I also heard from Immigration and Customs Enforcement."

"So this means that we now know when he entered the country, right?"

"Yes, it does."

"So, when?" Jack persisted. Tom seemed to be enjoying making Jack wait.

"He came in about two weeks before our body was found."

Jack exhaled. "Right about when Lillian was killed."

Tom agreed. "The time frame fits, but the big question of why is still there. Now, tell me about your little adventures in Hampton Beach."

Jack told Tom about his friend Dave, their visit to Mary and Lou's on Sunday night and how the bartender recognized the picture. Jack also told Tom about the store clerk on Monday who also recognized Franz.

Before Jack could go on, Tom stopped him, picked up the phone, and called the Hampton Beach Police department. "Sergeant Frazier please. Tom Scott from Rye calling." He paused, "Yes, I'll wait."

Frazier was a long time friend. It was only a few moments before Tom said, "Bob, Tom here. Yeah, things are great. Listen, you remember that body we found recently? Yeah, that's the one. Well, there is someone staying down in the south beach area who we want to talk to." He paused, "One of our locals, a guy named Jack Beale .... Yeah that's him, he runs down there with his friend Dave Wheeler. Oh, you know Dave? Well, they've been down there looking for this guy we want to talk to. His name is Franz Stokel. He's from Switzerland, and there is quite a bit of circumstantial evidence that seems to link him with this case. I just got his fingerprints, and we're having them compared to some we lifted from that car we found. I'm also sending them out to New Mexico where we have what seems to be a related crime, and they have some mystery prints as well. If there's a match in either place, then he goes from being a person of interest to a prime suspect. I sent you his picture a few days ago. Can you guys keep an eye out for him? Thanks, I owe you one."

Tom turned to Jack. "Bob's a great guy. If Stokel is down there, Bob will find him. You stay away and let us take care of this." Even though Jack had no intention of staying away, he agreed. Tom and Jack sat and talked some more before Jack excused himself. He wanted to go check on Max again and make plans for tonight.

As Jack drove out of the parking lot, he knew what he was going to do. First he'd go home, call Dave and see if he'd want to go for a run later. Then he'd spend the afternoon with Max and Patti making sure they got to work safely. He was sure they'd be okay while at work, while he and Dave ran around the beach looking for Scotch and Soda Man. This began a routine that would continue for almost a week with no success.

* * *

No more than an hour had passed after Jack's departure before Tom sent the fingerprints out. Now all he could do was wait. This was the toughest part of any investigation, waiting for other people to get back to you. As Tom sat there he did his own non-expert comparison of the prints to those they took off the car. To his eye they matched. He still would have the experts confirm the match, but for now his assessment was good enough. He was feeling a real rush of excitement. He took a deep breath and thought about his next step.

As soon as either the crime lab here or Martinez in New Mexico came up with a match, he would call Bob in Hampton Beach and make an official request to arrest, Even without the second confirmation it would certainly be enough to take him into custody.

But one big question remained. Why? Even if all of the prints matched, why would a lawyer from Switzerland travel all the way to the United States to allegedly murder two women with whom he had no known association? And more importantly, why was he still hanging around?

CHAPTER THIRTY-THREE

FINALLY...

A WEEK HAD PASSED since Tom had sent the fingerprints to the crime lab and New Mexico. During that time, against Tom's admonition, Jack and Dave had put in quite a few miles and consumed more than a few beers as they continued to scour Hampton Beach each night. Franz had disappeared.

* * *

Then, one morning, Jack arrived at Max's and found both she and Patti sitting on the couch staring at a Fed Ex box that was on the coffee table. "Hi, girls."

They both turned, and said "Hi Jack" at the same time with no emotion whatsoever, then they returned to staring at the mystery package.

"What's in the box?"

Without turning toward him, they said in unison, "Aunt Lillian."

After a few moments of stunned silence, he said, "I'm sorry. I didn't know."

"That's okay," said Max. "You had no way of knowing."

"Are you going to open it?"

"Of course."

"So open it."

Max and Patti continued to stare at the box. "This is creepy," said Max. Patti agreed.

"Would you like me to open it for you?", asked Jack.

"Would you?"

Jack opened the box and inside was a sealed brass urn. There was a flat spot near the base where a small engraveable plate could be attached. They all sat there looking at it. Max's eyes began to tear up.

"You okay, Max?" asked Jack.

"Yeah. I was just thinking about how little I really knew about Aunt Lillian and now I am the only one to remember her. What a way to die. Do you think we will ever know for sure why?"

"I have a feeling that we will," said Jack. Then to lighten up the mood he asked, "Any one up for some lunch?"

Jack decided not to tell the girls where they were going. A diversion was needed after all of the mysterious and sometimes deadly events of the past few weeks. The girls figured out that Kennebunkport, Me. was the destination when Jack took that exit off the highway. By the time the afternoon was over, they had enjoyed lunch, visited a few of the shops that were still open and were able to forget, if only for a few hours, all that awaited them back at home. Jack's plan had worked, and as they drove home, the mood in the truck was much lighter.

When they reached Max's, there was just enough time to change and get to work. Jack intended to take them to work, pick them up after, and bring them home. Max and Patti were adamant about driving themselves so a compromise was reached. The girls would go together in one car and would call Jack when they were ready to go home so he could provide an escort. He waited and followed them to Ben's. After they were safely in the building and had promised again to call him when the night was over, Jack went home to get changed for his nightly run.

* * *

While Jack was taking the girls out to lunch, Tom got word back from the crime lab. The fingerprints were a match to those on the car, so he called Bob Frazier in Hampton and asked him to pick up Franz. After placing that call, he opened the file and reviewed his notes. There had been plenty of time from when Franz had entered the country for him to go to New Mexico, kill Lillian, and return to Rye in time to kill Meredith.

The phone rang. On the second ring, Tom answered. He listened intently, then said, "Yes, thank you," and hung up. There was a heavy silence as he sat for a few moments before picking up the phone again. He made two calls. The first to Bob for the second time. "Bob, have you found him yet? ... No? ... Well I just got confirmation that his prints were also a match with some of those found out in New Mexico. He's definitely our prime suspect. I need to talk to him ... Thank you. Call me if you have anything." The second call was to Jack. Tom got Jack's machine and left a message, hoping that Jack would get it sooner rather than later. By late afternoon Tom was getting ready to call it a day. It had been a good one.

CHAPTER THIRTY-FOUR

BACK TO THE BEACH

WHEN JACK GOT BACK to his apartment, he noticed that there was a message on his machine. He hit the play button and listened as he began changing for his run. "Hi Jack. It's Tom. I just heard from both New Mexico and our crime lab, and both have positive matches to the prints I sent them. Franz looks like our man. I've called Hampton Beach and asked them to pick him up for questioning. Call me."

Now Jack knew. It was official. Franz was the number one suspect. He had been in New Mexico, he had probably killed Max's aunt, and now he was here. Jack's emotions overtook reason as he finished lacing up his shoes. He had to get to Franz first. Max wouldn't be safe until he was caught. No consideration was given to what Jack would do with Franz if, no, when he caught him. At this moment, it was all about the chase. Beyond that Jack didn't have a plan. Tom could wait. Jack would call Tom tomorrow. With steely resolve, Jack zipped up his jacket and headed down the stairs.

Halfway down, his phone rang. He stopped, afraid it might be Tom again. Jack let the machine answer and listened. "What the ..." he started to say as he heard Andy's voice, then he became quiet as he listened to what Andy had to say. It was an address for Scotch and Soda Man. Jack leapt up the stairs, straining to get to the phone so he could talk to Andy. By the time he picked up the receiver, all he heard was the steady hum of the dial tone in his ear and the pounding of his heart in his chest.

Stunned, Jack stood there looking at the receiver in his hand and hardly daring to breathe. "Shit," was all he said as he slammed down the receiver. He stood, staring at the machine, and pressed play. The machine spoke to him, "You have two new messages."

He answered the faceless voice, "Yeah, yeah. I know."

The voice continued, "Message one."

Tom's message began to play. Annoyed, Jack pressed the next message button.

"Message two."

Andy's voice came on, and Jack held his breath as he listened. He exhaled, pressed the button again, and listened a third time. By the fourth time, he realized that it wasn't going to change and smiled.

Scotch and Soda Man had just been given to him on a silver platter. Jack turned and almost fell going down the stairs. He couldn't get to Dave's fast enough.

The drive to Dave's was the longest fifteen minutes ever despite the fact that the roads were clear, there was little traffic, and Jack drove as fast as his truck would go. The possibility that he could get stopped for speeding never occurred to him. By the time he reached Dave's, the adrenaline rush was beginning to subside and was replaced by a calm determination. As he parked the truck, Dave came out to meet him. "Hey Jack, what's up?"

Jack told him about the two phone calls.

"I know where that address is," said Dave. "Before we go let me make a call. Come on in."

Jack waited impatiently while Dave used the phone. Jack could hear him talking, but the one-sided conversation was muffled.

Dave returned quickly and was now as excited as Jack. "I just called the store. Our guy bought his paper late this afternoon. Then I called Tony over at the bar, and he said that Franz was just there, read his paper, had his scotch and soda and left only five minutes ago."

"Did Tony say which way Franz was going?"

"Nah, only that he had just left."

"How close is that address?"

"Not far."

"Great. Let's go," said Jack as he pulled on his hat and gloves, and headed for the door.

"Hold on a second. Shouldn't we talk about how we're going to do this first?"

"What's to discuss? We know where he lives. Let's go get him."

"No. Jack, listen. Yes, we know where he lives, but he may not be home yet, and it's too cold to stand out front waiting for him to arrive. I'm sure if he saw us, he'd get spooked. Think about it, two guys in black spandex tights hanging out on a cold winter night?"

"Okay, what do you suggest?"

"How about we just do our regular run, only we'll gradually close in on the address. Maybe we'll get lucky and find him out on the street. It'll give him more time to get home."

"Okay. Let's go."

They started out running together, heading north on Back Street until they reached the Casino's parking lot. There they reversed directions, split up with each taking alternate streets, effectively running a basket-weave pattern while gradually approaching the address that Andy had left on the answering machine. This allowed Jack and Dave to cover more territory more quickly and keep in touch with each other at the crossing points. The pace was easy, the air cold but calm. It was a beautiful night for running. This weaving pattern eventually took Jack and Dave into the last neighborhood at the southern end of the beach.

As Jack took his last turn before beginning to run back over the same route in the opposite direction, he saw someone coming out of a house. It wasn't the address he had been given, but it was close and this was the first person Jack had seen during the run. The possibility that the man was Jack's quarry caused his heart to race. He tried to keep his pace steady and innocent, despite his urge to give chase. Jack had to make sure. As he came up on the man walking, he appeared to be about the right size and the overcoat looked familiar. Jack was thinking about how to make his move when a car turned down the street toward them. The headlights caught the man's silhouette and Jack was sure it was Franz. Jack had to run past Franz so as to not raise any suspicion. Running by turned out to be the right decision because the car was a police cruiser.

"Probably looking for Franz," Jack thought as he remembered Tom's message. As Jack turned at the next corner, he risked a look back and saw the cruiser's taillights disappearing around a corner. Franz had also disappeared. "Damn. Where did you go?" Jack mumbled under his breath. He saw Dave approaching and began to slow his pace. As they came together, both stopped to talk.

"I just passed him," said Jack.

"Where?"

"Back around the corner, only he's not there now."

"What do you mean?"

"Just as I was coming up behind him, a police cruiser came toward us so I had to just run past him; I couldn't risk a look. As I turned the corner, I glanced back and the cruiser was almost out of sight but Franz had also vanished. I'm assuming he was avoiding the cruiser."

"Makes sense if it was him."

"I know it was him. It had to be."

"So what do you want to do?"

"Let's keep going in the direction we were going and go around the block again. If he's there, one of us should spot him."

"You got it."

With that, they began running again, the distance between them rapidly increasing and quickly each was alone. As Dave reached the corner, he nearly ran into a lone man who emerged from the shadows.

A patch of ice caused Dave to slip, and they nearly collided. In that moment, he got a glimpse of the man's face. It was Franz. "Sorry man," said Dave as he regained his balance. There was no response, so Dave continued on as if nothing had happened. Dave's pace quickened as he raced to get to Jack with the news. When they met, Dave was gulping for air as he said, "It's him."

A calmness came over Jack. They had found him. "I'm going after him. I'll keep going this way so I can come up from behind. You continue the way you were going; this way we'll be able to contain him."

They separated. Jack quickly picked up his pace. As he rounded the corner, he could see his target several hundred yards down the street, still walking. "You're mine now," Jack muttered under his breath as his stride lengthened and he began to rapidly close the distance. The pavement was clear and his footsteps silent. He didn't even feel out of breath. As Jack came up behind Scotch and Soda Man, he was hunched down inside his wool overcoat, his collar pulled up around his ears in an attempt to shield himself from the cold. Jack slowed nearly to a walk. There was no indication that Scotch and Soda Man even knew Jack was behind him. Then Jack said, "Franz"—not loud, just in a matter-of-fact tone. Jack could see Franz's shoulders tense as he heard his name called out of the darkness. He stopped and turned suddenly. Before Jack could say anything else or even get out of the way, they nearly collided. Face to face, their eyes met. Even in the dim light of a winter's night, Jack could see the surprise in Franz's face as he recognized Jack.

That's when Jack's head jerked back as he felt a sharp pain in the center of his face, fell backward, and landed on his ass. It felt like an eternity, but in reality, only seconds passed while the surprise and cobwebs cleared from his head. He looked around just in time to see Scotch and Soda Man running in the direction that Jack had just come from and disappearing around the corner. "Shit. Great plan, genius,"

Jack berated himself as he stood up. Something warm was running down his face. At first he thought it was sweat, then he realized it was blood. He picked up some snow, put it on his nose to try to stop the bleeding, and began jogging slowly back in the direction that Scotch and Soda Man had fled. As Jack reached the corner where he assumed Franz had turned, Dave caught up.

"I thought we had him between us," said Dave.

"We did, until he sucker-punched me and ran back this way."

"Hold up a second. Let me see your face."

Jack stopped and took the snow in his hand away from his nose.

Dave chuckled. "Oh, bro. He nailed you good."

"Ha ha, very funny," said Jack.

"So are we gonna go after him or what?"

"We're gonna go get him," said Jack as he threw the bloody snow onto the ground and began to run. Dave was working to keep up when they saw Franz heading for the beach. Jack began to sprint after him. Two thoughts flashed through his mind. First, he hoped the cruiser he had seen earlier was not around. A bloody-faced man dressed in black chasing someone certainly would attract attention. Secondly, he was amazed at how fast Franz could run. Jack was gaining on him slowly as the end of the street came into sight.

A snowbank separated the end of the street from the beach. "That will slow him down," thought Jack. Dave wasn't far behind Jack by the time Franz reached the snowbank; Dave saw Jack and Franz scramble over it and disappear into the dark of the beach.

Jack could hear Franz's labored breathing over the soft swooshing of the surf. He was slowing rapidly, and the soft sand allowed Jack to close the final few yards until Franz was within reach.

"You're mine now," said Jack as he reached out his arm and gave Scotch and Soda Man a push. It wasn't a hard push, but it was enough to knock Franz off balance and fall. Jack also lost his balance and went down. Dave saw them both go down, and before either one was able to get up, Dave was on top of Franz, pinning him down.

"I've got him. You okay Jack?"

"Yeah," Jack honked. His nose was still bleeding, and he was pinching it with his fingers. "Thanks."

Jack stood up. Dave looked up at him and, as dark as it was, could see that Jack was a bloody, sweaty mess. Dave chuckled. Not so much because anything was funny, but more as a release of all the tension that had built up leading to this moment—and Jack did look pretty funny.

Jack chuckled also as he looked down at Dave sitting on Scotch and Soda Man.

Then they heard a muffled voice ask, "Would you please get off of me?"

Both Jack and Dave stopped chuckling and looked down at Franz. Dave shifted his weight off Franz, twisted Franz's arm behind his back, and said, "Get up."

With some effort Franz did; the three men stood there. Franz was facing Jack with his arm twisted behind his back, held by Dave. Looked straight at Jack, Franz asked, "You're Max's friend, aren't you? Now what?"

"Yes," Jack said, still honking slightly. "Now we are going to have a little talk. Then, I'm going to turn you over to the police who have a warrant out for your arrest. Let's go."

Dave jerked on the arm he held twisted behind Franz's back, and they began to walk to Dave's. Little more was said as each man was lost in his own thoughts.

CHAPTER THIRTY-FIVE

REVELATIONS

BY THE TIME they had walked the ten minutes it took to get to Dave's, all three were shivering from the cold. "Sit," said Dave as he guided Scotch and Soda Man to the table in his kitchen. Silently Franz sat down and watched as Jack went into the bathroom to clean up. Dave cracked a beer.

Jack looked in the mirror at his blood-covered face and clothes, and he thought rationally about what he and Dave had just done for the first time. "What were you thinking?" Jack asked himself as he began to wash off the dried blood. Finally, he joined Dave and Franz in the kitchen.

"You cleaned up well," said Dave as he handed Jack a beer. "How do you feel?"

"Fine. Who would have thought that a simple bloody nose could make such a mess."

Franz looked up at Jack. "Sorry about the nose."

Jack looked down at him. "Yeah, well, you may be sorry about the nose, but there are a few other things you should be more sorry about. You do know that the police have a warrant out for your arrest."

"It doesn't surprise me."

"And you do know that I am going to turn you over to them."

"Yes, I suspected."

Franz's demeanor was beginning to make Jack a little nervous. Franz was too calm, almost resigned. "Was he planning something? Why was he so subdued?" Jack wondered. Then a chill went through him as he realized that neither he nor Dave had searched Franz for a weapon. "Shit. What if ..." He didn't get the chance to finish the thought.

Scotch and Soda Man shifted in his seat, then reached into his pocket. Jack's heart skipped a beat, and he tensed as he stared at Franz. In that second, a thousand things flashed through Jack's head. "What if Franz pulled out a weapon? Could I react fast enough?" Jack tightened his grip on his beer, holding it ready to throw if necessary.

Franz slowly withdrew his hand from his pocket; Jack didn't see a weapon. Then Franz put something down on the table and sat back. It was a ring. It was gold and had a distinctive twist to it. Instantly, Jack knew it was the ring that had belonged to Max's aunt. Stunned, Jack stared at it, then slowly he lifted his eyes and gazed at Franz in disbelief.

In a soft voice Franz said, "That's what you are looking for, isn't it?"

Jack didn't move or say anything. He just stared.

It was Dave who first reacted. He walked over to the table, picked up the ring, and looked at it closely. "Cool ring."

Jack found his voice and said softly, "That ring belonged to Max's aunt who was killed out in New Mexico. Meredith, her aunt's life partner, was wearing it when her body was found in the ice out in the harbor. But the ring disappeared by the time her body was brought up."

"Oh," said Dave. He had heard the story. As he went to put the ring back on the table, it slipped out of his fingers and fell on the floor. Two sets of eyes focused on Dave, then all three sets of eyes looked down at the ring. It didn't roll as might have been expected; instead it spun around a few times, then lay there. Dave bent down and quickly picked it up, blushing with embarrassment. "Sorry," he said as he placed the ring on the table and stepped back.

Franz looked at Jack and said, "Aren't you going to ask me how I got it?"

Even though Jack was sure he knew the answer, he played along.

"Okay, how did you get it?"

"It was quite simple. That night out on the ice, as they brought the body over to the rocks by the parking lot, I recognized her. I climbed down to help. There was so much confusion that it was not hard to do. I saw the ring on her finger, so I took it and walked away. It was easy with all of the commotion."

"So why are you still here? You got what you wanted."

"No, I didn't. There is something else that Max may not know that puts her in great danger."

"What the hell are you talking about?"

"You know those two women, the ones who were killed?"

"Yes," Jack said warily as he stared at Franz.

"I didn't kill them, and I'm afraid that Max may be next."

Jack sat down across from him. He couldn't believe what he was hearing. "That is such bullshit. The evidence that the police have links you to both killings, and now I'm going to hand you over to them."

"So why haven't you called them?"

Jack was silent.

"You want me to call?" Dave's voice cut through the silence.

"No, wait a minute," said Jack.

Franz looked back at Jack and said in a quiet voice, "You have this all wrong. I did not kill those women. I only wish to protect Max."

That statement was so outrageous and yet spoken with such sincerity and quiet force that Jack looked at Franz in disbelief. Silence filled the room. Dave looked first at Jack and then at the man seated at his table. Franz Stokel continued to look straight into Jack's eyes, and Jack sat back studying his face. Jack was the first to break the silence. "OK, convince me."

Franz asked for a glass of water. Dave handed Franz one. He took a sip then began, "My name is Franz Stokel, and you must know I am a lawyer from Bern, Switzerland. I took over my father's law practice after he died several years ago. It is a small but well-respected practice that my grandfather started. I share the same name as both my father and my grandfather. Max's great-grandfather, William Jacob, and my grandfather were close friends. When William's daughter, Max's grandmother, Ruth, was born, he did two things. First, he commissioned a local goldsmith to make a special ring that would be given to his daughter on her wedding day." Franz paused and picked up the ring, "This ring." He then placed it back down on the table before continuing.

"Second, with my grandfather's help, a lockbox in the Bern Bank was obtained with my grandfather listed as the owner of the box. The political situation in Europe made this arrangement necessary. After my grandfather died, the responsibility for the lockbox was passed to my father and eventually to me. We were never told what it contained. I have my suspicions. Going back, shortly after the war, William died, and my grandfather visited his daughter Ruth in the United States. He passed on to her two letters from her father. In my grandfather's presence she opened the first one. It was a final good-bye, and it gave her instructions for claiming the contents of the lockbox. With my grandfather's help she would need to present the second letter and the ring to the bank. I was never told what the contents of the second letter were. I'm not even sure that my grandfather knew. I only know that it must be presented with the ring. After the bankers were satisfied as to her identity and the authenticity of the articles presented, she would then be given the box." Franz paused and took another sip of his water.

"That's a touching story, but you haven't given me any reason to believe that you didn't kill those women."

"I'm getting there. Growing up, I knew that often my father would become the guardian of people's estates. It was just one of those services that a good lawyer would provide. Other than its existence, I never knew anything more of Herr Jacob's box until my father told me this story when he was near death. Many years had passed, no one had approached me about this matter, and I had almost forgotten about it, until recently."

Jack was listening but was not hearing what he wanted to hear; although sensing Jack's impatience, Franz continued at his own pace.

"Now remember as the war spread over Europe, many other members of the Jewish community also set up lockboxes in banks all over Switzerland. As I'm sure you know, many of these boxes have never been claimed. The banks, bound by centuries of Swiss banking tradition, have held onto these boxes in the fading hope that someone would claim them."

Jack's impatience was increasing. "Thanks for the history lesson. Get on with it."

"Quite by accident it was discovered that someone had been discretely looting some of these boxes in the Bern Bank. Fearful of scandal, the bank kept this knowledge quiet and started an internal investigation. I was contacted by the bank as part of that investigation. Since my father's death, I had become the new custodian of the Jacob box. I verified that it had not been violated, and the bank moved it to a new location where access was even more limited. I didn't know who had the ring or the letter. I just assumed it would have been one of the heirs and it wouldn't matter until someone showed up to claim the box. I thought that would be the end of it. It wasn't. The bank contacted me again. Their investigations had come up with some names of looting suspects, and I was asked if I recognized any of them. I did. I recognized that of a schoolmate of mine whom I hadn't seen in many years."

"You are really trying my patience. I don't care about your old schoolmates. How does all this relate to Max? Get to the point."

"I will. Listen to me. This schoolmate was from a poorer background. I found his company exciting; he was in his first year, and I was in my last year. I was assigned to be his ... I'm not sure what you call it, he would come to me for help and I would show him around.

As it turned out, he showed me far more than I could ever show him. He was mischievous, always in trouble. As I tried to help him, I ended up getting pulled into his schemes, and I found them exciting. The result was that we had many misadventures. After we graduated, we went our separate ways. His friends outside of school were not the kind you would want to associate with, but as much as he was like them, he was also different. He preferred to use his head rather than his fists. You would call him a conman. We called him a caméléon, like one of those lizards that changes colors to suit its environment."

Jack's agitation with this long narrative finally overcame his patience. Dave watched in surprise as Jack pushed his chair back, stood and walked deliberately around the table, stopping behind Franz. Then Jack leaned forward, took Franz by the shoulders, and hissed in his ear, "I don't give a damn about your childhood friends. Tell me what I want to know about how this affects Max, or we are going to the police now and you can rot in hell."

Franz held up his hand. "Let me continue, and I think you will see."

"Okay. Go on, but make it quick," said Jack as he took his seat again.

"My old friend …"

Jack interrupted again. "Cut the dramatics and get to the point."

"You Americans, always in such a hurry. Okay, his name was André Bonhomme." With this pronouncement, Franz stopped and looked at Jack.

Jack looked back and said, "So?"

"So. When I knew him in school, he was André Bonhomme. You may know him by his more American name of Andrew Goodman."

It took a moment for this to sink in. Jack looked at Franz and said, "Andy?"

"Yes, Andy."

Jack felt as if he had had the wind knocked out of him. He took a deep breath.

Jack and Dave sat in stunned silence, and Franz continued. "Out of some twisted loyalty to my old friend, I did not say anything to the bank about knowing him. I decided to let the bank continue its investigations while I searched for André on my own. Maybe, I thought, I could change him. I don't know. I hired an agency to help me find him. It took some time. Eventually they discovered that he had worked in the banking industry as an independent auditor, which gave him access to many old records. He had used this information to discern which boxes he could break into. He was patient. He stole only a small amount each time. Working in many banks all over Europe, he was able to quietly loot these seemingly dormant boxes without arousing any attention. It was quite by accident that the discovery of the thefts was made.

"The reality is that he is a common thief who recognized the virtue of patience. It seems that over the years, he created two lives. In Europe, he was the respected banking auditor, and if he felt things were getting too hot, he would disappear to the United States where he could be whomever he wanted. It was on one such trip that he met Max and so began his on-and-off relationship with her. I don't think he knew who she was at first. But at some point, he learned of her family history and realized she might possess the key to a very valuable lockbox. I don't know how much of the story he knows. I'm sure he knows of the ring, but the rest … I just don't know. More importantly, I'm not sure what she knows. Understand, it has taken me many years to find all of this out and much is still speculation."

The room was silent as Jack and Dave sat in stunned disbelief.

Franz took a sip of his water and continued. "As I learned about more and more of André's activities, I became convinced that he was using Max for the sole intention of getting that particular lockbox. Remember, I had no direct proof of any of this, so I continued to watch him, hoping he would slip up.

"There were only two remaining living heirs of Herr Jacob: Lillian and Max. I went to New Mexico to see Lillian first, she being the oldest. By the time I found her, it was too late. She was already dead; her companion had vanished and her place had been torn apart. I knew Andy had to have done it and that he was desperate. I feared for Max's safety. I didn't want to involve the authorities, at least not yet, so I fled and came here to find her. I didn't know what she knew, if anything, about all of this, so I decided to just watch over her in case Andy showed up, and he did."

Jack interrupted him again. "You are so full of shit."

Franz looked over at Jack, startled by the interruption but he quickly went on.

"You don't believe me."

"Why should I? You must admit this is a pretty wild story."

"I suppose it is."

"So why didn't you just go directly to Max and tell her what you knew?"

"I intended to. I was trying to decide on the best way to tell her. Remember, other than sitting at the bar watching her, we had never met. You can't just walk up to someone you don't know and tell her that you found her relative dead, that her lover was also killed but no one knows it yet, and that she is in grave danger from the man she has been seeing for the past several years."

"I suppose that would be a little tough, when you put it that way."

"Andy really doesn't treat her very well does he?" asked Franz, changing the subject.

This question took Jack by surprise and he answered before thinking, "No, he doesn't."

As soon as Jack said that, he wished that he could take it back, but it was too late.

"You know," Franz said with a pause, "you're the one."

"The one what?"

"The one Max really belongs with."

Jack stood, glared at him, then turned and walked away from the table. He didn't like the way Franz had changed the subject from himself to Jack and his relationship with Max, and he needed a moment to compose himself. An uneasy silence filled the room. After what seemed like an eternity, Jack turned back.

"That's nice of you to say, but we're not here to discuss my personal life. We're here because I'm giving you a chance to explain yourself before I turn you over to the police, and I'm beginning to lose patience. How did you know about Meredith's death before anyone else?"

"After leaving New Mexico, I came out here. It was during that really cold weather. I couldn't sleep, so I had gone out for a walk. I don't mind the cold, and sometimes a late-night walk alone under the stars helps me think. I do this often at home in the Alps. As I was walking, I saw two cars stopped by that little bridge over the creek. The driver from the second car, a man, was standing next to the first car. At first it appeared innocent enough, and I remember thinking maybe they were two lovers saying a last good night. Then I could see their body language change and their voices grew louder. He pulled her out, and she screamed. I watched, not wanting to get involved, as she tried to get away from him. He grabbed her, and they struggled. She broke free, and ran around the car, but he caught her. My view was blocked for a moment by one of the cars, then I heard a splash and his voice swearing. He made no attempt to help her. Then he returned to his car and drove off. He never saw me."

Jack interrupted him, "Great story Franz. How do you explain your fingerprints on the car? And that scratch on your cheek? I think you got it while you fought with her before pushing her in the creek."

Franz looked up, confused for a moment by Jack's accusation. "No.

No. It wasn't me. I began running to see if I could help her, and my face was scraped by a tree branch." Franz reached up and touched his face.

"Right. You want me to believe that you were running to help her. You said 'he', who's 'he'? Did you get a look at him?"

Franz seemed a little put out by these questions. "I was not so close as to be able to see who it was clearly, but I could hear their voices. The man's was Andy's. I didn't recognize the woman's. As I ran, I prayed it wasn't Max. It was too late by the time I got there. She was gone. I noticed the car had New Mexico license plates so I knew she wasn't Max. I should have gone to the authorities, but I panicked and just couldn't. The next day in the bar, I decided to quietly stay in town and keep an eye on Max. I wasn't sure what she knew about the ring or the letter, and I guess I thought I could catch André myself. You know, sometimes events cloud one's judgment and you do stupid things. I was very stupid. Part of me wanted to catch him, and I guess I saw Max as the key. Another part of me thought I could protect her as well."

"Okay so you decided to stick around, hoping to catch him and protect Max"

"Yes."

"What happened that night when Andy came into the bar and you spoke to him? What did you say to him?" asked Jack.

"When he first came in, I saw him but, he didn't see me. From the way Max acted, I could tell she didn't want to see him. From the way he acted, I guessed he did not yet have the ring. When he became loud and abusive, I went up to him and said, 'I know what you've been up to and we need to talk.' Our eyes locked. In that moment, he recognized me. When he did, I could see his surprise quickly turn to confusion. He said nothing. He just turned and left. I followed him out. He was gone by the time I got outside, so I also left. I couldn't go to the authorities yet. I had no proof. I had to confront him first."

All during Franz's narrative, Jack had been standing by the window looking out, his back turned to Franz. Now he turned and said, "Franz, you tell a good story, but you can't honestly ask me to believe you when the police have hard evidence that you are the murderer."

"Except that I'm not. Let me continue," he protested. "As I said, things rapidly became both clearer to me and more complicated as events unfolded. I continued hanging out at Ben's as a way to keep watch over Max. When the body was found, I saw the ring on her finger, and in all the confusion, I took it. No one noticed. I knew Max was safe as long as she didn't have the ring."

"So you're telling me that Andy is after Max because after killing her aunt and her aunt's friend and not finding the ring, he now thinks Max has it. Of course she doesn't know any of this, but because you have it, you are protecting her."

"Yes."

A cold fear went through Jack. If this story were true, Max was in serious trouble. "Why should I believe any of this? You could just as easily be setting up Andy for your own purposes. Who would question you?"

"Yes, it does look so, but then why would I have given you this?" he pointed at the ring on the table.

Franz's story did seem to make some sense and as Jack looked down at the ring, he caught sight of the clock on Dave's wall. It was later than he realized. He should have been at Ben's to get the girls by now. He hoped they were still there. He asked Dave if he could use the phone. He dialed, and on the first ring, Peggy answered. As soon as she heard Jack's voice, she said, "Hold on, Patti needs to talk to you."

"Jack. Max is gone, and he's got her," her voice was quivering and sounded a thousand miles away as she spoke.

"What do you mean she's gone and who has her?"

"She's gone. She just went out back to dump the trash. She didn't come right back so I went to see where she was. She's gone. Then I got a call. It was from a man, I think it was Scotch and Soda Man. He said that I … we had what he wanted and that he'll trade Max for it. He said I was not to call the police and that he'd call back in an hour with instructions. I tried calling you, but I couldn't get you. Jack, I'm scared."

Guilt and rage overwhelmed him. While he had been out running, Jack had left his phone in the truck—that's why she couldn't reach him. "When did this all happen?" Jack tried to sound calm.

Between sobs Patti managed to say, "No more than ten minutes ago."

"Patti, stay there. I'll be there as fast as I can."

Dave and Franz had heard Jack's side of the conversation. Their looks asked the question as Jack hung up the phone. "He's got her, and he wants that"—pointing at the ring on the table.

CHAPTER THIRTY-SIX

MISSING

"I'M COMING WITH YOU," said Dave as he and Franz began getting their coats on while Jack made another call.

"Tom, I'm sorry for calling you so late. Max has been taken. I'm down in Hampton Beach. I came down to run and to look for Scotch and Soda Man. ... Yes, I know you told me not to. I have him here, and he's not our man. Andy is, and he has Max. He called, and talked to Patti, and told her we should not call the police. I'm leaving now, heading for Ben's. Meet us there, and I'll explain everything." Jack hung up the phone cutting off any further response from Tom.

With Franz in Jack's truck and Dave following, they covered the eight-and-a-half-mile distance to Ben's even faster than Jack did earlier when he was on his way to Dave's. But it just wasn't fast enough; it felt like an eternity.

"I'm sorry Jack," said Franz. "Perhaps I should have gone to the authorities in the beginning, but I wanted to protect the honor and reputation of my father. I was stupid."

"Shut the fuck up. None of this would be happening if you hadn't tried to be a hero. You can explain yourself to the authorities. Right now all I care about is getting Max back. After she's safe ... well, I don't really care what happens to you." They rode in silence the rest of the way.

When they pulled into Ben's parking lot, there was no sign that anything was amiss. Tom's car wasn't in sight. Jack, Franz, and Dave walked in the front door, not knowing what to expect. Peggy walked toward them, concern etched on her face. "I'm so sorry, Jack." Her look of concern turned to confusion when she saw who was with him.

"Thanks. Where's Patti?"

"She's in the bar with Tom."

The three men brushed past Peggy and hurried down the hall toward the bar. Her gaze followed them and she muttered under her breath, "What the hell?"

When Jack turned the corner, he could see Tom and Patti talking. Another officer from town was there as well. As Jack walked into the room, all heads turned toward him followed immediately by silence when Franz appeared with Dave.

As soon as Patti saw Scotch and Soda Man, she froze, a look of panic and confusion on her face. Jack stepped toward her, and she ran into his arms. He could feel her trembling. "Jack, I'm so sorry. ... What's he doing here? ... Who has Max?" she sobbed into his chest.

"It's okay, Patti," said Jack as he stroked her hair. "Max will be fine. Franz isn't the bad guy. Trust me. He's going to help us get Max back."

She pulled back, her eyes questioning his sanity. "Jack, there's blood on your clothes. You look awful, and you really stink. What happened tonight?"

"I'll tell you the whole story later."

Tom was already moving toward Franz, a hand on the gun holstered on his hip. Jack released Patti and sidestepped into Tom's path, blocking his way. Tom paused, and their eyes met. In that instant Jack could see the anger on Tom's face and knew there would be hell to pay if he didn't defuse the situation fast. "Tom, it's not what you think. We have to talk."

"You got that right." Then turning to the officer at the bar, Tom said, "Take him into custody."

"That won't be necessary," Jack said, staring into Tom's eyes. "He's not going anywhere. Franz come meet Tom Scott."

Franz moved forward as Jack turned toward him. "Tom, I'd like you to meet Franz Stokel."

Franz extended his hand, "Hello …"

Tom did not return the gesture, instead he only offered a long icy stare punctuated with a single command. "Take him." With that, the officer at the bar moved toward them. Turning toward Jack, Tom said, "What the hell were you doing? I explicitly told you to let us find him." He paused, then added, "And you involved someone else?" as he glanced at Dave.

"I know Tom. Can we talk in private?"

"I think that would be a good idea."

The officer moved past Jack and Tom, and grabbed Franz's arms.

"Tom. Wait," said Jack.

"No, it's all right," said Franz.

As Tom and Jack began to leave the room, Jack turned toward Patti and said, "Patti, this is Dave, one of my running buddies. He'll explain." She crinkled her nose as she extended her hand to Dave. Like Jack, Dave hadn't yet showered and still wore the aroma of their evening's run. "Hi Dave."

Turning to the officer, Tom said, "Keep an eye on him. I'll be right back." Then Tom pointed at Franz and said, "I'm not finished with you."

"Of course," said Franz.

Then Tom turned to Jack, motioned toward the door, and said, "Let's go."

* * *

While following Tom out of the room, Jack glanced back. Franz had been escorted to a table, and Jack saw the officer sit down across from Franz. Patti was over by the bar talking with Dave. It was at that moment the full effect of the events of the last few hours hit him. He paused, took a deep breath, then turned, and followed Tom to the small dining room that Peggy had prepared for them. Jack knew what was coming. Tom was waiting, and as he closed the door, Tom glared at Jack. To say it was tense would be a gross understatement.

Tom's steely voice broke the silence, "What the fuck were you thinking? Didn't I specifically tell you to let us do our job?"

"You did, but I couldn't just sit by and not do something. Besides Dave knows the beach better than anyone. I thought I could help." Then softly, he added, "I had to try."

Tom continued to glower at Jack. As a friend, Tom understood Jack's actions and sympathized, but now that Max had been taken those feelings were irrelevant. The stakes had been raised; Max's life was at risk, and there were procedures. Tom's frustration spilled out. "You might have screwed everything up."

That last statement snapped Jack out of his funk. "I might have screwed things up? Bullshit! I found Franz. He has valuable information and was with me when Max was grabbed. He didn't do it."

"So who did, Mr. Detective?"

Emotions were beginning to take over the conversation, and Tom's and Jack's voices were getting louder.

"Andy."

"Andy! What are you talking about?"

"If you'd shut up and listen to what I have to say—and more importantly, listen to what Franz has to say—you might thank me."

"Jack, watch yourself. If we weren't such good friends …"

Jack cut him off. "Listen, Tom. We're on the same side. Hear me out. Please."

Tom paused, exhaled loudly, then said, "I'm listening."

Jack described how he and Dave had been searching for Scotch and Soda Man for several days and that they had had some success.

When Jack told Tom about the phone message Andy left earlier in the day, Tom went ballistic.

"You got a call from Andy, and he told you where Franz was staying, and you didn't call me!"

"I couldn't."

"What do you mean you couldn't?"

"I just couldn't. It was personal. I had to find Franz first."

"Wrong answer. This was not a time for you to be thinking with your dick. You should have called me. He's already killed twice. Things could have been very different tonight."

"I admit I wasn't thinking clearly, but now it's over. We have Franz, and he has a lot to tell. Besides he's not the killer."

"You didn't know that when you went rushing off. You were lucky you only got a bloody nose," noting Jack's red swollen nose and the dried blood on his clothes. "And what do you mean he's not the killer?"

"Just that, and he gave me this." Jack withdrew the ring from his pocket and held it out for Tom to see.

"Is that what I think it is?"

"Yes."

Tom reached for it, but Jack closed his fist around it and pulled his hand back.

"Jack, give it to me."

"No."

"Jack, it's evidence."

"That may be, but I'm keeping it. Andy called me. He must have known that Franz had the ring and that I would get it. Andy used me. He has Max and wants this ring. I'm not letting it out of my possession until she's safe."

"Jack, you're playing a very dangerous game. I could arrest you."

"I know that, but you won't. You need me."

"I need you? Why?"

"Because you do."

"Explain. I'm listening."

Jack gave Tom a quick synopsis of what Franz had said about the ring. When Jack finished, Tom looked at Jack and said flatly, "Andy?"

"Yes, Andy."

"And you believe him?"

"Yes, I do."

"Son of a bitch. I suppose Max doesn't know any of this about the ring."

"I don't think so."

"That may be good."

"Why?"

"It's easier to deny knowledge if you don't have any. ... Okay. Jack, you've convinced me that our friend out there may not have been behind any of this, but the evidence still points to him. I'm going to hold him until we get Andy and can sort all of this out."

It was at this moment that there was a knock on the door. Jack opened it. It was Peggy. "There's a phone call for you. I think it's him."

Jack rushed out of the room.

* * *

Jack picked up the phone.

"Hello, Jack." The voice oozed contempt. Andy had made no attempt to disguise his voice.

It took all the self-control Jack could muster not to start screaming and threatening. Tersely Jack responded, "Hello, Andy." Then he listened, only speaking as necessary. "Yes I understand. ... She's telling the truth, she doesn't have the ring. I have it."

This last statement silenced Andy. Jack waited. He could only imagine Andy's reaction, and judging from the silence on the other end of the line, he wasn't prepared for Jack's statement.

"Let me talk to Max," Jack said. "I need to know she's all right, then we can talk." He could hear rustling, movement, muffled words, then, "Jack."

"Max, are you okay? Has he hurt you in any way?"

"Jack, I'm fine." He could hear the fear and strain in her voice. "He hasn't hurt me. Just do what he says; I don't need the ring."

Before she could say anything else, Andy came back on the line. "That's enough. I'll be in touch with instructions soon." Then the line went dead.

* * *

Jack hung up the phone. Tom looked at Jack. "What did Andy say?"

"He'll call back soon."

"Max okay?"

"Yeah."

Tom looked at Jack. "Don't get any ideas, we're doing this by the book."

"I understand. Andy said he'd call back soon. I'm going to go home, and get showered and changed. I'll be back in thirty minutes. I don't think he'll call back that quickly."

Tom nodded his assent and added, "Remember what I said. Don't get any crazy ideas."

"I know. By the book. I'll be right back." He went over to where Dave and Patti were sitting. He thanked Dave for his help, assured Patti that Max would be fine, and walked out of the bar. Jack shivered as the frigid night air hit him. As he drove the few hundred yards to his place, he kept thinking about what Max had said and what he didn't tell Tom. "What did she mean she didn't need that old ring? What had Andy told her?" Jack wondered. For the second time today, he began to consider what he would do.

Showered and changed, Jack felt like a new man as he closed the door behind him and walked to his truck. He could feel the snow crunch and squeak under his feet. Just as he reached for the door handle on his truck, he was struck by the near silence. If he strained, he could barely hear the sound of the ocean meeting the land. The air was calm, not a branch or bush rustled. The only light was from the stars that covered the sky, and as Jack looked up at them, he felt the ring in his pocket as words from a childhood rhyme suddenly popped into his head. "Star light, star bright, make my wish come true tonight," and Jack thought of Max. He opened the door, climbed in, and turned the key.

As he walked in the front door at Ben's, no one was in sight. Turning the corner into the bar, he saw only Tom, Franz, and the other officer sitting at a table talking. "Where is everyone?" Jack asked.

All three heads turned and looked up at him. Tom stood up and walked over to Jack. "Dave left and Patti went with him. I sent the rest home as well. There was no point in having all those people here."

"Has there been any word?"

"Not yet. Franz here just finished telling us his story."

"And?"

"It's interesting. There's a lot to corroborate, but now all we can do is wait."

Tom returned to the table where Franz was sitting calmly. Jack wanted to be alone. Too much had happened. He couldn't leave—he had to wait for Andy's call and instructions—so he sat down several tables over. He needed to think. Taking the ring out of his pocket, first he studied it, then he absently began tracing its unique shape over and over with his finger while staring out the window at nothing in particular. Twice around and he'd have touched the inside and the outside of the ring without ever breaking contact. Two sides and yet the same side. His thoughts drifted. What was he missing? Franz's story made so much sense, if it were true. Then it came to Jack. He glanced over to where Tom and Franz were still talking. The letter. The ring and the letter were part of the same whole, just like the two sides of the ring that were one. Tom didn't say anything about the letter, and Jack realized he hadn't mentioned it to Tom either. Did that mean that Franz didn't tell Tom about it? If not, why not? Why did he tell Jack?

These and other random thoughts about Andy, Max, Lillian, and Meredith swirled around in Jack's head, just as his finger continued to move around and around the ring. The ring, the letter. Both were necessary. He knew that, but besides Franz and Dave, did any one else? It seemed not. Why did Franz give up the ring so easily?

The phone rang, and the four men in the bar were instantly snapped out of their thoughts. On the second ring, Jack stood and began to move toward the phone. Franz merely watched, but his eyes flashed with anxiety. Tom intercepted Jack as he was about to pick up the phone. "Wait. Take a breath. Calm down."

Jack took a deep breath, exhaled, and picked up the phone, "Hello."

As Jack listened, the strain of the moment was apparent on his face. "Andy ..." was all he was able to say before he turned and slowly hung up the phone. The silence in the room was broken by the simultaneous swoosh as each person's held breath was released. The call had lasted but a few seconds.

"I've got to go," said Jack as he began putting on his coat.

"Whoa. Slow down. You're not going anywhere."

"No, Tom. I am. I have the ring. He wants it, and he's willing to trade. With me. No one else. It's that simple."

Before Tom could say or do anything else, Jack turned and ran out the door.

His departure was so sudden that by the time Tom reacted, Jack was gone. "Shit," Tom hissed. He reached for his radio to put out a call to try and stop Jack when Franz's voice broke the silence. "You should let him go."

Incredulous, Tom turned toward Franz. "What did you just say?"

Franz shifted uneasily in his seat. "I said you should let him go."

"Who are you to tell me what I should or should not do?"

"You're right. It's none of my business, but …"

Tom cut him off. "You're damned right it's none of your business."

Tom reached for his radio again.

"Of course, you're right."

Tom paused and glanced back at Franz, who now had the slightest smirk on his face as he spoke to no one in particular.

Tom turned, glared at Franz, put his radio down, and walked out of the room fuming.

Franz smiled.

CHAPTER THIRTY-SEVEN

PURSUIT

WHILE TOM WAS DECIDING what he should do next, Jack drove north along the coast in the first light of the new day. Halfway to his destination, he looked east just as the sun rose over the edge of the world. Its brightness hurt his eyes, and he squinted at the road ahead. Any other day, he would have found this moment to be magical. Today all he felt was apprehension.

All Andy had said was, "Science Center, Odiorne Point." Located about four and a half miles north of Rye Harbor, where Route 1A begins to curve away from the coast, the Science Center was in Odiorne Point State Park overlooking Portsmouth Harbor. The point was part of the coastal defense system during World War II. Now, the Science Center, devoted to marine ecology and biology, was the focal point of the park. Surrounded with miles of trails for cross-country skiing in the winter and hiking in the summer as well as with picnic areas, little remained of the defense system's network of bunkers and gun emplacements.

As Jack guided his truck into the parking area, he could see the Science Center in the distance. The atmosphere was perfectly clear. No clouds had formed yet, leaving the sky a perfectly unmarred blue. The sunlight reflecting off the glass of the building made it shine like a gemstone in the distance. Jack didn't feel the cold, but he saw it as his breath bathed his face in a cloud of vapor as he walked toward the building. Other than the lonely cry of an unseen gull, the world was silent. As he approached, he could see something taped to the door. His pace quickened as fast as caution fled. He grabbed the note, tore it open, and read the instructions. They were simple: "Prescott Park—by the plaque at the gundalow's berth—time is wasting."

Jack pressed the note into his pocket and hurried back to his truck. As he drove off, he was grateful that his heater was beginning to warm the cab. He hadn't noticed the cold when he was retrieving the note, but now he was shivering. There was little traffic, which allowed him to drive faster than would normally be possible, but he couldn't be reckless. The last thing he needed was to be stopped for speeding or some other violation. He felt for the ring in his pocket. It was there, and with it came thoughts of Max and how truly special she was to him. He was still just reacting to circumstances and didn't have a plan for when he met Andy.

As Jack began to drive through Portsmouth on his way to the park, his thoughts wandered: "Could Andy really be this stupid? What was he thinking? Was Franz telling the truth? What makes Andy think he can get away with it? What's in it for Franz? As soon as the swap was made Andy still would have to get out of the country. That would certainly become much more difficult since he would then be a fugitive. Suppose he does get out of the country; what about the letter? Does Andy know about it? Does he already have it?" Jack didn't have any answers. Plus something didn't feel right, but he couldn't put his finger on it. Before Jack was able to give it any more thought, he made the last turn onto Marcy Street and began the final approach to the park. All he wanted to do right now was to make the swap and get Max back safely.

The city was coming to life. Jack hadn't realized how busy the streets would be so early in the day, and he saw he would not be alone. Pet owners walking their dogs before work; each had little plastic bags attached to the leash ready to pick up and take home souvenirs of Fido's last meal. There were runners trying to get in some miles before work. Jack could tell the ones who were just starting from the ones who were finished. The former looked cold, their expressions questioning why they had left a warm bed to do this. Those who had just finished had steam coming off their heads, visible in the cold air like loaves of bread right out of the oven. These runners had expressions of accomplishment.

Jack parked on a side street, got out of the truck, and looked around. There was a breeze coming down the river that was cold and biting, and clouds were beginning to form. He turned up his collar and tried to scrunch down into his coat, like some kind of giant turtle pulling its head into its shell. His actions made Jack think how quickly the weather changed. He spotted the plaque near the gundalow's berth.

From a distance he didn't see anything. He hurried over. There was nothing there. Panic began to set in. He rapidly walked back and forth, looking around the plaque and along the chain-link fence hoping that maybe a note had blown off the plaque and been caught by the fence. Nothing. Then he saw one of the street people who hung out by the park bend over, pick something up, look at it carefully, shove it in his pocket, and begin to walk away. Jack ran toward him. It only took seconds for Jack to catch him. Jacke grabbed the man's arm and spun him around while shouting, "Stop! What did you just put into your pocket?"

Fear was in the man's eyes. It was the same look that a beaten dog had when cornered. As Jack caught his breath, he let go of the man's arm and spoke more calmly. "I saw you pick up a piece of paper and read it. May I have it?"

"Fuck off, asshole," the man replied as he began to turn away.

Jack fought to keep his panic under control. He tried again. He grabbed the man's arm again and, facing him, said, "There has been a kidnapping. I'm following instructions, and the next one was here at the park. I need to know if the paper you picked up is what I need."

The man looked at Jack and again said, "Fuck off." This time the man didn't turn away.

Jack tried again. "I'll give you ten bucks for that paper in your pocket."

The man's eyes narrowed, and he said, "Twenty."

"Okay here's twenty. Let me have the paper," Jack said as he held out the cash. The man slowly withdrew the paper from his pocket and handed it to Jack while taking the money. The note read: "Rest stop—I-95—York, Maine

The note didn't say whether this was where the swap would be made or what Jack was to look for. He had to assume that whatever he was looking for would be obvious when he got there. He turned to leave. After a few steps, he turned back and shouted to the homeless man, "You didn't happen to see who left this here this morning?" All Jack got in response was another "Fuck you" as the man continued to shuffle away. Jack turned and ran to his truck.

As he got back into his truck, he realized he was shaking, not from the cold or the run back to the car but from the realization that he had almost failed. He took a deep breath as he started his truck and headed out of Portsmouth. He cranked the heat on all the way, and it felt good. Getting out of Portsmouth wasn't quite as easy as getting in. The morning traffic into town was increasing. Leaving Prescott Park, he passed under the Memorial Bridge and turned right onto Bow Street. As he drove past the theater, he could see the I-95 bridge in the distance. Another right turn took him to Market Street past the salt piles and toward the highway. His frustration at being slowed by the endless line of trucks lined up for salt only increased his anxiety for Max's safety. Jack finally made it onto the highway, and as he drove north, he replayed everything again in his mind.

CHAPTER THIRTY-EIGHT

The Trade

ONCE JACK WAS ON THE HIGHWAY, it didn't take long to reach the rest area. His heart was racing as he slowed and drove in. He glanced at his watch and noted that only ten minutes had elapsed since he left the park. He thought how lucky he was that he hadn't been pulled over for speeding. That euphoria was quickly replaced by a feeling of foreboding. The rest area was nearly deserted. The snowbanks from the recent storms were darkening with road grime and formed a barrier against the outer world. Patches of sanded ice were scattered around the parking lot. There were few cars or trucks in the front parking lot due to the early hour of the day. He cruised past them and turned into the back parking area. Nothing. He wasn't sure where he was to look or if Andy would even be there. He looked at the note again.

"Rest stop—I-95—York, Maine"

All Jack could do was drive around the rest area. "Where are you, you bastard?" he asked himself. He had assumed Andy would be there and that was where the swap would be made. Panic began to set in as he completed his first circuit. He hadn't seen anything. He began again. The early sun was in his eyes as he turned into the rear parking area for the second time when he thought he saw movement. Someone had walked out from behind a snow bank on the back side of the parking lot. Jack couldn't tell if it was Andy but hoped it was. He could feel his heart pounding in his chest as he drove closer to the figure. When he was maybe thirty yards away, he stopped. It was Andy, and he was alone. Jack scanned the area looking for Max. He didn't see her. Panic caused his vision to tunnel until all he could see was Andy.

Andy motioned for Jack to get out. He shut the engine off, slowly opened the door, and cautiously slid out of the truck. As soon as the icy wind hit his face, his senses returned. All he could hear was the sound of the wind whooshing through the trees and the whine of tires on the nearby highway. He looked around for some sign of Max. He didn't see her. He began to walk toward Andy, ice crunching under his boots. He saw that Andy kept one hand in his coat pocket. Jack's imagination did the rest: "Hand in pocket, gun, not good." When Jack was close enough to talk, he stopped.

"Hello, Jack."

Jack didn't return the greeting. He just stared at Andy.

"Did you bring it?"

"Yes," Jack answered.

"Let me see it."

Jack reached into his pocket, removed the ring, and showed it to Andy.

"Give it to me."

"No. Where's Max?"

"She's safe. Give me the ring."

"You know I won't do that until I know that Max is safe." Then Jack put the ring back into his pocket.

"Fair enough. Let's go for a walk. This way." Without removing his hand from his pocket, Andy motioned to walk in the direction from which he had just come. As Jack got closer, Andy stepped to the side, allowing Jack to pass, and fell in behind him.

As they walked, a parked car came into sight. Jack could see there was someone in it. He was so focused on the car ahead that he didn't hear Andy say, "You know Jack, you have this all wrong."

After a few more steps, the sharp bark of Andy's voice broke the silence, "Stop. Don't move." Jack stopped and stood there looking at the car, trying to make out through the frosted windows who was inside.

Andy walked around Jack toward the car. When he reached the door, he knocked on the window. The door opened, and Max got out. Andy grabbed her arm, and before she could move or say anything he said, "Okay Jack. Here she is. Now, give me the ring."

Jack reached into his pocket and felt for the ring. Staring at Andy, Jack took hold of the ring but did not withdraw his hand immediately. Time seemed to stand still as they stared at each other, motionless, neither willing to make the first move.

For the first time Jack felt completely exposed. It was one thing to rush off on a quest; it was completely another to actually face your quarry. Now he wished he had listened to Tom and hadn't rushed off on his own. What had seemed the right thing to do now seemed really stupid. Jack had to hope that as dangerous as Andy was, he would uphold his end of the bargain.

"No. Max first, then I'll give you the ring. But first answer a question for me. What makes you think you will get away?" Jack asked.

Before he could answer, Max interrupted. "Jack, give him the ring. It's okay. It doesn't matter. Just do it so we can get out of here."

Her outburst took Jack by surprise. He looked at her with questioning eyes and said, "What are you talking about, Max? Of course it matters. He killed your aunt, he killed Meredith, and he kidnapped you."

"No he didn't, Jack. Give him the ring, trust me, and I'll explain as soon as we are away from here."

Jack grasped the ring more tightly in his pocket. His head was beginning to spin. What was Max talking about? Why was she defending Andy?

Before Jack could reply, Andy said, "Jack, listen to her. Give me the ring. She's all yours, and I'll be gone. I don't want to hurt either of you. I only want the ring."

Jack continued to stand there, unmoving.

"Jack." Max's voice broke the silence.

"Max, what do you mean he didn't kill your aunt and her friend? He sure as hell kidnapped you."

"He didn't. Jack, trust me. I'll explain it all to you. Please, give him the ring."

Jack's confusion increased. "I don't understand what's going on here. Why should I trust him?"

"I'm not asking you to trust him. I'm asking you to trust me. Please, give him the ring so this can be over," pleaded Max.

Jack took his fist out of his pocket, opened it, and looked at the ring. Then he looked up, first at Andy and then at Max. Her eyes pleaded with him as her words echoed in his head, "Trust me."

"Oh, what the hell," he muttered under his breath as he tossed the ring to Andy.

"Thank you," said Max. She glanced over at Andy as he caught the ring. He nodded, and she ran to Jack. Jack pulled her behind him to shield her and said, "There, you have the ring. Now go and leave us alone."

As Andy turned to go, he said, "Thank you, Jack. You did the right thing. Max, explain it to him. I have to go before it's too late."

* * *

Jack didn't hear Andy's last words. His only concern was for Max. He turned to her and took her in his arms. She pressed her face into his chest and wrapped her arms around him. In that instant, a sudden sense of peace and calmness washed over him.

The roar of an engine followed by the sound of wheels spinning in the loose sand and ice returned him to the present. Andy was gone and so was the ring, but Max was safe. Jack loosened his embrace slightly, and Max looked up at him. There were tears in the corners of her eyes, and she was beginning to tremble. Gently, he cradled her face with his hands and wiped the tears away with his thumbs. He brushed her forehead with his lips, inhaled, and then gave her the gentlest of kisses, just barely touching her skin. His heart was pounding.

Neither one dared breathe as they gazed into each other's eyes. Then, Max sighed. Jack leaned down and slowly, tentatively brushed her lips with his. It wasn't a kiss, it was more. Every nerve ending in his body was alive. His stomach fluttered, and there was a stirring of emotion deep within that he hadn't felt in so many years. The relief of having Max safe within his arms was almost overwhelming. Max closed her eyes and stretched up toward him. Their lips met and they kissed. Softly, gently at first. Little kisses. Tiny kisses that rapidly grew in intensity until passion overcame them and their mouths became one. Days, weeks, months, years of denied feeling came rushing out, and they stood there, holding on to each other, in the cold, desolate parking lot of the I-95 rest area in York, Maine.

"Hello, Jack Beale," she whispered.

"Hello, Max," he said softly as he gently wiped more tears from her face and kissed her again gently on the forehead.

"Come on Max, you're shivering. Let's get into the truck and you can begin to tell me what this is all about."

CHAPTER THIRTY-NINE

ANOTHER STORY

AS WARM AS THE CAB of his truck was, Jack turned the heater switch to high. Over the roar of the heater fan, he looked over at Max and asked, "Are you all right?"

She paused before answering, "Yes."

He continued looking at her, thankful she was all right. "What happened? Do you want to talk about it?" he asked softly.

She nodded. It was too warm so Jack turned down the heater, and the sudden silence seemed deafening. Max looked at Jack, staring deep into his eyes.

"Jack. He's innocent. He's been set up," she began.

That was the last thing Jack expected to hear. "What did you just say?" He was incredulous.

"He didn't do all those horrible things," Max repeated.

Still not believing what he was hearing, Jack said, "What are you talking about?"

Max looked down. Her hands clasped together, she took a deep breath and began. "It's complicated. I think I understand it though, so be patient with me. Last night, as work was finishing, I went out to put some trash in the dumpster. Just as I closed the lid, Andy came up behind me. He scared the living shit out of me. Before I could shout or move, he grabbed me and put his hand over my mouth. I couldn't move, and he said, 'I need to talk with you. I won't hurt you, but you have to come with me. Please, you must trust me.' There was something in his voice that made me believe him so I didn't resist, and besides, he didn't give me much of a choice. I had to go."

"You heard something in his voice and so you went with him. Were you nuts?" Jack cried out.

"I'm sorry Jack. I know it was a stupid thing to do, but I had to." She continued. "He eased his grip and guided me to his car, and we drove off. He didn't say much at first, he just drove, but as we got farther from Ben's he began to talk. He began by reminding me of all the good times we had in the past. I agreed with him and pointed out to him that the operative word was 'past.' His longer and more frequent disappearances had really hurt me, and I couldn't go through it again. It was over between us. He said he understood. There was a real sadness in his voice. He apologized again, only saying they were necessary, and that he hoped that I would understand and maybe someday forgive him. It was weird." She paused.

Jack didn't say anything. It was all he could do to sit there. Anger, disbelief, relief, all rushed through him at the same time. He had to force himself to focus on what she was saying and not scream out.

She continued. "This is difficult. I hope I get it right. His real name is André Bonhomme, and he is Swiss. He and Scotch and Soda Man, whose real name is Franz Stokel, went to school together. André … Andy was a troublemaker, and for some reason he and Franz became friends. Franz, whose father was a lawyer, grew up in a very proper environment. Andy did not."

Impatient, Jack blurted out, "I know all that."

"You do? How?" Now it was Max's turn to be surprised.

"We caught Franz last night, and he told us."

"You did? Thank God."

"Yes, Dave and I did, and he's now being held by Tom while his story is being checked out."

Jack noticed an immediate change in Max. She seemed relieved.

"Can I go on?" She was more animated.

Jack nodded.

"From what Andy told me, it seems their friendship grew because each needed something the other had. Franz was introduced to the seedier side of life, and he loved the danger and excitement. Andy saw a glimpse of a better world he didn't know existed, and he wanted to be a part of that world. One day they were caught breaking into a house. This was more than Franz had bargained for, and it ended their friendship. Fortunately Franz's father was able to get the charges dropped, and Franz and Andy hadn't seen each other until recently."

Jack interrupted again, "So far you haven't told me anything that Franz didn't tell us."

"Let me finish."

"Fine."

"So after Franz's father bailed them out, they went their separate ways. Andy continued to long for a more respectable life. He became a security consultant and worked quite often in the banking industry. He was looking into some thefts from old dormant lockboxes that dated back to World War II. A lot of Andy's work was undercover, and quite by chance, he ran into Franz. As they caught up on old times, Andy began to realize that Franz might be behind those thefts. There was no proof, but Andy had a feeling. Then one day, Franz told Andy what he wanted to hear and even suggested that they work together. Andy agreed because he still needed proof. This was when we met. Franz had this obsession with one particular box: the one my great-grandfather had set up with Franz' father. While doing research, Andy found out about me, and well, the rest you know. He never really told me what he did. I … uh … we all thought he was just a free-spirited drifter, and I fell for him."

"So he was just using you?"

"I guess so."

"And you are still defending him?"

"Jack, it may have started out that way, but there was more."

"And you know this how?"

Max was near tears at this point. "I just know."

Jack began to feel guilty. He could see she was getting upset, and the last thing he wanted was to cause her more pain. Reaching out, he touched her, and said softly, "I'm sorry."

"They knew about the ring. Andy was to get close to me and get the ring if I had it, while Franz pursued my Aunt Lillian. When Andy and I became close, he and Franz had a falling out. Franz was afraid that Andy's feelings would get in the way of their objective. Threats and promises were made between them, and they went their separate ways. All this took place over the last few years. Then when Franz showed up here, Andy did too, and the rest you know. Franz murdered my aunt, then Meredith, and now he's after me. Andy saw the only way to protect me was to kidnap me, find the ring, and give it to Franz so he would leave me alone. Andy never killed anyone."

"You believe this story?"

"I do."

"Max, he's a conman. He wanted that ring, he killed for it, and he's convinced you that he didn't. You are damned lucky he didn't kill you. I think he's still playing you."

"I can't believe that."

"Nearly everything you told me matches the same story Franz told us; just reverse the names. The only difference was that Franz had the ring. He took it off Meredith's hand when she was being carried from the ice to the parking lot. He thought if he had the ring, he could make a deal with Andy to stay away from you. Remember in the bar when Andy was being such a jerk, Franz said something to Andy, and he left?"

"I do, but what does that have to do with anything? It's not like they were still friends."

"No they weren't, but it does make sense if he were telling Andy that he should leave if he wanted to get the ring."

"I still don't buy it. I know Andy. He's not like that."

"Did he ever ask you about the letter?"

"What letter?"

"The letter that was given to your grandmother along with the ring."

"No. He never mentioned a letter."

"Franz told us that along with the ring, his grandfather had given your grandmother a letter that explained how to use the ring to claim whatever was in the lockbox. Franz knew these details, Andy didn't. Franz never told Andy about them."

"I still don't believe Andy could have done any of those things."

Jack was finding it hard to keep his emotions in check. "I think he did. Andy is full of shit. I've never trusted him and I don't understand how you can."

"Well I do trust him and you'll see."

"Maybe . . . " Then, after a moment of silence Jack suddenly cried out, "Oh shit ... Tom. Max, we need to get out of here and let Tom know that you are safe. I kind of took off on him this morning. You know he's going to want to question you."

* * *

The clear sky of the dawn was now becoming overcast and gray, foreshadowing the arrival of more snow. The increasing gloom matched Jack's dread of calling Tom. Even though Max was safe, Jack knew he had been foolish undertaking her rescue alone and that things could have turned out quite differently.

"Jack, you are the luckiest son of a bitch I know. What you did was just plain stupid. You had no idea what Andy would do. Almost anything could have happened."

"I know, but nothing did."

"That's not the point. You and I are going to have another conversation a little later. Now, how's Max?"

"She's fine. Tired and hungry. We're going to get something to eat."

"I'm glad to hear that. Will you bring her to the station? I need to talk to her."

"Listen, Tom, we're both exhausted. Any problem if I take Max home and we come down to the station later to talk with you?"

"I guess a couple hours won't make much difference. No idea where Andy may have gone?"

"None. He never said anything about his intentions, but I have a hunch he's not finished with Franz."

"Not to worry. We have him. Now you get some rest, and I'll see the two of you later in my office."

"Thanks Tom."

There was a pause on the line, then Tom said, "Jack, good job. Take care of Max." Then the line went dead. Jack hung up the phone and returned to the table just as breakfast arrived.

Max looked up at him, "Everything all right?"

"Yeah, Tom's a little pissed at me, but he's relieved that everything turned out okay."

Weariness and hunger kept conversation to a minimum while Jack and Max ate. As Max finished her last bite, she looked at Jack and said, "I want to look for that letter as soon as we get to my house. Will you help me?"

"Of course."

"Jack, is it really over?"

"Well, Franz is being held by Tom. Andy is out there with the ring, but I don't think it'll be long before he's caught." Jack paused, then said, "Yeah, it's over."

"It doesn't feel that way."

"Max, I won't let anything happen to you. Let's get out of here."

CHAPTER FORTY

HOME AGAIN

THE COLD GRAY DAY didn't seem quite so cold and gray as Jack and Max walked to the truck. The morning traffic was increasing as the world around them began a new day.

As Jack drove toward Max's, he began to realize just how tired he was. He glanced over at Max and could see she was fading fast. With a sleepy voice, she asked him, "When I apologized for getting you involved in this, you replied that you were already involved. What did you mean?"

Before answering her question, Jack thought about it for a few moments. He was ready to answer when he glanced over at her and saw she was sound asleep. He smiled and said very softly, "Max, I'm involved because I love you." She didn't hear.

The drive to Max's took less than thirty minutes, but it seemed like an eternity. Jack's eyes were getting heavy, and he had to fight to stay awake. When he pulled into Max's driveway and stopped the car, he looked over at her. She was asleep, and so relaxed and peaceful that he didn't want to disturb her. But he gently nudged her. She didn't move. He touched her shoulder and gently rocked her while saying in a soft voice, "Max, wake up."

She jumped. She stared at him with wide unseeing eyes as her brain tried to catch up. "Hunh? ... Where? ... What? ... Oh ... Jack ... . Where are we? What are you doing here?"

Jack said to her, "Come on Max, we're home. You're safe. Let's go in."

With a sleepy, dreamy voice, she said, "Okay," and reached for the door handle. The blast of cold air completed the process of waking up.

"Come on Jack. Let's get inside. It's freezing out here."

Moments later they were inside, and as the door closed behind them, they both felt a rush of relief. Jack took their coats and draped them over a chair. Max slowly walked around, looking at everything, touching everything—the chair, the table, a lamp—reassuring herself that she was really home. Jack watched her, and when she returned to where he was standing, he extended his arms toward her. She moved into them and slumped against him, wrapping her arms around him as she lay her face against his chest. Jack felt her warmth and smelled her hair. He cupped her face with his hands, lifted it toward his, and kissed her.

She returned the kiss and then, still holding his hand, she moved toward the couch. Nothing was said. She sat down and leaned back as Jack stood over her. She stretched out her legs and motioned for Jack to come to her. He knelt down between her outstretched legs, leaned forward, wrapped his arms around her waist, and lay his head on her chest. As he listened to her heartbeat, she rubbed his back with one hand and held his head to her breast with the other.

He looked up into her eyes and she into his, and they kissed again. This time it was neither tentative nor tender. The mix of emotions and fatigue created an urgency they both felt. Four arms, four legs, two bodies, and two hearts were becoming one when the moment was shattered by the ringing of the phone. They let go of each other gasping for breath. They separated, their faces flushed, and laughed. Max signaled for Jack to answer the phone. His heart was pounding wildly. He took a deep breath before answering the phone on its third ring. "Hello," he said, forcing himself to keep his voice even and nonchalant. "Hi Tom. What's up?"

"I just wanted to make sure that you made it home okay and to see how Max is holding up."

Glancing over at Max, Jack saw that she had curled up on the couch like a cat and was fast asleep. Jack smiled and said, "She's fine. I'm going to stay here while she gets some sleep. I don't plan on leaving her alone until Andy is caught."

Tom counseled Jack to be careful and said good-bye. Jack hoped to get some sleep as well, but there wasn't room on the couch for two, so he shook Max's shoulder to wake her. She didn't move. He rocked her again; no response. She was out.

Gently, he reached under her and picked her up. She stirred just enough to wrap her arms around his neck and put her head on his shoulder; she let out a soft moan. As he carried her into her bedroom, he whispered, "Come on Max. Let's get you to bed." He put her down on the bed, took off her shoes, placed them on the floor and covered her with a down comforter. Her eyes opened for just a moment as she snuggled under the comforter, and in a groggy voice, she said, "Thank you, Jack."

Before leaving the room, he stood there, looking down on Max, lost in his thoughts. Then he was hit by the same overwhelming fatigue that had overtaken her. He left the room, made himself as comfortable as possible on the couch, and was asleep in an instant.

* * *

While Jack and Max were sleeping, Tom busied himself with co-ordinating the search for Andy. Calls were made to local, county, and state police departments. Pictures were distributed. He called Immigration and Customs Enforcement. All this took the rest of the morning. By the time he finished, he too was exhausted.

As he drove home to get some well-deserved rest, he kept going over Franz's and Andy's stories in his mind. Essentially they were the same story, only with different conclusions. Depending on who told it, the other was the guilty one. No doubt, one was a liar and a murderer while the other was somehow complicit in the scheme to get the contents of the lockbox. For two men to risk so much for an unknown reward seemed strange to Tom, but greed was a funny thing.

He thought about Max. She had been threatened, kidnapped, and had a relative murdered all the while unaware that she may possess the key to all of this madness.

Then there was Jack. Tom knew he could count on Jack to protect Max but also that Jack wouldn't sit idly by, waiting for something to happen. That was evidenced by his capturing of Franz. "At least we have one of them," Tom thought as he arrived home. It was his turn to get some sleep.

CHAPTER FORTY-ONE

THE LETTER

JACK OPENED HIS EYES to a nearly dark room. He sat up with a start, thinking the sun had set and he had slept all day. Looking toward the windows, he saw the shades were drawn. A quick glance at his watch reassured him he hadn't slept all day and it was only early afternoon. He moved to the window and looked out. The clouds that moved in earlier had thickened and the first flakes of snow were beginning to dance about.

The house was silent. He went to Max's door, quietly pushed it open, and peeked in on her. She was still asleep. He smiled as he looked at her, and as he did, his stomach rumbled. Backing away, he pulled the door shut and headed for the kitchen to see what there was to eat. There wasn't much in the fridge. He had a craving for Chinese, so he made a call and placed an order. It would be close to an hour before the food would arrive, so he lit the fireplace, opened a bottle of wine, and poured a glass.

He was trying to be as quiet as possible as to not wake Max when he heard a noise. He looked toward the hallway that led to Max's bedroom and there she was. She was standing in the doorway, watching him, and holding a shoebox.

"Max, I didn't hear you get up," he said.

"All that clanking in the kitchen woke me up. I decided to look for this before coming out," she motioned toward the shoebox.

"What's that?"

"A box of letters and papers that belonged to my mother. I took them with me after she died, but I've never looked at them."

"Do you think it's in there?"

"I don't know. I wanted you to be there when I looked."

"I've just opened a bottle of red wine, the fire's lit, and I ordered Chinese. I hope you don't mind."

Her face lit up. She walked across the room, went to Jack, and gave him a kiss. "Jack, you are so sweet."

"Ah shucks, ma'am," Jack replied with a goofy kind of voice, then more seriously, "Should we open it now?"

"No. Later. I'm not ready to just yet."

"I understand." He took the box from her, put it on the table, and asked her if she would like a glass of wine. "Yes, but in a few minutes. I want to go take a shower first," he heard her say as she disappeared back down the hall. He was grinning as he turned to throw another log on the fire.

While she was in the shower, the Chinese food was delivered. By the time she reappeared, Jack had the table set, and two glasses of wine poured and waiting. She returned wrapped in a thick, luxurious, dark green bathrobe. Her hair still was damp, and she had that pink glow on her cheeks that one gets from having just come out of a very hot shower. He must have had a stupid grin on his face because she looked at him and asked, "What?"

"Nothing. Dinner's ready."

She walked to the table, and as she bent over to look into the containers of food, her bathrobe gaped open just enough that Jack could see most of a bare breast. "Chinese food be damned," he thought. At that moment his thoughts were inside the green robe. Then his stomach rumbled, and Max said, "Jack, you remembered."

"Remembered what?"

"That I love crab rangoons and kung pao chicken." She began spooning some onto a plate. He could still see her breast peeking out from behind the fold of the robe, and his heart rate began to rise—as did the rest of him. Max finished putting food on her plate, stood up, and saw Jack looking at her. The look in his eyes must have been obvious. She looked down, blushed slightly, and with one hand, pulled the robe a little tighter. Then she said, "This looks great. I'm starving. Let's eat. We'll open the box after."

Jack nodded his assent and began filling his plate. He wanted to open something, and it wasn't that shoebox. His first bite returned him to the present as he realized just how hungry he was. As they sat eating in front of the fireplace, their conversation stayed light and trivial. It was as if neither wanted to be the first to bring up the last twenty-four hours. When they had finished eating, their plates were in the sink, and the leftovers put in the fridge, that moment had to be faced. There weren't any other distractions. Well, there was one, but that would have to wait.

Max walked to the table where the shoebox was, picked it up, paused, and looked at it. Then she walked to the couch and sat down with the box in her lap. Despite the fire in the fireplace, she felt a chill and pulled her robe closer around her. Jack sat next to her, his leg pulled up so he could face her. "It's time, Max," he said quietly.

"I know," she replied as she slowly lifted the lid off the box. The box was filled with envelopes, pictures, and memories. Some of the papers were faded and brittle; the photos were mostly black and white, many with well-worn edges. Slowly and with shaking hands, Max began removing each item from the box. Letters were opened and read, each picture studied as she relived her family's story. Bits of a dried flower, its reason for being there long forgotten, were mixed in among the pages like potpourri and accumulated in the bottom of the box. Then, near the bottom of the box, they found it. Carefully shaking off those bits of dried flower, Max gingerly picked up the envelope and stared at it. She slowly turned it over in her hands, studying it. The paper was yellowed with age, thin and brittle with a wax seal that had never been broken, still protecting its secrets. On the face in a flowery and perfect script was written, "To My Daughter Ruth." Max looked up at Jack as if asking permission. "Go ahead. It's okay," said Jack softly.

Max took a deep breath then slid her finger under the flap, breaking the seal, and removed a carefully folded sheet of paper. Silence filled the room, save for the occasional crackling of the fire. Max unfolded the letter carefully and began to read.

My Dearest Ruth,

The day that you were born was the happiest day in your mother's and my life. I resolved then to leave for you a most precious gift. It is in a lockbox in the Bern Bank, and the only way to access it will be with the help of my most trusted friend and lawyer, Herr Stokel. When it is time for you to collect this gift, and you will know when that moment is, take this letter and the ring I gave you to Herr Stokel. Together they will verify your identity, and you will need both to retrieve the box and its contents. He has the first six digits of the pass code; the remaining digits of the pass code are RJ1918143. The bank will release the box only to the person presenting the correct pass code. Inside you will find another sealed box. This box can only be opened using the ring I gave you. It is the key.

Your Loving Father,
William

Jack watched Max reading the letter. When she finished, she handed the letter to Jack and waited for him to read it. As he finished, he exhaled slowly and said nothing. He just looked at Max then said, "Now we know why Andy wanted the ring."

Max returned his stare, "No, now we know why Franz wanted the ring."

"I don't buy it. Andy was the one who kidnapped you for the ring. Now he has it."

"I suppose so, but Andy said he was protecting me."

"That was Franz's story as well."

"I know," Max turned away, wiping her eyes with her sleeve.

"Max, I'm sorry. All that really matters is that you are safe. I'm sure Tom will find Andy and soon enough the truth will come out."

She turned back toward Jack, her eyes still moist. "I don't know what to think anymore."

He slid over closer to her and put his arm around her. She leaned her head on his shoulder and shuddered. Softly he kissed the top of her head and held her. The room was silent, save for the soft crackling of the fire. No more words were necessary, and Jack could feel her relax.

"Jack?" she said his name in a small muffled voice.

"Mmm."

"What do you think is in the box?"

"I have no idea. Didn't you once tell me that your great-grandfather was a diamond merchant?"

"He was." She inhaled, "Do you think ..." Her voice tailed off.

"Could be. We'll just have to wait until we get the ring back."

Jack stopped talking; she couldn't see his embarrassment as he realized what he had just said.

"Did she notice? 'We'?! Why did I say that? The ring was hers, not ours," he thought. His heart was pounding in his head, and he felt like the room was closing in on him. It seemed like forever, even though it was only a split second.

"You're right. We'll just have to wait."

She said "we" also.

Changing the subject, he said, "I should call Tom."

"No, not yet," was her reply.

* * *

She got up from the couch. "I have to go pee."

Then she stopped and bent down to pick up her empty wine glass. As she did, her robe opened slightly giving Jack another teasing glimpse of her breast. Looking deep into his eyes, she handed him the glass. "I'd like some more wine," she said softly, and then she turned and padded out of the room.

His heart began to pound in his head again as he watched her leave. "What just happened?" a voice in his head asked. The answer came as a warm, pleasant feeling of pressure filled his lap. Another voice answered, "Jack, don't be a fool, you know where this is going. You love her. Don't blow it."

"No," he said to himself, forcing that second voice back as he filled their glasses and threw another log on the fire. It worked, the activity calmed him. Then, he sat back down on the couch. With its overstuffed cushions and lots of pillows, it was the kind of couch that would swallow you up. As he sank down into the couch, the combination of the warmth and flickering light from the fire; his relief that Max was safe; fatigue; and the effects of the wine allowed him to slip into an almost trancelike state. He smiled to himself, and that's when the second voice returned, "She's right. No need to call Tom right now."

He was snapped out of his reverie when Max returned and sat down next to him. He handed her glass of wine to her. She took a sip, and Jack watched her. She held the glass with both hands—cradling it delicately and yet firmly like it was something precious—and looked at him. The moment was magical and intimate. Her red hair flowed over her shoulders onto the deep green robe, which had opened slightly allowing the soft curve of her breast to be exposed again. Jack tried not to stare. He felt that urge begin to rise again. He sipped his wine; he looked at the fire and around the room. But no matter what he did, his eyes were drawn back to Max. The moment was about to overwhelm him when Max broke the silence. "Do you really think Tom will catch him?"

That simple question brought Jack out from that other place where his emotions ruled for the second time. "I have no doubt."

That was all it took, and they sat there and talked. They talked about the letter and what it could mean. They talked about all that had happened. They drank more wine; they talked about nothing, and they talked about everything.

When the bottle was empty and their glasses drained, conversation stopped for a moment. Jack leaned forward and kissed Max. She responded, then abruptly sat up and said, "Would you like some more wine?"

"Sure, that would be good."

Max got up to get another bottle. As she moved away from the couch, he watched her and noticed there was a slight unsteadiness in her gait. He threw another log on the fire. When she returned, Jack was sitting on the rug in front of the fire, and he motioned for her to join him. As she bent down to sit next to him, her robe gaped open again, this time slightly wider than before. Again Jack began to feel that warm and pleasant pressure, and this time he didn't try to quell the feeling. "Max, it's been a long, trying day. Would you like me to massage your shoulders?"

"Mmmm. That sounds nice." She stretched out on the floor face down, her robe riding up, past her knees, exposing her bare legs. Jack smiled and inhaled softly. His heart pounded as he admired the sensuous curves of her backside, imagining what hid beneath the robe. He poured himself a little more wine and took a sip. Then without thinking, he straddled her, sitting on the backs of her thighs. She didn't react nor could she see his momentary embarrassment as he realized what he had just done.

He began to rub her shoulders. His thumbs worked on her neck, his fingers the tops of her shoulders. He was kneading her like a happy, contented cat. He worked his way down her back, his thumbs continuing to work the muscles along her spine. After he reached her lower back, he would go back up to her shoulders and start again, working his way slowly, deliberately down toward her tush.

Max moaned, "That feels good. Don't stop." Her voice was heavy and sensuous like honey dripping off a spoon.

Having finished her back, Jack turned his attention to her legs. He slid down to her feet and began there. First the right foot. She giggled and wriggled it out of his grasp. "Stop. That tickles."

"Okay, but stop wriggling. You're getting all tense again."

He let go of her foot and began to rub her calf. He started at her heel, and while holding it in both hands, he began kneading it, applying the pressure alternately with his thumbs as he moved up toward her knee. She moaned. After reaching her knee, he would slide his hands back to her foot with his fingers applying the pressure. He repeated this several times. Her calves were firm and smooth, and when he finished with one, he turned his attention to the other.

After the calves, he gently ran his hands up the back of her thigh, applying pressure with his thumbs to the center, and then as he reached her buttocks, he would slide his hands back down with his fingers applying pressure simultaneously to the inside and outside of her thighs. Each time his hands moved up her leg, the robe seemed to creep a bit higher, exposing more leg. It was a slow tease that awakened memories and feelings Jack hadn't felt for years. He kept expecting Max to move, to say something, to stop him, but she didn't—which only heightened those feelings.

She moaned once, or at least he thought she moaned. He couldn't be sure because about all he could hear was the sound of his breathing and the pounding of his heart. Then he thought he felt her spread her legs slightly farther apart. He paused. He needed a sip of wine. As he stopped and reached for his glass, Max moaned in that soft honey voice, "Don't stop."

Resuming the massage on her legs, it seemed that no matter how hard he tried, more and more leg was exposed with each stroke. He didn't want to be presumptuous, but he wasn't sure he could remain a gentleman for much longer. When he stopped for another sip of wine, Max pushed her shoulders up until she was resting on her elbows, looked back over her shoulder at him, and said, "Will you go to Switzerland with me?"

The question took him by surprise, but his answer was instantaneous, "Of course I will."

The phone rang. They looked at each other, and Jack began to get up. It rang again. "No. Let the machine get it," said Max.

He hesitated then sat down next to her and let the machine pick up. It was Tom. "Jack. Max. Pick up." Then a pause and more faintly as if he were no longer speaking to them "Shit. They must still be asleep." Click, he hung up.

"See, you didn't have to get it," Max purred. Then she rolled onto her side, her robe gaped open a little more, she stretched her legs, and she said to him softly, "Come here, Jack Beale."

He looked down at her, and the phone call was immediately forgotten. With his heart pounding, he stretched himself out and lay down facing her. She rolled a leg over him, wrapped her arms around him, and kissed him. That's all it took. It was as if a dam had burst, releasing a torrent of repressed emotions. Any questions he had were answered in that moment.

Under her robe, she was already naked and ready, and she wanted him as much as he wanted her. Primal instincts took over. Their kisses were almost savage in their intensity. She pulled at his clothes and he at hers until none remained. They became one in the flickering shadows of the firelight. Slow, fast, rough, and gentle, neither could get enough of the other. The air filled with the musk of sex, and their bodies glistened with sweat. The moment was pure. No inhibitions, no talking, none of the vagaries or vanities of modern life. It was desire at the most elemental level. After, as they lay together exhausted, they came together one more time and made love in front of a dying fire at the end of a very long day.

CHAPTER FORTY-TWO

Escape

TOM GOT THE CALL shortly after getting home. He tried calling Jack and Max immediately, but there wasn't any answer at either of their houses. He could only assume they were asleep. Sleep. Wouldn't that be nice? A car had been dispatched to check on their houses, while he went back to the station.

"Tell me again. How did Franz get away from you?" Tom snapped, his anger still evident. Before the other man in the room could open his mouth to speak, Tom looked at him. "Never mind. Get out of here."

"Yes, sir," was the muted reply.

The door clicked shut, and Tom stood alone in his office. His head hurt. The shadowless whiteness of the institutional fluorescent lights on the ceiling hurt his eyes. Crossing to his desk, he turned on a small, green-shaded light, then, he walked back and turned those harsh ceiling lights off. In the semidarkness of the room he leaned against the wall and closed his eyes and took a deep breath before returning to his desk. He sat down and tried to focus his thoughts.

He shuffled through the papers on his desk and began a conversation with himself. A little self-recrimination can be cleansing. "Stupid. Stupid. Stupid. I should never have let Jack get involved the way I did. I knew it would screw things up... . True, he did find Franz. True, he did retrieve the ring. And true, he did get Max back. But, now Andy is gone and has the ring. Franz is gone. Now we're right back where we started with nothing but two dead women, a missing ring, and few answers. On the brighter side, we still have two suspects, even though they are out running around due to our collective efforts." He laughed at the irony of the situation.

The radio on his desk crackled to life. It was the cruiser reporting in. "It appears that they are at the woman's house. His truck is there. Everything looks normal. Do you want me to go to the door and check on them?"

Tom didn't reply immediately. His fatigue slowed his response and clouded his judgment.

"Sir? Did you copy?"

"Yes, yes I heard."

"Shall I?"

"No. That won't be necessary. Just drive by the house regularly tonight. Let me know if anything changes."

"Copy that," and the radio went silent.

At least now Tom knew where Jack and Max were. Tom had been up for well over twenty-four hours, and he wasn't going to accomplish much else tonight. Leaning back in his chair, he closed his eyes and instantly he was asleep. All of a sudden, his head jerked and he sat up with a start. It took a moment for the disorientation to clear. He looked at his watch. It had been less than a minute, but it felt like an hour. "I've got to get out of here and get some sleep," he thought.

CHAPTER FORTY-THREE

A MISTAKE

THERE HADN'T BEEN ANY SIGN of either Franz or Andy for nearly two weeks. They had completely disappeared. Tom started every day by contacting all the other agencies involved, and each day the answer was the same: nothing. He could tell that enthusiasm for the case was beginning to wane and that he was starting to be perceived as a pain in the ass. A break was needed. Soon.

Jack's concern for Max and her safety consumed him. He would take her to work every day. The only times he would leave her alone were when she was at work. It was during those times that he would stop at his place, feed Cat, and maybe putter around his shop. Cat was not at all happy about this arrangement, and she let him know it.

Every night Jack would wait for Max and take her home, where they would sit up late talking—rather Max would talk while Jack listened. Jack loved listening to Max talk about her past, her future, and her hopes and dreams. Occasionally he would even open up and talk about his past. These late-night sessions were good for both of them as they came to grips with all that had transpired over the past month.

Patti had moved out since Jack had replaced her at Max's, which was fine since she and Dave had become almost as inseparable as Jack and Max.

It had been two weeks to the day since Max's kidnapping and rescue, and the day had been a particularly busy one at Ben's, so it was later than usual when Jack picked Max up and they returned to her house. Exhausted, and cold, there would be no long talks this night. By the time Jack had checked everything and locked up, Max was already in the bed. The comforter was pulled up to her chin as she struggled to get warm. As soon as Jack climbed in with her, she snuggled up tight against him. In the dark, Max couldn't see his smile. Her bare legs, so smooth and silky, draped over his. He noted that as cold as the bed was, she wasn't. Unfortunately, he could also tell by her breathing that she was already asleep. It didn't take long for fatigue to win out over more carnal stirrings. Soon his eyes closed, and he too was asleep.

Jack woke first. Max was still wrapped around him, sound asleep. He looked down at her and smiled. He hadn't been dreaming. A ray of sunlight shone on her face, and she stirred. "Good morning sleepyhead," said Jack. Max looked up at him, "Good morning. What time is it?"

"It's early."

"I've got to pee." Max slid out from under the covers and padded to the bathroom. He climbed out from under the covers and stretched, his back to the door. He was about to reach for his clothes when he heard a sound in the doorway. He turned and saw Max standing in the doorway. She still was wearing the old, very large sweatshirt with the collar cut out that she slept in. It was hanging down off one shoulder draping over the swell of her breast. It was obvious she had been there for more than a few moments. "Nice, very nice," said Max with a teasing voice.

Jack blushed and continued dressing. "Like what you see?"

"Not bad," teased Max.

"Not bad? What do you mean not bad?" asked Jack, feigning indignation.

"Okay, it's better than not bad."

"Thanks for the vote of confidence," he said as he pulled up his pants.

Max continued to watch him, and then she spoke with a glint in her eye and a tone in her voice that Jack picked up on immediately.

"I don't have to be at work until noon. Do you have to leave right away?"

Jack felt the beginnings of a warm stirring sensation in his pants. "Yes I do."

Then with a slight pout, she stepped toward him and said, "I have this really stiff neck." As she raised her arms to rub her neck, her sweatshirt rose just enough to give Jack a peek at a tuft of reddish hair.

He inhaled. The pressure in his pants increased, and he said, "I'm sorry, but yes, I do have to get going."

"Awww," Max teased.

"I'll rub those kinks out tonight." Changing the subject, he asked, "Patti picking you up?"

Defeated, Max replied, "Yes."

"Good. Remember to keep the door locked and don't open the door for anyone except Patti."

With a touch of annoyance, she said, "I'm not a little kid you know. I'll be fine."

"I know you will." He took her face in his hands, gave her a kiss, and said, "I've got to go. Lock the door as soon as I leave. I'll pick you up around five." He headed out the door.

"Fine. I'll see you then. Love you."

Jack didn't hear those last softly spoken words as he closed the door behind himself.

* * *

Jack spent the rest of the morning in his shop working on several unfinished projects. As he worked, he kept a running dialogue in his mind between flashbacks of Max in that sweatshirt and the not-so-subtle invitation to rub her "neck." "Why did you leave? You must be the dumbest man in the world. Damn, she is something else. Admit it, you are hooked on her."

The more he debated with himself, the more frustrated he became with himself. He was glad she was working the lunch shift because he probably would have gone back and embarrassed himself trying to salvage a nooner. "I really blew it," he said over and over.

Something kept happening to him whenever he was with Max, and he wasn't sure what it was or how to handle it. All he knew was that he liked the way it made him feel. He decided he needed a run. It would do two things: One, it would burn off some of this energy in his pants, and two, it would let him think.

The day was relatively mild and the roads clear. He decided to run south on the boulevard for twenty minutes and then return. He wasn't going to worry about how far he was running. Today forty minutes would be about right, and it was. When he returned, he felt relaxed and refreshed. He still had a few hours until Max would finish work, so after his shower, he stretched out on his couch. Cat planted herself on his chest, ecstatic to have him to herself. With the sound of Cat's loud purring and her paws kneeding softly, he fell asleep. By the time he woke up, the sun was dipping below the horizon and he realized he had slept longer than intended. He'd have to hurry if he was to get to Ben's when Max got off work.

By the time he walked into Ben's, it was dark out. He said hi to Peggy as he turned to go into the bar. There was a impish grin on her face as she returned the greeting. Jack didn't pay much attention to it, although he did notice that some of the other waitresses gave him looks as well. He didn't see Max behind the bar, only the night bartender. Patti came in right then and said hi with the same kind of glint in her eye that Peggy had when he first arrived.

"Hi, Patti. Is Max here?"

"No," she replied. "You weren't here when she got off work, so she borrowed my car to run home for a minute. She went to get her passport to show us her picture. She'll be right back."

"What?" Panic began to creep into Jack's chest. "You let her go by herself?"

"Jack it'll be okay. She's a big girl. She just left, and she'll be right back."

"That's not the point. The deal was that she didn't go out alone. Period."

Patti could see Jack's agitation so she tried to change the subject. With a teasing tone to her voice, she asked him if he could rub her neck; it was feeling really stiff.

He looked at her as if she had three eyes and said, "What are you talking about?"

Patti replied in that same teasing tone, "Oh ... nothing."

That's when Jack got it. He tried to maintain his composure, but he could feel his face start to flush. He looked at her and thought, "What was it about girls? They just love to share the juicy details of things that should remain private." Then he asked, "Could I use the phone?"

"Why?" was the teasing reply.

He surrendered a little. "Because I want to call Max to see how long she'll be so I know how long I will have to put up with this."

"Oh Jack, you're no fun. You know where the phone is. Go on."

He wouldn't admit it, but deep down he was enjoying the attention. He punched in her number. It rang. And rang. And rang. When she didn't pick up after a few more rings, he began to worry. Why wasn't she picking up? She should still be there. He looked at his watch. Something didn't feel right. As he hung up he wondered if maybe it was just his imagination.

"Patti, did she say she was going anywhere else besides home?"

"No. She said she was going to get her passport and come right back. Why?"

"No reason." Jack tried to sound unconcerned. "I'm going to head over to her place, maybe I can catch her." With that he headed out the door.

"She's coming right back," Patti said to no one. Jack was already out the door.

CHAPTER FORTY-FOUR

THE PASSPORT

SINCE HER KIDNAPPING and rescue, Max had resisted Patti's and the others' attempts to find out what was going on with Jack. They knew he stayed with her, but they didn't know any of the details. Today, Max filled Patti in. The kiss, the massage, and her invitation to him to go to Switzerland with her. Patti was beside herself with excitement. It was so romantic, and she had endless questions for Max, who answered as many as she could—or would.

Max had just received her passport in the mail, and Patti wanted to see it.

"Go get it and bring it back. I want to see it," pleaded Patti.

"I can't. Jack's not here yet."

"You don't need Jack. Take my car. You'll only be gone a few minutes. If he shows up, I'll explain. Here." She tossed Max the keys.

Buoyed by the excitement of the moment, Max caught the keys and, without further thought, said, "Okay, I'll be right back."

As she ran out and climbed into Patti's car, one thought flashed through her head: "Jack is gonna be pissed." Jack had made her promise never to go out alone until Andy and Franz were caught. That thought lasted but a second. There had been no sign of either of them since the "incident," as she referred to it, so she turned the key and the engine roared to life. She smiled and turned the radio on. It had been a while since she had gone anywhere alone, especially driving alone. She felt like a teenager who had just been given the car for the first time after getting her license. Caution was forgotten as she turned up the radio, shifted into gear, and hit the gas.

She arrived home just as the last light of day faded. The bare trees around her house cast even darker shadows on the already dark landscape. The front light was not on. The ebullience that had possessed her when she left Ben's was suddenly gone. Since the kidnapping, Jack had always been with her, making her feel safe. Now, alone, with only the light from the car's headlights shining on her dark house, she began to have second thoughts. She sat and stared at the dark house. "It's okay. There's nothing to worry about. Leave the car running with the lights on, walk up to the door, unlock it, go in, and turn the lights on." She was talking out loud to herself; the sound of her voice made her feel slightly braver.

She took a deep breath.

"Go on," she thought as she pulled on the door handle and the car door opened. The sharp cold of the night air hit her like a slap in the face, suppressing any fears she had as she hurried to the house. It only took a moment for her to insert the key into the lock, and with a quick turn of the wrist, the latch clicked and the door opened. She stood in the doorway for a moment and took another deep breath. Her shadow stretched across the floor as Patti's car lights shone behind her. She reached for the light switch and turned it on. Suddenly all of her anxiety disappeared as she looked around the room. Everything was as she had left it, all warm and cozy. She stepped in and closed the door. "See, nothing to worry about," she said as if someone else were with her.

She continued to speak out loud. "There's no one here. Everything is just as you left it this morning." Crossing the room, she began to feel a little silly for talking to herself, even though the sound of her voice made the house feel not as empty and gave her courage. Then the furnace started. She jumped, and with her heart pounding in her chest, she felt her face flush with embarrassment. She stopped and scolded herself, the sound of her voice once again giving her courage. "Stop that. Stop being such a girl. Get the passport and go."

Hurrying down the hallway that led to her bedroom, she thought she felt a draft of cold air. But since the furnace fan had just turned on, she ignored it. Then she felt the cold air again. Deep inside her, a little voice screamed, "Leave!" while another, louder voice convinced her it was only the furnace. The door to her room was shut. She was so focused on getting her passport that she didn't give it any thought and didn't notice the light that shone from under the door.

The knob turned in her hand, and as she opened the door, she was hit by a blast of cold air. "I don't remember leaving the light on," she thought.

Paralyzed in the doorway, time stood still as she tried to make sense of what confronted her. The curtains were waving gently in front of the broken window. Glass was all over the floor. The bed had been pulled apart, the mattress askew. Each drawer in her bureau had been pulled out, and the contents dumped out. Her closet was open; clothes, stripped off of their hangers, were scattered all over the floor.

She couldn't breathe. She couldn't scream. She could only stand there looking at the mess, feeling violated and helpless. That little voice had been right, and now it was screaming at her, "Get Out!" But she couldn't move. That's when she saw the feet sticking out from behind the bed. Whose feet? Dead? Alive? Would she be next?

Her voice returned in one long primal scream. Before she could turn and run, a hand came from an unseen party behind her and clamped over her mouth, stifling the next scream, and another arm wrapped tightly around her. She was pulled back against her attacker as fear and confusion filled her head. She couldn't move; then a voice said something. Because of her panic, she only heard sounds, not words. She tried to move but couldn't. The arms holding her tightened their grip, and the words were repeated. This time she understood. "You have what I want, and you're going to give it to me."

Those were the same words that she had heard on the phone.

The phone began to ring.

"Jack!" Her silent scream echoed in her head.

Her attacker was breathing heavily, and she felt the warmth of his body and his hot, moist breath on her neck as he hissed in her ear those words again. "You have what I want, and you're going to give it to me."

This time she heard more than just the words, she heard the voice, and it was familiar. With this realization, came a moment of calm as reason began to overtake her fear and questions flooded her mind.

That moment of calm quickly changed as she realized that yes, he probably would kill her. After all, he already had killed Lillian and Meredith. A rage began to build within her. It didn't matter who was holding her or who was dead on the floor. What mattered was that she was probably next. Her rage turned to anger and that anger to an act of desperation.

She sagged in his arms, forcing him to adjust his grip, and as he pulled her upright, she crashed her heel onto his instep as hard as she could. Almost simultaneously she threw her head back, driving it into his nose, and jabbed her elbow into his ribs. He screamed in shock and pain, and his grip loosened. She twisted free.

Before he could react, she spun around him and ran for the front door. By the time she reached the door and was turning the knob, he had recovered some and was running toward her. The door opened and she flew out, slamming it behind her, hoping that it would slow him down. It did, but only for a second. He was right behind her.

Patti's car was still in the drive, engine running, but he was too close, she had to run past the car or be caught. She strained to stay ahead of her pursuer. Her lungs hurt, and her breathing became labored. She could hear him breathing behind her. Her only hope was to make it out into the road and maybe, just maybe, there would be a passing car. She saw the glow of lights on the road ahead as she ran down her drive and that gave her hope.

Her lungs burned, and her legs felt like lead as she reached the road. She looked for the car whose lights she had just seen. It wasn't there. The road was dark. Despair began to set in when she realized he hadn't yet caught her. Without looking back, she turned left and continued her sprint down the center of the road, away from her house, away from her pursuer, hoping that another car would pass. She had gone nearly a quarter mile down the road before her legs and lungs gave out.

She slowed to a stop. Hands on her knees, she bent over, trying to catch her breath while expecting to be grabbed by her pursuer, but nothing happened. She looked back. She was alone. No one was chasing her.

Tears began to well up in her eyes as all of those adrenaline-fueled emotions began to release. She was alive. Something terrible had happened, but she was alive. She began to shiver, both from the cold and from her relief. She started walking down the center of the road—away from her house, away from what had just happened—when she was lit up by the headlights of an approaching car. She stopped, and the car slowed and stopped, its lights shining on Max. Blinded by the lights, she could hear the car door open and then a voice said, "Max. Is that you?"

The voice was familiar. "Tom?" her voice squeaked.

"Max?"

"Tom!" she cried out as she ran to him and collapsed into his arms. "Thank … God … it's … you," she sobbed

"What do you mean, Max? What are you doing out in the middle of the road like this?" He held her as she cried.

"I … went … home … to … get my passport to show Patti." Slowly her sobbing stopped, and she began to speak in hyper-speed. "He was there. He had broken into my house, only I didn't know it when I went in. The window in my bedroom was broken, and the room was torn apart, and there were two feet sticking out from behind the bed."

"Whoa. Slow down."

She was beginning to shiver again. "O-Okay," was her answer. Tom escorted her to the car, and they got in. He pulled over to the side of the road, stopped, called for backup, and then turned to her. "Now, start again, slowly. Tell me what happened."

"I went home to get my passport. Patti and I were talking about my going to Switzerland with Jack, and she wanted to see my passport. I didn't wait for Jack. It was going to be quick. I was only planning to run in and out. Anyway, I got to the house, and it was dark. I had forgotten to leave the outside light on before going to work so I left Patti's car in the drive, running with the lights on so I could see. I went in, and when I got to my bedroom to get my passport, I found that the window had been broken and the room was torn apart. That's when I saw the feet sticking out from behind my bed."

"Whose feet?" interrupted Tom.

"I don't know. I don't know whether that person was dead or alive. I screamed, and was about to turn and run when I was grabbed from behind. He said I had what he wanted and I should give it to him. I don't know who it was, I never saw him. Anyway, I managed to get free, and he was right behind me as I ran down my driveway. I don't know why he stopped chasing me."

"Son of a bitch," Tom said, remembering he hadn't seen any one else when he found her in the middle of the road.

* * *

As Tom and Max approached her drive, they saw Jack's truck parked on the road. "What's Jack doing here?" Tom asked.

"I didn't know he was here. I never saw him," replied Max. They turned up the drive. Patti's car was still in the drive, running with the lights on. The front door to Max's house was open, and all the lights were on. Just as Tom stopped his car, a cruiser pulled up, blues flashing. He looked at Max and said, "Stay here," as a second cruiser arrived.

Unholstering his gun as he got out, he met the other officers who also had guns drawn. After a short conversation, one of the officers moved around the house toward the back. Tom and the other officer began cautiously approaching the open front door. Tom had his gun arm extended in the ready position as he spun into the doorway. He stopped, and Max saw him lower his arm and holster his gun as he went in, followed by his backup. She couldn't sit there anymore. She left the car, and ran up to the house, and followed Tom in.

Jack was inside, sitting on the couch. Tied up in the chair across from him was Franz, dried blood covering his face. "What the hell?" asked Tom.

"Hi Tom." Before either could say anything else, Max came barging in, "Jack!" He jumped up, and she ran to him, throwing herself into his arms. For Max and Jack, time stood still and the world was silent. The only sounds, their hearts pounding together. Max sobbed, "Oh Jack." He held her tightly and whispered into her ear, "It's over. It's over." They pulled apart and kissed, tears streamed down Max's cheeks, Jack wiped them away with more tender, gentle kisses.

While Jack tended to Max, Tom and the other officer took Franz into custody, secured the house, and called for the ambulance. Finally, Tom was able to turn his attention to Jack and Max. "Jack, what happened?"

"I got to Ben's to pick up Max after work only to find out that she had borrowed Patti's car to come over here. I was pissed that she did that so I drove over to get her. Just as I drove up, I saw her come running out of her driveway. She didn't see me since she turned the other way. Then I saw a man chasing her. I couldn't see who he was, and he didn't see me. Let's just say I got him before he got Max. It turned out to be Franz." Jack looked at his hand, which was visibly bruised. "We had a little conversation, and I dragged him into the house and tied him up. Andy's dead," he said looking at Max. She gasped and held onto him a little tighter.

Tom looked at them and said, "What you did was both incredibly brave and stupid."

Jack looked down at Max with a little grin and said, "I had no idea that you could run so fast."

"Thanks Jack, you would too if you had a killer chasing you."

"Jack, what else?" interrupted Tom.

"Well there isn't really much more to tell. From the conversation I had with Franz and as best I can understand, he had come over here looking for the letter and Andy followed him. Apparently they argued, over what I don't know, and, well the result is on the bedroom floor." Max began to shiver, and Jack pulled her close. Noting this Tom said, "Jack, I've got to take care of things here. You two go and get out of here; we'll talk later."

"Sure Tom, later."

The ambulance arrived, and with a backdrop of flashing blue lights and yellow crime-scene tape, Jack and Max slipped away. It had been an exhausting night, and maybe now it was truly over.

CHAPTER FORTY-FIVE

HOME AGAIN

"YOU'RE BACK!" Patti squealed as she gave Max a huge hug. "I can't believe you're back. I thought you weren't coming home until next week."

"We were, but we missed you," said Max with a giggle, and she looked over at Jack.

"Speak for yourself. She's the one who wanted to come home." Then turning to Patti, Jack held out his arms and said, "So what am I, chopped liver?" Patti pulled away from Max and gave him his hug.

Hugs finished, Patti said, "Come on." She took their hands and tugged them toward the bar. Patti was so excited she was talking a mile a minute. "I need to hear all about it. How was the trip? Did you get it? Were the Alps really beautiful?" Each question followed the previous so quickly that answers were impossible. Max and Jack looked at each other and grinned as they followed Patti.

"You're lucky, we were about to lock up. Ten more minutes, and we would have been gone."

It wasn't until they turned the corner into the bar that the "we" became apparent. Dave was sitting at the bar. As soon as he saw Jack and Max, he got up and all the greeting and hugs hello started all over again.

"So Patti," Max said with a wink and a nod in Dave's direction.

Patti blushed and changed the subject. "What would you like to drink?"

"I'll have a draft," said Jack.

"A halvsie would be perfect," said Max. "I can get it."

She began to walk behind the bar, but Patti blocked her way.

"Sit. You must be exhausted. I'll get your drinks."

Max, Jack, and Dave sat at the bar. Patti drew two beers and handed them to Jack and Dave. They toasted and then began a serious guy conversation while Patti made halvsies for her and Max. Max sat there watching Patti make the drinks, and when Patti handed Max her drink, she looked at Patti and said, "So?"

"So what?" asked Patti as nonchalantly as possible.

Max rolled her eyes in Dave's direction. "You know damned well what."

Patti blushed, "Dave came over to help me close."

"Right. I see." Max drew out her response and winked at Patti.

Patti blushed again. "No, really he did." Her protest was weak, and she could tell Max wasn't buying it, so Patti quickly changed the subject. "Tell me about your trip. Did you get it? What was Switzerland like? Is it really like what you see in magazines and movies?" Before Max could answer, Patti grinned and turned the table on Max. "Was it romantic?" Patti asked as she glanced over at Jack and Dave who were still talking.

"Yes, yes, and yes."

Max began telling Patti about the trip. As she did, the guys grew silent. Everyone was focused on Max. She told how Franz's law firm was still in shock about what had happened and couldn't do enough for Max to try and make things right. "The lawyers accompanied us to the bank where, after introductions, we were escorted into a small room. The password was verified, and the lockbox was brought in. I remember feeling a chill as it was placed on the table. As soon as it was on the table, the bankers and lawyers excused themselves and left us alone with the box."

Max paused to take a sip of her drink while Patti, Dave, and Jack watched her. Feeling their stares, Max giggled and said, "I feel like we are at summer camp and are up late telling ghost stories."

"So what happened?" asked Patti.

"We opened the box." Max took another sip.

"Max! Will you hurry up and tell us. What was in the box?"

"Just what was supposed to be in the box. Another box, just as the letter had said."

"Did you open it? What was in it?"

"Patience. We couldn't open it. It was a small, plain metal cube with no visible seams or marks, save one—an engraved circle on one of the sides. I shook the box, but couldn't hear or feel anything move inside. That's when Jack handed me the ring. The letter said the ring was the key. It looked like it was the same size as the engraved mark on the box. I held it against the engraved mark, a groove appeared, and the ring fit inside of it perfectly. I pressed it all the way in, there was a click, and the box opened, or rather it split in half."

"What do you mean it split in half?" asked Patti.

Before Max could answer, Jack spoke up. "The cube was made of two pieces, each made of three sides." He held both of his hands in a C shape and then rotated one ninety degrees and slid them together. "Like this. That's why there were no visible seams."

"Cool," said Dave.

"So what was inside?" Patti was getting impatient.

Max continued the story. "I pulled the two parts apart and a small velvet pouch dropped onto the table. I picked it up; it didn't weigh much, and it felt like a pebble or something was inside."

"What was it?" Patti blurted out. "Stop teasing, tell me what was inside."

Max giggled. "Should we tell her?" she asked Jack with a grin.

He nodded.

"Damn it. Tell me."

"Okay. It was a huge, uncut diamond." Max said this quickly and without emphasis, and then sat back to watch Patti's reaction.

"Did you just say a large, uncut diamond?"

"Yep."

"Define large."

Max made a circle with her thumb and index finger, leaving a hole large enough to put your thumb through, raised her hand, and looked at Patti through it.

Patti stared at her in disbelief. "You're shitting me."

"No, I'm not."

"Jack?" Patti turned toward him for confirmation.

"It's true."

There was a long silence. Then Patti asked, "So where is it? I want to see it."

"You can't," said Max as she took another sip of her drink.

"Why not?"

"Because I don't have it. It's still in Switzerland."

"Why is it still there?"

"It's getting cut, and that will take time. Franz's law firm introduced us to a diamond cutter whose father knew my great-grandfather. He's going to split it, and make a pair of earrings and a pendant for me. He will keep the rest as his payment."

Patti's voice betrayed her disappointment. "Oh."

It was silent for a few moments, then a cold current of air passed through the room. They looked at each other, no one moved; that's when they heard the first footstep in the hall. "I thought the door was locked," Patti said to no one in particular.

"It was," replied Dave.

Before anyone could move, Courtney breezed in all tanned from her vacation in the tropics. Without even a "how do you do?," she said, "I'm back. Did anything interesting happen while I was gone?"

CHANGING TIDES

BY K.D. MASON

CRANG. CRANG. CRANG. CRANG. The sound of his footsteps pounding on the aluminum ramp shattered the quiet of the early morning as he ran down to the floats to which his boat was tied. His heart was pounding and the voice in his head kept saying, "It can't be. You'll see." But he would see, and that voice would be wrong.

* * *

Jack Beale started his day standing in the parking lot of Ben's Place looking out over Rye Harbor. It was around 7 am and the sun had been up for almost two hours. He looked east, toward the jetties that created the entrance, and could see the early fishermen casting their lines and settling in for a day of patient waiting. He turned his gaze back across the harbor to the north where he could see the main road as it crossed over the creek that led out into the salt marsh. The endless stream of summer traffic had not yet begun in earnest and the early morning runners, power walkers and roller bladers could be seen crossing the bridge along with an occasional car.

The sky was that perfect shade of blue that you only see in the early morning of a summer's day, unbroken by clouds not yet formed. The water was a mirror with two of each boat, connected at the waterline, waiting for the first hint of breeze to appear that would break the glass. The last remains of the evening's coolness lingered as the sun's warmth was beginning to be felt. This was the mid-July Monday morning that greeted Jack.

Jack had sailed into Rye Harbor more than 25 years ago on his now vintage sloop, the *Irrepressible*, and lived across the street from Ben's Place. Ben's, a landmark watering hole, catered to both tourists and locals throughout the year, but it was the summer when the real money came. With their spacious outdoor deck, live reggae, and drinks flowing freely, it was always a full house.

Jack was early into his second half century although you would never know it save for a few gray hairs at the temples. He ran to stay in shape, had an easygoing disposition and spent as much time as possible working on or sailing his boat. For as long as he had lived in Rye Harbor, he only had a few really close friends, although he seemed to be on good terms with just about everyone.

Courtney, who owned Ben's place, was one of those few close friends. She and her sister had inherited Ben's from their uncle and lived across the street in a cottage that they had renovated. Tom, Jack's oldest friend and the town's detective, had convinced him to come to New Hampshire those many years ago when it seemed his life was falling apart. Jack had suffered a terrible loss when his lover, Marie, was killed accidentally when they had been living on their boat in Martinique.

Courtney had been wanting to build an apartment above the barn behind her cottage, and when Tom told her about Jack, it was a perfect match and a way for Jack to get away from a painful past. Jack would build the apartment and it would become his home. His other close friends were Dave, his running buddy, Patti, a waitress at Ben's who was dating Dave and happened to be Max's best friend. Patti worked as a waitress but her real talent was photography.

Max was the bartender at Ben's and she and Jack had been friends ever since she came to work at Ben's in the mid-nineties. It took his dramatic rescue to save her from a ruthless killer after the murder of her aunt last year for Jack to finally admit the obvious: that he was in love with Max and had been for some time.

A private man, Jack masked his past in an openness of the present.

Few people knew anything specific about his past and that suited him just fine. By all appearances he was quite well off, source unknown. He was always busy helping someone, doing something, and not having a job—in the sense of a nine to fiver—had led to much speculation with the locals about his lifestyle.

Standing there, overlooking the harbor, he was mesmerized by the peace and calm that the start of the day always brought. His eyes scanned the harbor noting which boats were still on their moorings and which were out. Finally, his eyes returned to the pier that began in the corner of the parking lot and extended north out toward the commercial wharf.

At the end of the pier, tied to the floats, was in his opinion, the most beautiful boat in the harbor: the *Irrepressible*, and she was his. Her bow rose up from the water in a gentle curve that projected a sense of graceful strength and power. The soft lines of her sheer as her deck sloped back toward the stern was like the sensuous curve of the back of a beautiful woman lying in the sun. Her single mast was just the right proportion, not one of those tall, bendy racing spars that were all the rage, nor was it too squat like you see on so many cruising boats. *Irrepressible* spoke to him. Freedom, adventure, security, comfort, the happiest and the saddest days of his life were all rolled up into that beautiful hole in the water.

The tide had turned and was beginning to ebb. The current of water flowing from the marsh had begun to deposit a mat of sea grass and other floating marsh debris between the bow of his boat and the float. Normally he wouldn't have even taken notice except that there was something else bobbing in that pinched space. It appeared larger than the expected collection of discarded coffee cups, small pieces of driftwood and scraps of line and other reminders of man's existence that had washed out of the marsh. "What the hell is that?" he thought as he stared. Whatever it was, he had decided that it was large enough that it should be cleared away before it could either damage his boat or any others should it break free and drift out into the harbor.

As he walked the length of the pier, his view was blocked and he began considering the possibilities of what it could be. By the time he reached the end of the pier he had decided that it was probably a large billet of rigid foam, the kind that would be under a float or raft.

He stopped before heading down the ramp and seeing it clearly for the first time knew it wasn't a piece of foam. It wasn't anything that should have been there.

"Shit," he said under his breath as he froze. It seemed his heartbeat grew louder. It pounded in his ears as he stood looking down on the collection of flotsam caught in that narrow space. Amid the sea grass, a paper cup from the local donut shop, a scrap of cloth, and a paper plate, there was a body.

He didn't remember running down the ramp as he stood at the edge of the float looking down on the lifeless figure as it bobbed and shimmied in the water. It was a man, floating face down. He had on khaki cargo shorts and a striped t-shirt. Only one sandal remained on a foot. There was a tattoo of a snake on his tricep and bits of sea grass clung to his hair.

The tide was flowing out from the marsh with increasing force, simultaneously pushing the body into that small wedge of space between the float and the bow of his boat while at the same time trying to force it free. Jack didn't move for what felt like an eternity. He just stood there, under that perfect blue sky, feeling the first gentle caresses of breeze as it broke the mirror that had been the surface of the harbor, fascinated at how the body seemed to have a life of its own as it shimmied and pulsed with the rhythm of the out flowing water.

The cry of first one gull followed by a chorus of cries from the rest of the gulls brought him back to the present. He stepped back, not taking his eyes off of the body and reached for his cell phone.

* * *

Jack's first call was to the police station to report his discovery. Tom wasn't in yet although he was on the way and expected soon. Jack filled the dispatcher in on what he had found and was told to wait there and not touch anything, so he climbed on board his boat to sit and wait, all the while keeping an eye on the body. It was one of those sights that you didn't want to see, yet you couldn't take your eyes off of it.

He placed a second call, this time to Max, knowing that he would wake her this early in the day, but if he didn't call her with this piece of news he knew that she'd never forgive him. The phone rang several times before Max answered. "Hello?"

He could tell that she had been deeply asleep. She sounded groggy, barely awake. There was a bit of a soft moan that gave her voice a sexy, smoky quality that is only possible when just awakening. "This had better be good, Jack Beale."

Jack's memory flashed back to a time not so long ago when he didn't need a phone to hear that voice. He forced that thought away as he responded with a too cheerful and enthusiastic, "Good morning, Sunshine."

Jack continued in his teasing way, "Hey Max, I just wanted you to know; I'm down on the boat and it's a glorious morning. The sun is out, the sky is blue, the birdies are chirping …"

"Jack!" She cut him off. "What are you babbling about?" Now it was his turn to cut her off. "Max. Listen to me. I called to tell you that there is a body floating in the water next to the boat."

There was silence on the other end of the line and then Max's voice returned, this time much clearer, fully awake, that sexy, just barely awake timbre gone. "Did you just say that there is a body floating next to the boat? You better not be messing with me, Jack."

"No really, there's a body floating next to the boat. I've called the police and they are on the way, I thought that you'd like to know."

Before she could say anything else Jack saw that the body was beginning to dislodge itself from where it was wedged between the boat and float. "Max, I gotta go." He snapped his phone shut and jumped off of the boat.

He got to the end of the float just as the current had begun to pull the corpse free. It almost looked as if it were starting to swim away as the rushing waters buffeted the limp form. Not wanting it to get away, he lay down on the float and with his arm fully extended, he managed to grab a foot. To keep from being pulled into the water, he hooked his feet over the other side of the float, and then began to think about what he was going to do next. That's when he saw a cruiser speeding over the bridge and heard the sirens of the rescue team in the distance.

That caught the attention of the few people across the way at the commercial wharf and they quickly became spectators to the drama unfolding. While some remained on the commercial pier, satisfied to watch from afar, others began to walk or run over to Ben's to get a closer view.

To Jack, it felt like an eternity before anyone got down to where he was. The first to arrive was the patrolman who had answered the call. He just stood there looking at Jack, lying on his belly, holding onto the swimming corpse. Then in his by-the-book cop voice he asked, "What seems to be the trouble here?" Jack could only look over his shoulder in disbelief and thought, "You dumb shit, I'm lying here holding onto a dead body by its foot as the current tries to take it away and you have to ask me what's going on?" What he said was, "Officer, give me a hand, grab one of those lines on the boat so we can tie him off, it's getting really hard to hold on."

By the time they got a rope around the corpse and secured him so he couldn't get away, the fire department's rescue team had arrived, followed by Tom, then Max, then Patti with her camera, and then the rest of the town, or so it seemed. Jack moved out of the way as the rescue team pulled the corpse out of the water and up onto the float.

Yellow tape began to go up to keep the crowd away from the area, but not before Max and Patti joined Jack on *Irrepressible*. Coffee seemed in order so Jack went below and started some water heating. Instant would have to do. By the time the coffee was ready, Tom had arrived, and given his instructions, and joined them on the boat. Jack brought four cups up. If it weren't for the fact that there was a water-logged corpse lying on the float it would have been the perfect morning to just sit with coffee in hand watching the harbor wake up.

"Thanks. So, Jack, what happened?" said Tom as he took his cup from Jack.

Jack took a sip then glanced over to where the corpse was lying on the float like some big fish and said, "All I did was come down to the harbor early to watch the sunrise and to enjoy the early morning quiet."

At that Max and Patti rolled their eyes. Neither one of them could grasp the concept that the day began much before ten a.m. Jack went on, "I was up in the parking lot just looking over the harbor thinking about what I would do today. It looked like it might turn out to be a good day for a sail. I noticed that some junk from the marsh had washed into the gap between the bow of my boat and the float. There was something large in with all the grass and garbage. I couldn't tell what it was, but whatever it was, I thought that it was large enough that it could either damage *Irrepressible* or someone else's boat if it escaped out into the harbor. So I came down to check it out." He looked over toward the corpse, now covered with a blanket as it lay on the end of the float. "When I got close enough to see it more clearly I realized it was a body, so I called the department. By then the tide was really beginning to run out hard and it—he—had come free and I was just able to grab his foot."

Max and Patty in two-part harmony sang out, "You touched it??

That's disgusting." Max then added quietly, "I hope you washed your hands before making the coffee."

Jack shot her a look and continued. "That's when Officer what's-his-name showed up. He helped me get a rope around the body and we tied him off. Then everyone else showed up and here we are."

"Do you recognize him?"

"No, but I've only seen his back. He was face down in the water."

"Come with me and see if you recognize him." Tom said. Jack followed Tom off the boat, coffee in hand and went over to the body that the rescue team was preparing to carry up to the parking lot. Max peeked out from behind the dodger on the boat, not really wanting to get up close and personal with a corpse. Patti, on the other hand, grabbed her camera and followed.

She possessed the artist's gift of a great eye and an ability to get to the core of a subject. Tom saw her following them as they approached the body and he knew that it would be useless to try and keep her away. He remembered back to the pictures she shot last winter when she found the body in the ice as he heard the first "ka-chick" from her camera. He also knew that her photos would be professional and that from her artist's perspective they might be more revealing than the ones already taken by the police photographer, so he didn't say anything.

He pulled the corner of the blanket away from the body's head revealing a calm and peaceful face staring up at them. Jack studied the face. His skin was the color of light coffee; there was a band of faint freckles across his nose. His lips did not have an Anglo severity, but rather a slight sensual fullness to them. His eyes were blue and his short cut hair was tightly curled against his head. Jack thought he looked Haitian or Jamaican. Whatever his heritage, he was (or had been) a handsome man. Jack continued to stare at him, thinking, remembering.

Finally he said to Tom, "I know him."